SADDLEBUM

Center Point
Large Print

Also by William MacLeod Raine
and available from Center Point Large Print:

Courage Stout
Clattering Hoofs
The Black Tolts
Long Texan
The Trail of Danger
Square-Shooter
This Nettle Danger

**This Large Print Book carries the
Seal of Approval of N.A.V.H.**

SADDLEBUM

William MacLeod Raine

CENTER POINT LARGE PRINT
THORNDIKE, MAINE

Library of Congress Cataloging-in-Publication Data

Names: Raine, William MacLeod, 1871-1954, author.
Title: Saddlebum / William MacLeod Raine.
Description: Center Point Large Print edition. | Thorndike, Maine :
    Center Point Large Print, 2018.
Identifiers: LCCN 2017057149| ISBN 9781683247272
    (hardcover : alk. paper) | ISBN 9781683247319 (pbk. : alk. paper)
Subjects: LCSH: Large type books. | GSAFD: Western stories.
Classification: LCC PS3535.A385 S34 2018 | DDC 813/.6—dc23
LC record available at https://lccn.loc.gov/2017057149

CHAPTER ONE

FROM THE HILL LEDGE where the rider drew up he caught his first glimpse of Powder Horn. It lay in a fold of the land waves, and even from that distance gave promise of fulfilling its reputation as the most charming town of the territory. In this great waste of baked brown terrain it was a picture pleasant to the eye, an oasis green with the foliage of trees through which rambled a winding river like a jeweled ribbon flinging off sparkles of light.

He lingered a moment for the sheer gratification of watching the restful scene before reining into the dry water-run that in the wet season must sometimes bank a raging torrent. The many hoofprints showed that cows used this steep descent to get to the river from their grazing ground above and left it presently when the way grew too precipitous, so making the rock-strewn path of switchbacks along which the roan now picked a slow and careful footing. Though the gelding was tough and strong, its head drooped, and its hoofs dragged the dust. Sweat-stained shoulders and hips were confirmation of a long, hard day.

The sun beat fiercely against the bare hillside. With the sleeve of his cotton shirt the rider wiped perspiration from his forehead. As men do who live much alone in the open spaces, he spoke his thoughts to the horse. "Rest for the weary soon, Cap," he drawled. "For you and me both."

Long hours in the broiling heat and the fine dust had dehydrated his system, had left throat and nostrils dry as a lime kiln. There must be a water hole in the river near town where boys bathed. The thought of plunging into it was a delight.

Before he reached the valley, Powder Horn had disappeared behind a spur jutting into the plain and did not come into view again until he topped the promontory above it. The nearer panorama of the town was entirely satisfactory. He rode close to the river, cool and sweet, its ripples gurgling over stones with the pleasing music of a stream in not too great a hurry. A meadow lark flung out its sudden joyous melody. The comfort of this pleasant journey's end went to his soul like water to the roots of thirsty trees.

The houses along the wide street were of log, well kept, with gardens in which roses and nasturtiums bloomed. A breeze had begun to stir, and the shade of cottonwoods and poplars blanketed stretches of the road along which he moved. The business street into which he turned, the only one of the town and a connecting link between the cattle country to the north and the settlements nearer the southern border of the territory, had none of the gaunt rawness of the usual frontier town. There were few false fronts and no sod houses. A clear little stream ran down one side of the road to the river and watered the shade trees growing in front of the stores. Powder Horn was proud of itself and showed it.

This was puzzling to the rider, for he had heard reports that the place was inhabited by thieves and riffraff. Powder Horn was the capital of the little men's kingdom, the nesters, the homesteaders, the rustlers, and the nomad wanderers of Cattleland.

In front of Gann's combination hotel and saloon a man sat under the shade of a cottonwood, chair tilted back against the wall, his eyes resting on the rider moving up the street. The seated man was heavy-set, not tall, hard-eyed, and tight-mouthed. He wore a wide, low-crowned black hat, an open vest without a coat, and corduroy trousers thrust into the legs of a cattleman's high-heeled boots.

Another man came out of the saloon end of the building, nodded to the first, and took an adjoining chair.

"Howdy, Mr. Dunn," he said. "Hot as hell with the lid on."

Chris Dunn accepted the other's presence with a glance half scornful. Soft-bellied and slack-jawed, Cad Withers's appearance advertised him for what he was, a village hanger-on ready to cadge drinks from whoever turned up. When he sat down his fat overflowed in the chair.

Dunn wasted no words on him. His gaze was already back on the approaching rider.

"Stranger," Withers commented. "Doesn't belong in these parts."

The training of the range told Dunn a great deal more than that. He noted the long, lean, loose-jointed body, the unshaven bony face streaked with dust and sweat, the down-at-the-heel worn boots, the checked trousers, ragged and discolored. His keen eyes took in the double-cinch rig of the saddle and the fatigue of the horse, the torso-slumped heaviness of the man's seat. From a corner of the nearly closed lips Dunn murmured judgment in two words.

"Texan. Saddlebum."

The rider drew up at the drinking-trough, swung a long leg over the rump of the animal, and came to the ground stiffly. Dunn observed that the roan dipped its nose deep into the water, a sure sign of exhaustion. For the present its master let the horse drink sparingly, then tied to the hitchrack. With a bandanna he mopped the perspiration from his face.

Grinning amiably, he turned to the men sitting on the sidewalk. "We'd call this hot in my country," he croaked from a throat dry as chalk. "For this spring season."

Cad Withers agreed to that. He was hoping there might be a drink in this for him soon. Dunn let the man's friendliness pass without an answering smile. Just now any stranger was under suspicion, though this one looked harmless enough. He seemed as eager to please as a stray mongrel wagging its tail to insure a welcome. Chris still felt he had the fellow rightly placed as a fiddle-footed cowboy on the chuck line. But there were details that needed explaining. One was the JB brand on the right shoulder of the roan; another was the rifle resting in the boot beside the saddle.

"Texas can get hot, too," Dunn mentioned.

The saddlebum's face lit with pleased surprise. "How did you guess it?" He found the answer to his own question. "Sure. The double cinch."

Dunn said, without stress, "You're a long way from home."

"Me, I'm one of those guys who want to see what's over the hill." The stranger took off his big hat and rumpled his unruly hair. "Gents, I feel a drink coming up. On me."

Cad promptly unhooked his heels from the rungs of his chair. "Fair enough," he said.

Dunn gave no sign that he had heard the invitation, but as the others passed through the swing doors he rose and followed.

"A pair of overalls," the stranger ordered, his foot on the bar rail.

The bartender put two glasses and a bottle of Overholt rye in front of them. Noticing that Dunn had come into the room, the Texan said, "Make it three."

"I'm obliged," Dunn said, "but I'm not drinking today."

The lank man took no offense but said cheerfully, "Good for what ails you." To Withers he urged, "Drink hearty."

Three men were playing pitch at a table near the rear. Another lay on a bench asleep. The game did not stop, but it hung suspended in the air a moment while the dealer took in the newcomer. The others turned in their chairs and looked at the seedy Texan. They were small-fry cowmen who had settled along the creeks and were trying to build up herds. None of them looked prosperous, but they were not drifters like this fellow at the bar. They sized him up as the sort of man who was always looking for work but did not want to find it.

The bartender offered a comment. "You've come quite a ways today, I judge."

"Y'betcha. From Johnson's Prong. Fellow told me it was forty miles. I'll settle for sixty."

"Been working for the JB spread," Dunn suggested.

"No, sir." The puzzled look on the Texan's face lifted. "You noticed the brand on Cap. Fact is, my horse was plumb wore out, and I traded with Mr. Baxter for one of his *remuda*, giving him twenty bucks to boot."

A couple of men had dropped into the saloon from the hotel end of the building through a side door. "Everything quiet around the Prong?" one of them asked.

"Didn't look like any Fourth of July to me," the stranger replied, with his ready, vacant smile.

The card players had resumed their game. "I'll bid a weak-minded two," one said.

"Shoot the moon," announced the man on his left.

He slapped down an ace of clubs. The next man played a six of diamonds and complained resentfully. "Never saw the beat of it. You've shot the moon three times and me without a trump."

The bidder followed with the king of clubs and drew from the third player the queen. He next led a queen of spades and lost to the king, but no ten fell. The fourth trick he took with the four of clubs, which was low. The club jack took the fifth and the jack of spades the last.

"High, low, jack, and game," the bidder whooped. "Pay cheerfully, you poor boobs."

From the hotel side of the building excited voices were lifted. One rising above the others demanded shrilly, "Dry-gulched?"

"That's what I said," the flat, tired answer came. "I want a beer. I'm spittin' cotton."

The side door opened. A tall middle-aged man in plain leather chaps and a floppy Stetson hat came into the saloon, his spurs jingling as he moved. Behind him trooped half a dozen others.

CHAPTER TWO

"WHAT'S THAT ABOUT A DRY-GULCHING, Jake?" Dunn asked.

"Young Jim Baxter. Killed on Dry Creek, eight miles above the Prong."

Angry surprise expressed itself in a crescendo of rising voices. Exclamations, curses, threats filled the room. Dunn beat down the tumult.

"Let Jake talk," he ordered.

Jake Hanson shouldered his way to the bar. "Gimme a beer, Casey. My throat is raw with the dust." While the bartender was drawing the beer he slipped out of his heavy chaps and handed them to the man nearest him. "Hang 'em on my saddle, Hank," he said.

Not until he had drained the glass did he pay any attention to the clamor of those surrounding him. He said, "That calls for another, Casey." But before he drank the second he gave information. "The killer waited for him under a bridge below Daly's place. Shot him with a Winchester, then to make sure went close and pumped a bullet from his forty-five into the back of Jim's head."

"My God, the killer must have got him while he was on the way home with that load of lumber he bought here day before yesterday," Withers cried.

"That's right," Hanson agreed.

"The lumber was to have gone into a new house," one of the card players said. "Jim was aimin' to marry Miss Amy Truesdale next month."

The roar of anger rose again.

"Do they know who did it?" someone asked.

"They think it's the phantom killer, as they call him," Hanson answered. "That makes his fourth in a year."

"Maybe we don't know who fired the bullet, but we know who paid to have it done," a huge fellow with heavy, rounded shoulders cut in with a savage oath. "Do we have to sit on our behinds and take this?"

"Duffield is right." Dunn nodded. "Jim was no rustler, even if maybe he killed a calf sometime or other for food. That's not why they murdered him. It was because they didn't want his fences shutting off the stock of the big ranches from the water of Sun Creek." The ranchman had not raised his voice, but there was a hard and bitter rasp in it.

One of the pitch players, Dick Stuart, thumped a fist on the table. "You've said it, Chris. This was a murder for profit. We know who gains by it. The Diamond Tail and the other large outfits ranging on the Sun watershed."

Cad Withers contributed information, pleased to be for a moment important. "Jim had a quarrel with Solly Moore when they met at Rillings's saloon account of someone setting fire to the first load of lumber he had took home. He claimed Morley must of hired it done."

Morley was the manager of the Diamond Tail and Moore one of his riders.

"Sure he did," Duffield cried. "Out of the treasury of the Wyoming Cattlemen's Association."

The saddlebum paid for the drinks he had ordered and moved toward the front door.

Dunn pulled him up short with a sharp question. "Where you going, fellow?"

"To finish watering my horse," the man said.

"Yore horse can wait. I've got some inquiries to make. First, what's yore name?"

"Jerry East."

"How long were you at Johnson's Prong?"

"Overnight."

"Did you hear about this killing?"

"Why, yes, I heard folks talkin'."

"But you didn't mention it to us."

"I hadn't got around to it. Seeing I didn't know him, why I—"

"When did you reach the Prong?"

"About five in the evening." The saddlebum smiled uneasily. "Now looky here. I'm a run-of-the-range cowhand and don't know a thing about this."

The noise in the room had subsided. Nothing

could be heard but the questions and answers of the two men. It was beginning to sink into the minds of these angry men that this stranger might have a good deal to explain.

"Where do you hail from?"

"My folks wagoned west from East Texas to the Brazos when I was a kid. They died there. I drifted around considerable. Came north with a herd drive, and seeing I was footloose I stayed in the North. I worked around the Walla Walla country—eastern Oregon—Nevada. Last fall I got into Idaho and worked for a big cow outfit owned by Buck Rollins. You must of heard of it. I don't know why I'm telling you all this. It's no crime to be a cowpoke on the chuck line, is it?"

Dunn hammered questions at him. How long had he worked for Rollins? When had he left Idaho? Did he know anybody in this territory?

East answered patiently, then protested mildly. "What's the idea of picking on me just because I'm a stranger? I'm no killer."

The bartender Casey thought this was probably true. Nobody would pick such a ramshackle drifter for his hired gunman. He had not the force, the craft, nor the ruthlessness. Nonetheless the anger of those gathered in the room had turned against the Texan like a hot, fierce fire. There was, Casey thought, a feeling of frustrated helplessness in it. They wanted revenge, and they

15

were eager to make the most of what evidence there was against the stranger.

Dunn kept at the man, flinging questions and charges at him. "By your own say-so you were at the Baxter homestead. You went to pick up information about Jim. You heard from his father that he was on his way back from here with the lumber. You ambushed him and then lit out."

"No," the Texan denied. "It was nothing like that."

"You probably ran into a bunch of Baxter's horses and roped one, leaving your fagged one in the herd."

"I swapped with old man Baxter, like I said."

"Why are you packing a rifle as well as a pistol? No cowboy needs a rifle."

"I did considerable wolfing for Mr. Rollins. I heard there are a lot of the critters around here and figured that since I'm kinda lucky at it I might take a whirl at wolfing." East added, with his anxious, lost-dog manner, "Why would I shoot a young fellow I had never met and had nothing against?"

"For five hundred dollars," Duffield explained harshly. "I'll bet he has got some of the money on him right now."

"How about that?" Dunn asked the Texan. "How much have you?"

The Texan hesitated, then answered reluctantly,

"About two hundred and twenty dollars. I let my wages pile up with Mr. Rollins till I quit."

Duffield laughed with sarcastic bitterness. "Sounds reasonable. How many men in this room have two hundred dollars in their pants? Don't all say yes at once."

That brought a laugh, but not one reassuring to the Texan. Most of them were poor as church mice. A saddlebum with so much money in his pocket could not have come by it chasing longhorns.

"No, sir," Duffield continued, fiercely exultant. "It's laid right in our lap. They paid him half in advance. The rest he was to get after delivering the goods."

The man who called himself East looked unhappy. "Write to Buck Rollins," he said. "Parshall, Idaho. He'll back up what I say."

"Sure he will," cut in Stuart. "He's a big cattleman, a friend of the skunks who hired you to bushwhack poor Jim."

Dunn took over again. He stepped forward and drew the revolver from the holster at the Texan's side. "A forty-five, like Jake said," he announced. "Dick, go bring his rifle in from the saddle."

Stuart pushed through the swing doors and returned with the weapon. "It's a Winchester," he cried.

The howl that went up disturbed Casey. It sounded too much like the cry of a wolf pack closing in on its prey. He was a man who prided himself on minding his own business strictly, but he did not like this at all.

A man had come into the room from the hotel, a well-dressed young fellow in English riding-breeches and boots. He had a clean-cut ruddy face, and he wore his clothes with the careless ease of one who had always had plenty. All of them knew him. He was one of the gay young lads who had come from Britain to make their fortunes in the cattle bonanza boom of the West. His brother and he owned a ranch called the Slash 72, where they had built a fine hunting-lodge and entertained their friends of the Cheyenne Club. Hal Carruthers had taken no part in the feud with the little fellows, but his social and financial position automatically ranged him on the side of the big cattlemen.

"I say, you mustn't jump at conclusions," he suggested, in the high, pleasant Oxford voice. "If nobody saw Baxter killed how do you know he was shot with a Winchester and a forty-five?"

The query took them by surprise. They resented it, because they resented Carruthers. The prejudice against the English was still strong, and especially so against the moneyed class to which he belonged. What right had he to come to America and buy land needed by natives? Raising cattle was to them a business of life and death. To him it was an adventure varied by big-game hunts and pleasant parties with those of his kind.

But he had posed a question that could not be ignored. Dunn turned to Jake Hanson, who rasped his bristly chin doubtfully before answering.

"Why, I dunno. Seems like I heard someone say it was a Winchester, and likely the killer would pack a forty-five same as most of us do." Even to Hanson himself this seemed a little feeble, but it was the best he could offer.

"Forget the guns," Dunn snapped. "Take the facts. This bird admits he was right around where the killing took place about that time. He is carrying a rifle and a six-shooter. He skedaddles out of the country quick as he can, in his pocket the dough he was paid for killing Jim. He's even riding a horse belonging to Baxter, probably one he stole for the getaway."

"He says he can give references," Carruthers urged.

Dunn swung on the Englishman. "References for what? To show that he worked for a big outfit. What does that prove?"

"I don't say you oughtn't to arrest and hold him," Carruthers conceded.

Duffield's jeering voice held anger. "We're not talkin' about arresting him, so as some lawyer can get him out. We all knew Jim Baxter. And we liked him. It's time we did something about these killings, and I aim to do it right damn now."

"When was Baxter killed?" Carruthers asked Hanson.

"Must have been about five in the evening. Happy Jack met him a mile farther down the road about a quarter to five."

Carruthers turned to the accused man. "Can you prove you were at Johnson's Prong at five o'clock?"

"Yes, sir. I turned my horse into the Ranchers' Corral before five. Three men were there when I came in."

"If he is telling the truth he is innocent," Carruthers said to Dunn.

"Do you know this man?" Dunn asked the Englishman coldly.

"Never saw him before."

"But you take a heap of interest in him."

"He doesn't look like a murderer to me."

"What does a murderer look like?" Dunn demanded. "Does he wear hoofs and horns?"

Carruthers laughed. "Dashed if I know. Never met one."

"You don't know who killed Jim Baxter?" Dunn inquired, insult in his manner.

The young cattleman flushed angrily. "How would I know?" he asked.

"Then perhaps you had better keep out of this."

Though an easygoing man, Carruthers was not one to be browbeaten. "Thought this was a free country where one could express his opinions," he said stiffly.

"Yore friends would like it so damned free that their hired killers could shoot down homesteaders with no objections," Duffield retorted. "It ain't going to be that way."

"No friend of mine hires murderers to kill settlers," Carruthers flung hack promptly. "Here and now I'll offer five hundred dollars for the arrest and conviction of the man who shot Baxter."

A loose-lipped cowboy known as Yorky, a drifter whom nobody knew by any other name, clapped his hands softly in ironic applause. "Fine," he said. "We've got the cat-eyed wolf corralled right here."

"Inside of twenty-four hours you can find out whether my story stands up," the Texan told them. "Ask the fellow at the Ranchers' Corral."

Leaning against the bar near the door was a slender, graceful man, dark and good-looking, with reckless eyes set in a sardonic face. He was better-dressed than most of those present. Up to this time he had said nothing.

"Four since last April." He spoke evenly, not raising his voice. "First Radway, while he was building a fence for a pasture. Next, Hank Carlton, shot down as he came out of his cabin in the morning before breakfast. Third, Chapin, on the way home with Christmas presents for his kids. Now Jim Baxter." He ticked the names off on his fingers, was silent for a moment, then asked, "Which of us do you reckon will be next, boys?"

"Right you are, Sanborn," Duffield cried, the savage anger hot in his brutal face. "The killer didn't give any one of them twenty-four hours."

Carruthers moved closer into the circle surrounding the Texan. "I'm not popular with you," he began quietly. "Put that out of your minds for a moment. A man's life is at stake. If you destroy it and he is innocent you will regret it all the rest of your lives. All you have to do is wait a little to make sure. It might happen to any one of you. Give him the chance to prove what he says."

The bartender broke a lifetime rule. "Sounds reasonable, boys," he said. "You can hang him tomorrow as well as today."

There were others present who felt as he did. They had been swept away by the passionate mob-instinct to kill, but in them was a lurking doubt as to whether they had the right man.

"I'm with Casey on that," one of them cried.

A man came through the swing doors. He was in his late forties, short and heavy-set, with the stamp of the outdoor West on his sun-wrinkled face and careless clothes. A sheriff's star was pinned on his shirt.

He did not need to be told what was in the air. "I'll take over, boys," he said briefly.

Dunn made a quick decision. "He's yours, Chuck, for tonight. But if he's the man we want he'll be ours tomorrow. Don't make any mistake about that."

The sheriff did not argue that point. No use crossing bridges until he came to them.

Duffield slanted a sour look at Dunn. "Thought you were hell-bent on stringin' up this fellow," he growled.

Sheriff Herrick said, "Take it easy, Duffield. If he's the man we want he'll keep nice in my jail."

"We didn't elect you to protect Morley's killers," Duffield told him angrily.

"You elected me to see justice done. No sense in pushin' on the reins, boys." The sheriff fastened handcuffs on his prisoner.

Dunn explained his position, cold eyes fixed on Duffield. "I'm in favor of hanging the man who killed Jim Baxter. I think this man did it, but I'm willing to give him a chance to prove he didn't."

"Different here," Duffield retorted. "My idea is the sooner the quicker."

CHAPTER THREE

THE TEXAN SAID, with his foolish, friendly grin, "Tomorrow you boys will all be wantin' to set the drinks up to me for scarin' me half to death."

"Don't go loadin' yoreself with the idea that we are through with you," growled Duffield. "We've just loaned you for a li'l while to Herrick before we put you out of business."

"I have the doggonedest luck," the stranger complained, ignoring the threat and still weakly playing to win their good will. "All the way down the trail from the ridge while the sun was bakin' me I was figurin' on asking some kid where yore swimmin' hole is so I could have a nice swim and cool off."

"Intending to drown yourself?" Stuart asked grimly. "No go. There's an old saying that a fellow born to be hanged can't drown."

"You're wastin' time trying to soft-soap us, fellow," Yorky cried. "We know you are guilty as hell."

"All I'm askin' is twenty-four hours to prove I ain't." The prisoner clung to his pretense that he was not worried at the charge against him. "Anyhow, my horse Cap ain't guilty. Will one of you gents see he gets to finish that drink and then

24

take him to a stable where he will be fed? I'll be obliged."

One of the pitch players offered to take care of the animal.

The tension eased. Carruthers walked back into the hotel. A poker game was made up. Duffield invited several cronies to join him at the bar in some serious drinking. The man on the bench sleeping off a drunk went back to his slumber. Casey busied himself setting out glasses and liquor. Sheriff Herrick was satisfied that the danger point was past. There would be no trouble tonight.

Dunn returned to his seat on the sidewalk. He watched the Texan walking beside Herrick to the jail. It was better, he thought, that the hanging had been postponed. They could hang the fellow later if it seemed wise.

Steve Sanborn joined Dunn. He did not take the vacant chair but leaned indolently against the door jamb. "Think he's the right duck, Chris?" he asked.

"We'll know tomorrow."

Sanborn agreed. "Time takes care of all our problems if we give it a chance." He added, as an afterthought, "Did it strike you this guy might not be so much of a saddlebum as he played?"

"He took it kinda easy," Dunn admitted. "That might be because he is too big a chump to realize how close he was to a rope."

"Might be," Sanborn nodded. "Still is close to one, I've a notion. Duffield is in there making war talk. About striking while the iron is hot. He has a nice bunch of riffraff with him."

"Duffield is always flying off the handle. I reckon they won't do anything but talk."

"I dare say." Sanborn continued, mockery in his careless voice. "Too many fellows being bumped off from the brush. I'll go hunt up Judge Jenkins and make my will." He misquoted a snatch of a Psalm. " 'As for man his days are as grass; as a flower of the field, so he flourisheth. The wind passes over him and he is gone.' There's a breeze stirring. It might turn into quite a wind. I've got to leave my debts to somebody. I'll think up some guy I don't like."

Dunn watched him go up the street, a jaunty debonair figure who seemed out of place in this raw frontier country. Most of those living in and near Powder Horn Dunn understood pretty well. Storekeepers, office holders, small ranchmen, nesters, nomads, rustlers. He had them sized up shrewdly, knew which of them were entirely honest, guessed at those who had slipped over the line occasionally to brand as his own the calf of a big outfit, and had tabbed mentally the out-and-out scoundrels. But Sanborn was not so easily read. One could not call him a professional gambler, though he was decidedly the best player in the district and usually left

26

the card table a winner. A free spender, he could be excellent company. No better companion could be found with whom to go fishing or big-game hunting. Apparently he was a remittance man, the wild scion of some family in the East which preferred to forget him except quarterly. When he had money any drifter with a hard-luck tale could borrow from him. Though not a particularly silent man, he never referred to his past. Usually easygoing, if a fight was forced upon him he was dangerous and once had beaten up a desperado under circumstances entirely justifiable. Ordinarily he did not drink, but at rare intervals he went off on a binge that lasted for a week or two. Most men responded to his charm when he took the trouble to turn it on. Even his insolent audacity had the justification that it was backed by a daring spirit willing to accept the consequences.

After searching the prisoner the sheriff put him in a room with heavily barred windows and a strong iron-studded door. Herrick was a kindly, tolerant man. He had been elected by the group opposed to the big ranches and was in sympathy with them in their fight, but he did not share the hot hatred that inflamed some of his constituents. As to this drifter, the chances were that he was innocent. The killer had been at his trade in this district for a year, and East was a newcomer known to nobody. A man could not ride these wide open spaces without making contacts.

"Don't worry, son, if you're telling the truth," the sheriff advised. "I'll get in touch with Johnson's Prong tomorrow and see if yore alibi is okay. Supper will be along soon. Eat hearty and sleep sound."

As soon as East was alone a swift change passed over him. His slack figure firmed and straightened, his jaw tightened, the lines of his bony face took on strength. From the first moment since he had struck town he had been playing the part of a weak saddlebum. Now he paced the floor with strong, easy strides, his mind busy with the situation confronting him. The hot anger of the men in the saloon that had beat upon him had not alarmed him much. Watching them carefully, he had realized that the rage of some of them had not been fused to the point necessary for a lynching. His slackness had been disarming. Those who employed gunmen to rid them of settlers in their way did not use feckless instruments such as he seemed to be. The men of Powder Horn would wait to make sure before they took drastic action.

Herrick himself brought East's supper to him. He sat on the cot and chatted with the prisoner while the man ate. The drifter seemed a simple chap. He talked freely without saying much, and he had a very bad memory for dates. Time did not appear to mean anything to him. The places he had been during the past few months he was sure of, but when he had been at any of them was very vague in his mind. The one exception was that he knew he had been at the Ranchers' Corral before five o'clock on the previous day.

"Duffield is taking it hard that he couldn't hang you," Herrick mentioned. "He's a tough old rhinoceros and he's tanking up with a few kindred spirits. I reckon they will cool down after a while."

"All they got to do is wait till tomorrow," the Texan said.

"Yes. That's all." The sheriff dropped the subject. He could do any worrying that was necessary without disturbing the prisoner. "Be seeing you in the morning."

Herrick became aware of a certain excitement on the street born of the talk among those gathered at Gus Rillings's saloon, The Good Cheer. He met Dunn at the hotel and commented on it.

"Duffield is talking big," he said.

"He's working his crowd up to a lynching," Dunn answered. "Your ramshackle calaboose won't keep them out ten minutes if they get started."

"With two—three good men I could hold them off," the sheriff said.

"I reckon." Dunn's poker face was not encouraging. "Where will you get them? Good men will fight shy of risking their lives for a scalawag who may have killed their friend for money."

"That young Englishman Carruthers?"

"Rode back to the Slash Seventy-Two an hour ago."

"Hmp!" The sheriff's level eyes held fast to the face of the other. "How about you?"

"Nothing doing," Dunn replied coolly. "I don't know this bird East. Something about him doesn't tie up with his story." He added advice. "Why don't you get the fellow out of town where they can't reach him?"

The sheriff had thought of that in case matters got any worse, but he did not tell Dunn so. He said, "I guess there won't be any trouble."

But Herrick's confidence did not increase. As the evening progressed there were fewer men on the streets. Good citizens had gone home. The more reckless were dropping into the saloons and drinking. When Herrick walked into The Good Cheer his advent brought at once an awkward silence. As soon as he was out of the place he could hear the heavy murmur of voices again. They were discussing something he was not meant to hear, some action in which the prime mover was Duffield. He made up his mind to be prepared. In case of an attack it would be better not to try to hold the jail. To have to kill some of his neighbors, as these hill men were in a sense, would be very bad.

He went to his house, roped two horses grazing in the pasture back of the stable, and hitched them to a light wagon. A woman came out of the house and joined him. She walked with the light, poised grace that always charmed Herrick.

"Where are you going, Charles?" she asked.

Nell Herrick was twenty years younger than her husband. They had not been married more than ten months. He had met her in Cheyenne where she had been running a boardinghouse and was in love with her from the first. She was beautiful rather than pretty, and in repose there was likely to be a haunting sadness in her lovely eyes, the stamp of some tragic experience buried in her past.

She was a woman so fully sexed that men were always aware of her. Herrick had thought admirable the aloof indifference with which she made it clear to her boarders that they were present on a business arrangement only. There were rumors that in spite of her reserve at least one man in the cowboy capital could testify to fires of passion banked in her. Herrick had heard some hint of this and brushed aside the story as unimportant. He wanted for his wife this mysterious woman, so vivid and yet so quiet, who set his pulses hammering as nobody else had ever done. The surprise of his life was that he had won her. He still wondered how long he would be able to keep her. There were hours when she seemed to be wholly his, and there were others when she was withdrawn and distant, when there was a gulf between them he did not know how to bridge.

"It's about my new prisoner," he told her. "I think I had better get him out of town. Duffield is stirring up some of the boys to make trouble. If they go to the jail and he isn't there nobody will be hurt."

"Where are you going to leave the team while you are getting him?" she asked.

"Back of the jail, I think."

"You can't tie there. No post. I'll go and hold the horses."

He told her that would not do at all. He did not want her getting mixed in this. There might be trouble, even shooting. It was not a woman's place. Anything was likely to happen.

"Not if I'm there." Her dark eyes were bright with excitement. "You can't leave me out of this, big boy."

Herrick did not argue. He knew it would be no use. She was bored, and this would give her a thrill.

"Will you do just as I say, honey?" he made condition.

"Of course."

He was conscious of the warmth of her rich

body close to his as they drove to the jail. Nothing so vital as this woman had ever before come into his life. He felt a surge almost of despair. How could he hold her, so gracious and desirable, against the admiration of many men?

"Wait here," he told her, and handed her the reins. "I won't be long."

He awakened the prisoner from a sound sleep. "Get up and dress," he ordered. "Fast."

East was out of the bed in one swift movement.

"Where are we going?" he asked as he got into his trousers.

"To Johnson's Prong. The boys have got ideas. If your story won't stand up, tell me now before we start."

"It will stand up."

"Fine. Johnson's Prong it is."

The saddlebum drew on his boots. "Ready," he said.

Herrick handcuffed him. They went out of the back door to the wagon. The prisoner stared at the young woman, greatly surprised.

"Get in," the sheriff said, without introducing his wife.

He helped the man climb awkwardly into the seat. To his wife he said, after they had started, "I'll drop you at the end of our street."

"I'm going with you," she told him.

"It will be a long, hard, dusty ride. You'd better not go."

"Yes," she replied, a quiet obstinacy in her voice.

Her husband gave way reluctantly. "All right. All right." As soon as he had consented he wished he had not.

To reach the Johnson's Prong road they had to pass through the town along the main street, now empty of life and dark except for the lights in front of the saloons. To them came the song of the river rippling over the smooth boulders in its bed. Powder Horn seemed peaceful as Eden.

"A nice quiet summer night," the Texan said. "Cool now the sun is down. I don't recollect ever being in a town I liked better, though the boys seem a little bit quick on the trigger, as you might say, seeing I'm harmless as Mary's little lamb."

The sheriff snapped, "Less talk." They were abreast of the first saloon lights, and voices came clear to them, through the swing doors. Herrick held the team to a slow trot, not daring to arouse suspicion by a faster gait. The wagon was not more than a stone's throw from the bridge at the end of the street when an eruption of men poured to the sidewalk from Gann's, excitement high in their jangled voices.

Herrick's whip rose and fell. The horses jumped to a gallop and rocketed past the hotel, the hoofs of the broncs flinging up a cloud of yellow dust. Somebody shouted for them to stop. The sheriff leaned forward, flogging the team. His prisoner caught the woman by the arm and pulled her from the seat to the bed of the wagon. Guns crashed, one bullet striking the axle. The wheels rattled over the bridge into the darkness beyond, the frightened animals going at top speed.

They traveled half a mile before the driver got them under control going up a hill.

Nell Herrick laughed as she patted her hair back into place. "A nice quiet summer evening, with the boys a little quick on the trigger," she said.

Her husband looked at her reproachfully. "I knew you oughtn't to have come. I was a fool for letting you."

"But I wouldn't have missed it for anything," she cried, bright eyes shining. "You can't have all the fun, big boy."

The sheriff swung into a draw that led them deep into a fold of the hills. He was reasonably sure that the would-be lynchers were already on their horses in pursuit.

CHAPTER FOUR

FROM THE HILL FOLD where the wagon was concealed the sheriff's party heard the sound of galloping horses. The beat of the hoofs died in the distance.

Nell Herrick laughed softly, eyes shining. "Gentlemen in a hurry," she said.

Her husband did not smile. His mind was still occupied with the job he had to do. "They'll travel quite a ways, figuring we are on the road ahead of them," he said. "I reckon for right now we'll forget Johnson's Prong. Think we'd better cut across to the Slash Seventy-Two and hole up East until we hear from the Ranchers' Corral."

"I'm a heap of trouble to you-all," the shackled man apologized.

"What I'm paid for," the sheriff answered shortly. He turned again to the woman. "I hate to keep you up all night, honey, but I can't send you home alone with all those crazy riders on the loose."

She said, with mock primness, " 'A wife's place is beside her husband.' "

"Like heck it is. You ought to be home in bed, and you would be if I wasn't soft in the head and let you push me around."

He knew it was the heart and not the head that

36

was soft. Nell was not a demanding woman, but she was given to deep silences that disturbed him, moods when he did not know what thoughts were passing through her mind. Almost old enough to be her father, at such times he felt a stranger to her. Life with him in this small town must be drab. She had not made friends with the women here. They held aloof, finding no sense of kinship with one who dressed well and wore her clothes with undulant grace, who could not walk down the street without being followed by the eyes of men. Since there was not much Herrick could give her, he was loath to refuse anything she asked.

"I can sleep any night," she answered. "I'll probably never have another chance to help a murderer escape." She had a low throaty voice that just now had a touch of amused insolence. Her head tilted toward the prisoner. "Or do you claim you were just an innocent bystander?"

"That's my story," he replied.

"Unfortunate if true. What do *you* think, Charles?"

The sheriff offered no opinion. It was in his mind that Nell's audacity could be embarrassing. She ought not to talk at all to this man, at least until he was cleared of the charge against him. Yet he was aware this feeling was inconsistent. He had married her because she was as she was.

If she had been less direct and honest he would not have fallen in love with her.

The sound of a horse moving through the brush reached them. Herrick picked his rifle from the bed of the wagon and waited. They heard the creak of saddle leather. In another moment the animal would come into sight round the bend.

"Get back of the wagon, honey," the sheriff ordered.

A pulse beat in the young woman's throat, but she did not move.

As the rider came into sight Herrick snapped a sharp command. "Hands on the horn."

The man pulled up his mount, dropped his hands on the saddle horn, and chuckled. "Smart as a whip I am," he said.

"Are you alone?" Herrick asked.

"I was till I met you. The others are high-tailin' it down the road hell-bent for a lynching."

The man was Steve Sanborn. He sat in the moonlight smiling at them cheerfully.

"Why did you leave your friends?" the sheriff inquired.

"Friends is not quite the word," Sanborn demurred. "I don't make friends with scalawags like that. About leaving them—why, I used my brains. Since you are not a fool, you would not try to outrun them for forty miles. You would duck into the first draw that would take you away from the road. This is it. So here you are—and here I am."

"What do you want?"

"The satisfaction of knowing I was right. The pleasure of good company."

"You started out to lynch this man," Herrick charged.

"I thought I would trail along on the chance you might be able to use another deputy." He bowed toward Mrs. Herrick. "In addition to the new one you already have."

Nell Herrick looked at the man steadily without speaking. Her slenderly full figure had stiffened at sight of him. The excitement of a thrilling adventure that had lifted her spirits was quenched.

"If you mean that, you can get down and rest your saddle," the sheriff said. "But don't pull any funny stuff."

"Like firing a shot to bring that drunken crowd back?" their new ally suggested. "It would not do any good anyhow. They are a mile away by now." He asked genially, "Where do we go from here?"

The sheriff said, "You move a little fast, Sanborn. A man who can swap sides once might do it again."

Sanborn glanced at the young woman. "You have known me quite a while, Mrs. Herrick. Do you think you can guarantee me to your husband?"

"I can tell him you wouldn't betray him to this bunch of drunkards, if that is what you mean," she answered, her level eyes meeting his almost in a challenge.

"We're thinking of heading for the Slash Seventy-Two," Herrick explained. "We would have to cut back along the road a quarter of a mile. Think we can make it before they come back?"

"If we get a move on us."

"Will they follow us along the road to the Slash Seventy-Two after they come back?" Nell asked her husband.

He shook his head. "I don't think so. The drink in them will be worn off by that time. They will call it a night and quit."

They turned back into the road, followed it nearly to the outskirt of the town, then went through a pasture gate and up a long hill crowned with small pines. Wagon tracks pointed the way along a little-used road to a second gate beyond which was the open range. For several miles the trail held to the ridge before it dipped into a wide valley with a floor uneven as a restless sea. The cattle of the Slash 72 grazed here, and from a rise the night travelers looked down on a dark huddle of buildings. The time was close to midnight, and the lights of the ranch had been put out except for those in the living-room of the lodge itself.

"Somebody still up," Herrick said. "Maybe

the Carruthers boys have guests. I'd better make sure."

He walked softly up the steps of the veranda and looked in a window. Two young men were in the room, one lying on a lounge reading, the other cleaning a rifle.

The sheriff knocked on the door. It was opened by Ned Carruthers. Briefly the officer explained why he was here.

"Of course we can put you up as long as you like," the young Englishman said.

This was Nell Herrick's first visit to the ranch. The lodge was of logs and had been built to accommodate half a dozen guests. She walked into a hall both large and high. At the top of a stairway was a gallery that ran the length of the house and looked down on the great living-room. The design was rustic but elaborate. At one end of the living-room was an immense fireplace built of stone, and on the walls were mounted heads of moose, elk, and buffalo. Plainly it was lived in by men alone, and the note was comfort and ease rather than order. Hunting rifles, shotguns, and revolvers were all over the place. But the bookcases were filled with books, and open on the piano rack was Johann Strauss's "Blue Danube."

Hal suggested brandy and soda for the men and a glass of sherry for Mrs. Herrick. A spot would be refreshing after their long drive and the excitement of the night. The offer was declined. The sheriff explained that all they wanted was a room for himself and his prisoner. Sanborn had offered to see Mrs. Herrick home safely.

Ned Carruthers protested that they had plenty of room for the whole party. Mrs. Herrick must be tired. Why not let her get to rest at once and save her the long drive back to town?

The sheriff hesitated. He found the situation awkward. As a public officer he had a right to ask the aid of any citizen to protect a prisoner, but to accept private hospitality from one of the large ranches was different. He had been elected on an implied platform of opposition to the big spreads, and though he felt no unkindness toward the owners of the Slash 72 he did not want to be under obligations to them.

"If you're not too tired, honey, I reckon you had better go back with Steve," he said to his wife.

"It is very good of Mr. Sanborn to offer to take me, but I don't think I'll trouble him," Nell said, a faint flush in her cheeks. "I'll stay with you, Charles, since Mr. Carruthers is so kind as to ask me."

"No trouble at all," Sanborn cut in with a smile. "A pleasure."

Mrs. Herrick did not answer him. She was explaining to her hosts that she did feel a little unstrung from the adventure.

Ned Carruthers was a tall, elegant man with a

keen aquiline face and an air of casual indolence. In Powder Horn he was known as the belted earl because of the mannerisms he had brought with him to the frontier. The Oxford accent, and the suggestion of superiority that went with his immaculate clothes, were an affront to the rough-and-ready settlers that made him much more unpopular than his younger brother. He was aware of this, and sometimes in his speech was the dry, caustic sting of a whiplash.

"Don't let our small differences affect you, sheriff," he said. "I understand the rule of the West is that night-bound travelers have the right of shelter. We are charmed to have Mrs. Herrick and Mr. Sanborn with us. No obligation incurred. Tomorrow you can still do your duty in protecting gentlemen a little free with the branding iron."

Angry color beat up into the face of Herrick. "I don't protect thieves," he said stiffly. "Any more than I protect those who have settlers shot down from ambush."

"A Roland for an Oliver," Hal said, laughing. "You asked for that, Ned." He turned to the sheriff. "All my brother means is that a night's lodging is not expected to buy any change in your feeling about the big ranches."

"Quite so," the older brother apologized. "I went too far. What I should have said is that you will still be on the other side of the fence from us."

"A good many honest men are," Herrick replied bluntly.

"And some not so honest," Ned retorted.

A clock struck twelve. Hal Carruthers suggested that since Mrs. Herrick was tired she might like to retire. He led the way to a room next to the one which her husband was to occupy with his prisoner.

Sanborn watched them go, a grin on his sardonic face. Nell Herrick had neatly put him out of the picture. To Ned Carruthers he expressed politely ironic regrets that he would be unable to accept the hospitality of the Slash 72. He had to return to Powder Horn and condole with Mr. Duffield and his friends over the escape of the killer.

CHAPTER FIVE

NELL HERRICK ATE BREAKFAST at the lodge with her hosts, but since her husband had in his charge a prisoner who might turn out to be a murderer, he thought it more fitting for them to eat with the ranch riders. The rumor had already spread that this man was the killer of Jim Baxter, who had been until the previous year in the employ of the Slash 72. Baxter had been a gay, popular young fellow, and the cowboys at the long table turned hostile eyes on the lank stranger.

A short bandy-legged man with a sullen face snarled a question. "Do we have to eat outa the same dish with a sidewinder?"

Herrick said amiably, his voice easy and friendly, "Nothing proved yet, boys. Mr. East claims he is innocent. I think he is."

"Sure he claims it. Anybody but a plumb fool would. The story we hear is different. What I say is, a hired brush killer had ought to be strung up pronto."

"I wouldn't push on the reins, Jody," the sheriff suggested. "We'll know in two—three hours whether the alibi of Mr. East is good."

"It better be," Jody growled.

"That's right," a big man with a scar on his chin

45

agreed. "It doesn't make a killer popular with me because he calls himself a stock detective, even if I do ride for a big outfit."

There was a murmur of assent. The Slash 72 punchers were faithful to the ranch, but their allegiance did not carry to an acceptance of the view that rustlers were vermin to be exterminated like coyotes. Most of them expected to be small cattlemen themselves some day and it was possible they might want to be a little free with the branding iron. A fellow never could be sure, since circumstances were liable to alter his way of looking at stray calves.

The saddlebum told them mildly, "I'm jest a cowpoke on the chuck line, harmless as a newborn colt, and I'll certainly feel a heap more comfortable when you find that out." The lost-dog, worried look on his face gave weight to his explanation of himself. It was a reasonable guess that he was not even a top hand, far less a cunning and ruthless killer. Even Jody, who had a bilious temperament that inclined him to think the worst of his fellow men, was of opinion that this slack drifter was a kind of Simple Simon.

The sheriff found his team hitched to the wagon and tied to a rack in front of the house. His wife and their hosts joined him on the veranda. They were telling her about the big hunting reserve their friend Dunraven had established at Estes Park in the Colorado Rockies, where they had spent several weeks the preceding fall.

A rider appeared on the hilltop from which a ribbon of road ran down among the scrub oaks to the ranch house. Hal Carruthers identified the approaching rider. She was the daughter of the ranch foreman Cliff Truesdale, who lived a mile farther down the creek in the old log house that had been the Slash 72 headquarters before the lodge had been built.

"It's Amy," Hal said. "Poor kid. Her heart must be sick this morning on account of Jim Baxter's death."

"Is she the girl he was engaged to?" Nell asked.

"Yes. He was hauling lumber for their new home when he was murdered."

Nell's eyes rested on the girl. She was dressed in gray jean trousers, a red-and-white-checked shirt, and a wide-brimmed floppy hat. She rode astride like a man, and her lithe, lean body was perfectly at home in the saddle. In front of the veranda she drew up to give the owners of the ranch a message from her father, that he was working today on the south fence of the big pasture and wanted four of the men sent there to join him.

The eyes in the sun-darkened face showed the effect of hours of weeping, but it was written in them and on the erectness of her slim figure that any grief she felt was her own business and any expression of sympathy would be rejected.

Though she was not at all pretty, Nell decided there was undisciplined character in the face. The wide cheekbones were probably an inheritance from a Slavic ancestor. They set the framework for a finely modeled face framed by a mass of blue-black hair disordered by the wind.

Hal suggested that the coffee was still hot and Pete could serve her flapjacks and sausages inside of five minutes.

"I've had breakfast." Her eyes were fixed on the handcuffed man standing beside the sheriff. News had reached her that the killer had been caught. It flashed to her mind that this must be the man. Her fist tightened on the saddle horn so hard that the knuckles whitened. Within easy reach dangled the small revolver she carried as a protection against rattlesnakes. She had not the remotest idea that in a matter of seconds she would fire it at a man.

"Who is he?" she asked.

The scar-faced man answered. "He's the fellow murdered Jim."

From her lips the color washed. The blood ran stormily to her heart. Words choked in her throat.

"What are you going to do with him?" she managed to say.

"Why, the sheriff is fixin' that up nice," Jody said viciously. "He is takin' him to town for to get an alibi."

Inside the girl cymbals clashed and drums beat.

A tumult filled her bosom. The world rocked wildly. She saw jagged pictures of the tragedy, of the assassin crouched behind cover waiting for his victim, of this villain standing triumphantly over the slack, lifeless body of her lover. And the turmoil swept her into action. Her fingers whipped out the revolver and fired it.

Hal Carruthers jumped for the girl's wrist and forced the arm down before a second shot could be fired. His grip was so tight that her fingers relaxed and the weapon fell to the ground.

"By God, she hit him," Jody cried exultantly.

"She sure did," the prisoner said. He held his left hand away from his clothes and watched the blood drip from it. The bullet had cut off clean below the upper joint the middle finger.

Amy Truesdale stared at him, astonishment in her wide eyes. Beneath her heart a cold knot tightened her stomach. She had shot a man on the wild impulse of a moment. If she had aimed straighter he would be lying dead before her. The shock of it made her limp and sick. Carruthers steadied her while she dismounted.

"I—I might have killed him," she murmured, white-faced.

Nell put an arm around her waist. "Be glad you didn't, Amy," she said. "We don't think he is the right man."

"Not the right man?" The girl's shocked gaze met that of the prisoner.

His smile was ironic. "Don't worry, miss. You meant well. Better luck next time."

Sheriff Herrick looked sternly at the girl. "If you are quite through and don't want another crack at my prisoner I'll take him into the house and fix up his hand," he told her.

All she could say was, "I must have been crazy."

Ned Carruthers answered coldly, "You had better not carry a weapon, Amy, if you don't know when to use it." Though he had been in the territory two years he still did not understand the lawless reactions of this frontier West. Even the women seemed to have murderous impulses.

Mrs. Herrick came to the defense of the girl. Her dark eyes swept the half circle of men derisively. "That's right. Blame the child. You men get crazy and try to lynch this stranger without knowing whether he did or didn't kill Jim Baxter. You tell her he is guilty and that my husband is going to turn him loose. And you are all horrified because she tries to avenge her lover's death. Men have a queer sense of justice."

The saddlebum looked at the blood dripping from his amputated finger. "You said it, Mrs. Herrick." He spoke with mild sarcasm. "There's an open season on me. Why blame the young lady for having a try?"

He followed the sheriff into the house to have his wound dressed.

CHAPTER SIX

A LONG, GANGLING MAN got off the stage as it was entering Powder Horn and followed a path beside the river to the sheriff's house. "I'm Tim Bowdre," he explained to Mrs. Herrick. "Came up to identify the fellow Chuck has arrested for the Baxter killing."

"You saw him do it?"

He shook his head. "No. I'm here to clear the man. That is, if he's the one showed up at my wagon yard before five o'clock the evening of the shooting."

Herrick came out to the porch in his shirt sleeves, a copy of the weekly newspaper in his hand. " 'Lo, Tim," he said. "Glad to see you. We've had a little excitement up here. Some of the boys got notions. You can set us right as to whether this man's story is true or not."

He dropped the newspaper to a chair and started down the steps. Nell made a suggestion. "If it turns out he is innocent bring him back here for dinner, Charles. The poor fellow must be ready for a little human kindness."

As soon as Bowdre saw the prisoner he said at once, "This is the man came to my wagon yard the afternoon of the murder."

"Before five o'clock?" Herrick asked.

51

"Maybe a few minutes before. Not later than five."

"That lets you out, East," the sheriff said. "Since a man can't be two places at once it's not possible for you to have shot Baxter."

"I had an idea all the time I didn't do it," the Texan drawled.

"You weren't alone in that opinion," the officer said. "Mrs. Herrick told me she was sure you didn't. By the way, she wants me to bring you back for dinner."

"It's right kind of her," East replied. "But I wouldn't want for to trouble her."

The sheriff smiled. "I'll be the one to get the trouble if I do not bring you. It was an order from my boss."

He had another reason, but he did not tell it to the young man. Amy Truesdale had ridden into the yard just after he left. He had seen her as they turned the corner into the main street. It was likely that Nell would keep her for dinner and she would probably like to have a chance to tell East again she was sorry for what she had done.

On the way to his house they walked through the business section. At the hotel he stopped and took the two men into the lobby with him and into the saloon. At each place he had Bowdre tell his story before the men gathered there.

"Fine," Cad Withers said. He was sitting in an armchair, his soft, fat belly resting on his laced fingers. "I never did think Mr. East guilty. Seems like we ought to have a drink on this happy outcome." He looked around expectantly for somebody to take the hint.

The Texan said he reckoned he would celebrate later. He was going to dinner with the sheriff and he didn't want to keep Mrs. Herrick waiting. Though he declined amiably, the vindicated man felt a lingering resentment. He had no wish to drink in comradeship with men who had wanted to hang him without giving him a chance to prove his innocence.

Amy Truesdale was setting the table for dinner when the sheriff and his guest walked into the house. She was as much surprised and disconcerted as the Texan. A warm color beat into her face. They stared at each other, for the moment dumb.

From the kitchen Nell Herrick walked into the room, salt and pepper shakers in her hand. She explained the situation pleasantly.

"I thought you two ought to know each other better, to clear up any misunderstanding," she said. "So that there won't be any hard feelings."

"We have a shooting but not a handshaking acquaintance already," East said. "Miss Truesdale didn't like me and she shot me. I can't complain about that."

The cool sarcasm in his voice hurt the girl. She said, humbly, "No use telling you I'm sorry.

I could say that if I trod on your foot while we were dancing." She added, while she set the knives and forks, "I ought to be whipped. Father says if I were a little younger he would give me the strap."

"Too bad you're not," the Texan drawled. "By the way, I'm going to send you my finger for a souvenir. But before you go out after big game again you really must learn to shoot straighter."

Amy put down the tableware and walked quickly into the kitchen. There were tears of anger and distress in her eyes.

East's hostess took him in hand. "I hope you are satisfied," she reproved. "The girl was crazy with grief when she saw you. The ranch cowboys egged her on by claiming you were guilty and were going to be turned loose. Several other settlers had been killed and nobody punished. Is it any wonder she lost her head and thought only that you had killed Jim and were going to be protected by the big ranchmen?"

"Of course if she was annoyed there was no reason why she should not pour lead into me," he said blandly.

"You might be more generous," Nell Herrick told him. "Can't you see the poor child is distracted because of her lover's death and very unhappy about wounding you?"

There was a touch of scorn in her voice that reached East. He did not want this charming, alluring woman to think him small. After all, what she had said in apology for Amy was true.

"You win, ma'am," he answered. "I'll go into the kitchen right now and tell Miss Truesdale I always found that finger in the way, anyhow." He grinned at his hostess, a little impudently, to let her know her criticism had not abashed him.

Mrs. Herrick watched him go, a sharp curiosity in her mind. She was convinced he was not the saddlebum he pretended to be. When off guard there was a careless ease about him that showed strength and confidence. She wondered why he wanted to seem less a man than he was. She felt sure he was not a fiddlefooted drifter. He was here for some concealed reason of his own.

Amy was standing by the window, apparently looking out, her slim body stiff and rigid. She was fighting down the dry sobs that rose in her.

"It's all right with me, Miss Truesdale, about that trifling little wound," he told her gently. "You don't need to worry about that any more. I'd like to shake hands and be friends."

He had thought her a homely girl, thin and scrawny, but the surprised face she turned to him was quick with life. Though not pretty, there was in the bone structure a promise of beauty, and in the dark eyes that looked at him so gratefully there was a lovely light.

"If I had—killed you," she murmured.

"But you didn't," he said cheerfully. "What's a

finger? And the one you lopped off wasn't even on my right hand."

"Is it healing all right?"

"Doc says that in a week I won't know I ever had a finger there."

She smiled weakly in apology. "I wasn't brought up right. My mother died when I was three years old, and I began tagging around after my brothers. I just growed up, like Topsy, wild and harum-scarum. It worried my father for fear I wouldn't be a lady, but there wasn't much he could do about it. And I'm not, of course."

"You're only a kid," he reminded her. "I expect this will be a lesson to you. Next time you won't be so impulsive."

"You're being awf'ly nice to me," she said.

"We haven't shaken hands yet," he reminded her. "I think I'm going to like you."

She offered her hand shyly, pink flowing into the cheeks beneath the tan.

"I don't see how you can after what I did," she said contritely.

"Miss Truesdale, I'm going to tell you something," he said, her small hand still in his. "This is for you only, not for general circulation in this neighborhood. When I was about your age I shot a man. Folks said I was justified because he was a bully and a killer. But I knew, deep in my heart, that if I hadn't had two—three drinks I might have slipped out of the store away from

56

his abuse. But I didn't. I stayed, scared some-body might think me a coward. So I had to kill him."

Nothing that he could have told her would have eased her heart more. He had made himself a fellow sinner beside her. It did not shock her that he had killed a man. One of her uncles had once been on a posse that had hanged a horse thief. To be trusted by East with a secret he would not have confided to anybody else in the territory warmed her soul. It was assurance that she had been forgiven.

The girl's eager eyes reflected her pleasure. "I'm so glad," she cried softly. "I mean I'm so glad you told me. It must have been awful for you—just a boy."

"I wasn't happy about it, but time heals most griefs. The man I killed was better dead. He would have continued terrorizing and killing. I knew that, yet it did not relieve my sense of guilt that I had destroyed him."

Nell Herrick came into the room and knew at the sight of Amy's face that all was well between them.

"We'll have dinner now," she said briskly. "Will you dish up the potatoes and the beans, Amy?"

East strolled back into the combination parlor and dining-room. Herrick took his guest to the back of the house where he washed his hands and face in a tin basin on a bench. Dinner was on the table when they returned to the women.

While they were eating Amy asked which one of the Herricks did the gardening. "I haven't seen any roses like yours in town," she said.

Nell told her that the sheriff did the spade work and she did the bossing.

Amy explained that her roses did not do very well. Maybe she did not know how to handle them, or perhaps she did not have the right varieties. After dinner Herrick took her into the garden to give her a lesson in rose culture. His wife detained East with a question.

She wanted to know if he had attended theaters often. Her guest looked a little surprised. He told her he had seen *East Lynne* and *The Black Crook*; perhaps nine or ten other plays. Among the actors whose performances he had attended were Eddie Foy, James O'Neill, and Lotta Crabtree.

She slanted a friendly, derisive smile at him. "Didn't take lessons from any of them?"

He shook his head. "I don't know what you are driving at, except, of course, that you are joshing me."

"Oh, no. I just don't think you are very convincing in your role. You do nicely for a time and then you forget and step out of it."

"My role?" he asked.

"The part of a saddlebum. You are good when you are good. For a while you had me fooled.

But not for very long. Occasionally an intelligent expression rubs out the vacant look in your face. I'm afraid you are not going to get away with it, Mr. East."

He grinned at her. "You are wonderful. I'm not a saddlebum. So what am I?"

"Apparently you are not the phantom killer." There was a dancing impudence in her eyes. "It's very rude of me to impeach your alibi. When a man in the West says he is East we don't challenge it."

"I see. You take my word for it that black is white—with your tongue in your cheek, unless your curiosity gets the better of your good manners—of your discretion, I mean."

She took it with a smile. "I deserved that." She nodded. "But you might let me off with the backhanded compliment that I mean well. Since I am not the only one watching your little play others may get inquisitive, too. Give me credit for warning you."

"I still don't know of what I am guilty."

"You are guilty of being more intelligent than you pretend to be."

"Is it your idea, Mrs. Pinkerton, that my alibi is a fixed-up one?"

"Your alibi is all right. You didn't kill Jim Baxter and you didn't steal his father's horse. I'm not asking any questions, Mr. East, or delving into your past. All I am saying is, be careful."

"Or I won't fool the boys. Thanks a lot, ma'am."

She detected a chuckle in his voice.

As he turned away to join her husband and Amy Truesdale in the garden she fired a last shot at him. "Isn't it rather a giveaway for you to call me Mrs. Pinkerton? You must have had the name on your mind. It might be you are a Pinkerton man yourself."

Jauntily he flung back a retort over his shoulder. "Just a plain saddlebum, lady."

Her personality stimulated interest in East. She was a strange woman to find in this back-country town, an alien who had been swept here by some freakish crosscurrent of fate. Why had she married Herrick, salt of the earth though he was? Granted his quiet strength, his inflexible character, nonetheless he was almost two decades older than she, with none of the flashy charm that might be expected to interest such a woman. Nell Herrick was no clinging vine. East guessed that back of her poise there was passion in her, hot blood clamorous for life regardless of conventions. He wondered if Herrick could hold her. She was a woman who might fling herself away with reckless abandon. In fact the thought was strong in his mind that sometime in her past a lawless urge had carried this woman close to tragedy.

CHAPTER SEVEN

THOUGH THE TESTIMONY of Tim Bowdre, backed by that of two other men who had been present when Jerry East arrived at the Ranchers' Corral, cleared the Texan of the charge of murdering Jim Baxter he was aware of still being an object of suspicion to the residents of Powder Horn. The men either ignored him or were grudgingly civil. He understood the reason for this. The county was in a state of armed tension. Any stranger was likely to be a secret employee of the Cattlemen's Association brought into the country to gather evidence against rustlers and the small ranchers.

The exploded cattle boom was partly responsible for this. A decade earlier the high plains had been regarded as a paradise where stockmen could grow rich by letting their herds breed and the issue grow fat on the abundant native grasses. The old-timers had been bought out on a book count—made from the books of the seller instead of by a check of the stock by an actual roundup— by companies organized in Edinburgh, London, and New York, and the large new outfits had mushroomed over several states with the result that the ranges had been heavily overstocked and the grasses cropped too close. The management was often both expensive and inefficient, and in order to produce dividends the ranches had been stripped of young cattle including even heifers. Bitter winters had decimated the unprotected stock, and rustlers had preyed upon the calves of the big companies as well as those of individual owners.

Unable to convict thieves in the courts, the members of the Association had made such reprisals as they could. Rustlers caught in the act had been shot or hanged, suspected nesters threatened and driven out, and cowboys who had homesteaded along the creeks refused employment. Many of the ranchmen kept their hands clean and knew nothing about the assassinations from ambush, but to poor settlers the big spreads were all lumped as enemies. It was enough that they were members of the Association. All stock inspectors were especially disliked.

"A detective for a big outfit is nothing but a hired killer," Duffield said angrily, slamming his fist down on the bar at Gus Rillings's saloon.

Sheriff Herrick took a mild exception. "You include too much territory, Hank," he said. "Cattle inspectors are as a rule pretty high-class. I've known some top-hole ones, square and decent men."

"What I said goes," Duffield insisted harshly, his lowering gaze on East. "If they weren't

wolves they wouldn't be in that low-down spying work."

East was on his way to the street. He moved past Duffield without paying any attention to what the man had said. The sheriff followed through the swing doors. He found East reading a printed poster tacked to the wall of the building. It read:

Powder River Farmers and Stockgrowers' Association

Roundup will meet at Carson's horse ranch, May 15. Will work up both sides of North Fork to the Rafter JM, then across to the Black Eagle Prong and up 17-Mile Dry Creek to Twin Buttes. Across to Sand Creek divide and up to head of Salt Creek to the Edson ranch. From there to mouth of South Fork working Middle and North Forks. Finish by combing Crazy Squaw Creek far north as the Spur.

Chris Dunn, Foreman

"It will make trouble," the sheriff told East gloomily. "The law gives the Wyoming Cattlemen's Association power to set the time and place of all roundups. This is illegal, and the boys are headin' for grief when they try to butt in with a roundup of their own. They ought to know that. Matter of fact they do, but they are tired of being run over by the big fellows."

"They have set this one two weeks ahead of the regular roundup," East mentioned.

"The big outfits won't like that," Herrick said. "They will figure it was put ahead to brand as many strays as they can in their own brands."

A big broad-shouldered man was tying a roan horse with white stockings at the hitching-rack in front of the saloon. "The little boys will sure get the cream of the crop," he said cynically. "Question is, will they get paddled later?" He was chewing tobacco, and his eyes idly searched for a spot to unload the juice. It landed unerringly in a sidewalk crack.

The sheriff introduced him and East. The man was David Daggs. East thought that it had been some time since he had seen so much man. Daggs stood six feet two, deep-chested, with big muscles tiger-smooth under the skin. Hair and eyes were black, lips full, jaw strong. When he moved to the sidewalk he walked lightly as if he were treading on eggs. His legs were slightly bowed, and the thighs looked hard as young hickory trees. He was a trapper, one of the few left in the country, and he lived in the foothills of the Big Horns, moving his camp from time to time.

"You don't get to town often, Dave," the sheriff said.

"Only when I need supplies." Daggs tilted his head toward the poster. "Something likely to bust soon," he suggested.

"Hope not," Herrick replied. "But folks will have to keep their heads and not go crazy."

"Fellow down the road told me there's been another killing."

"Jim Baxter. Shot from the brush on Dry Creek. While he was hauling lumber from here for his new house."

"Who is blamed for it?" Daggs asked.

The sheriff did not answer directly. Daggs knew as well as he did that all the enemies of the big ranches would lay the blame on a detective of the Cattlemen's Association. "The assassin is not known yet," Herrick side-stepped. "The killing wasn't in this county. Sheriff Yeager may have information he isn't giving out."

"Time somebody did something about these dry-gulchings," Daggs said bluntly. "It's getting so it is not safe for a fellow to own a homestead."

"The killer is pretty slick," Herrick said. "He doesn't leave sign to give him away."

"Did Jim have enemies?"

"None we know of."

"Was he supposed to be a rustler?"

"No. He was just a nice young chap expecting to be married soon."

"There used to be talk about old man Baxter's cows having so many twins," Daggs said. "That was quite some time ago before so many cowmen got honest."

Sanborn had joined the group. "Perhaps he was just lucky in his bulls," Steve said dryly. "Probably he specialized in those that had twins."

The eyes of the sheriff had returned to the poster. Strictly speaking, this roundup was not his business. He frowned at it, not certain what he had better do. "Think I'll ride out and have a talk with Dunn," he decided.

"Too late, sheriff," Sanborn commented. "It is out of Dunn's hands. This has been hashed over by the whole bunch. They claim the big ranches put this roundup law through the legislation in their own interest. The small fry are going to fight it."

Herrick knew this was true, but his conscience would not let him sit still without making an effort to avert the trouble likely to follow. He returned to his house, saddled, and set out for the Dunn ranch.

From the front porch Nell watched him go. He would not be back until suppertime. To get away from the thought of household tasks she picked up a copy of Tennyson's poems and walked through the pasture to the cottonwoods shading the riverbank. On a mossy spot she sat down and opened the book, riffling through the pages almost at random. A snatch of verse caught and held her eyes. She read the lines, and read no more.

> My life has crept so long on a broken
> wing
> Thro' cells of madness, haunts of horror
> and fear,
> That I come to be grateful at last for a
> little thing.

The words carried her back to the dreadful days when she had sat in a courtroom and felt the eyes of a hundred men accuse her. She had escaped from that past, though the fear of it still threw a shadow over her path. It had changed her life, carried her reckless feet for a time along forbidden ways. Yesterday was gone, but she could not be sure of tomorrow. The harbor she had found was not a little thing—if she could keep from being driven out of it. But how could one be safe from a danger that might rise again to destroy her? All she could do was to hold in a tight fist the good that each day brought.

The sound of a snapping twig drew her eyes to the path that ran along the stream. A man was moving toward her, and the sight of him stirred instant fear in her. She restrained an urgent impulse to rise. That Sanborn had seen her husband leave town and had come to meet her she was sure. The fishing-rod he carried was for the benefit of anybody who might chance to see him. No doubt he had watched her walk down through the pasture.

"Any luck?" she asked, trying to keep her voice casual.

"I can't complain," he answered with a smile and sat beside her.

With one swift movement her lithe body was erect. "One can fish better alone," she told him. "I won't disturb you."

He was up quickly, barring the way of escape. "But you do disturb me—damnably. We are going to talk this out."

"There is nothing to discuss." Her level eyes met his. "You are trespassing on another's property."

"No," he denied. "You are not his. You are mine, Nell."

The color deepened in her cheeks. "You are quite mistaken," she corrected. "I don't belong to either of you, but I am married to Charles Herrick. You are no longer in my life."

"Why did you leave me?" he demanded. "And why did you marry him?"

"I did not leave you to marry Charles. I had never met him then. Be generous, Steve. You came into my life when I was desperate, when all the world seemed against me, when all I wanted was a little kindness. But it was never right. I'm not a loose woman."

"You were happy with me."

"I was contented—for a time. At least I told myself I was."

"Can you say you weren't in love with me?"

"I don't know. You see I was so unhappy—and tired—and alone, after Jeanie's death. It was good to have you care for me. And I am a woman who needs a man. You gave me something. But—I couldn't go on—not for always."

"All Herrick means to you is a refuge, because you were afraid of loving me too much," he flung out.

"No. Let's leave him out of it, Steve. He is the man I chose—the one I want."

"Liar!" he charged. "You love me now. A woman like you can't run away from living, Nell. Herrick is too old and too tame for you. You lie awake nights and wonder how long you can go on with it."

A pulse of anger beat in her throat. "He has given me more—much more than you ever could. I am happy with him, when I forget."

"When you forget me," he amended.

"No. When I forget who I am and what I did."

"And when he finds out?"

"I don't know." She lifted a hand in a despairing little gesture. "I ought to have told him but I didn't dare."

What Sanborn had said was true. She had married Herrick for a refuge, but she knew that

69

now he meant to her something far different.

"He's what they call a good man," Sanborn said. "You are Caesar's wife. When he finds out—and he will—you'll see his door shut to you."

"You wouldn't tell him," she cried.

"Maybe I will. All's fair in love and war. He's bound to find out, anyhow. Why not take it now?" There was an urgency in his voice and face. "You hate your life here—this dull cow town—the women who don't understand you—the fear of discovery. Come with me, Nell. I'm the one man who knows all about you and loves you more because of it. We'll go to Frisco and have such a gay good time."

"No," she told him. "If you'll let me pass, please."

He took her in his arms and drew her close. He kissed her throat and eyes and mouth. She neither resisted nor responded but stood stiff and cold in his embrace. He pushed her from him. In her frozen stillness he had found no comfort.

He watched her walk through the pasture, the skirt clinging to her knees and remodeling the long thighs at every step. He did not know her heart was pounding like a hammer against her ribs and that her legs were so weak they could hardly carry her.

CHAPTER EIGHT

JERRY EAST WAS SITTING in front of the Gann House whittling a pine stick when Daggs came out of the saloon end of the building. He stood on the sidewalk hesitating whether to turn right or left. His eyes swept up the street, then down, came to rest on the Texan a dozen yards from him. The trapper walked across to join him, light-footed as a schoolgirl in spite of his almost two hundred pounds.

The grin on his face was friendly. "Fellow at the bar was just telling me they had you picked for Jim Baxter's killer," he said.

East stopped whittling and looked at the man. "Correct," he answered.

"But you proved an alibi."

"Yes."

"Good. You're out of it, then."

"Not quite. Sheriff Yeager sent word by my alibi witness that he would like to have me come down and see him. I'm waiting for the stage."

"What's he want you for—if you are in the clear?"

"The way Bowdre puts it the sheriff thinks, since I was almost the last man who saw young Baxter alive, maybe I might be able to give him some information."

71

The candid blue eyes of the trapper held fast to those of the Texan for a moment. He drew up a chair, sat down, and lit a cigarette.

After he had taken a few puffs he said indifferently, "What does he think you know?"

"Search me." East was wearing the saddlebum's face of empty innocence. "I was at Johnson's Prong when the killing took place."

"Did you meet anybody on the road before you got there?"

"Sure. I met Jim Baxter. That is, I met a guy hauling lumber. They say it must have been Jim."

"Anybody else?" Daggs asked casually. "Yeager may have the idea that you might have seen the killer—met him, or caught sight of him hanging around in the brush."

"So I have to travel forty miles at my own expense to tell him I don't know a thing," East said irritably.

"Why go, if you don't know anything?"

"I dunno. He has sent word for me to come. I've done been in one jam about this killing. If I act like I'm scared to go I may be in another."

"No sense to that," Daggs told him. "Unless you do know something you're keeping to yourself."

The eyes of Daggs still probed into those of East.

"I hadn't a thing to do with this," the Texan

insisted fretfully. "Do I have to spend the rest of my life saying that over and over?"

"Better go back to Texas, my friend," Daggs said scornfully. "You're not tough enough for this country."

The stage rolled up the street and stopped in front of the hotel. Passengers emerged from it to stretch their legs while the horses were being changed. The driver tossed down a mail sack. More carefully he unloaded a crate of eggs, a box of crackers, and a barrel of nails. Into the saloon the Wells Fargo guard disappeared, presumably for liquid refreshment.

Ten minutes later the stage was on its way again. It had taken on another passenger, Jerry East. He had found a corner seat next to a young woman from Philadelphia who had come out to teach school and wanted reassurance that the Indians would not attack the stage. Since she was clever and pretty the Texan devoted some hours to her education in the ways and customs of the West.

At Johnson's Prong a member of the school board and his wife met the new teacher and took her to their home. Before leaving she turned her brown eyes on her instructor's long, lean body and well-shaped head.

"It's been a pleasure to meet you, Mr. East," she told him. She did not say that she hoped their first meeting would not be the last, but he read that message in the lingering gaze. During the stage ride the Texan had not taken the trouble to play the part of a saddlebum.

"Goes double, Miss Fowler," he replied. "You'll like the West. It's big. But not so big but what we'll meet again."

The thought of her remained with him for all of five minutes, at the end of which time he was walking into Sheriff Yeager's office. That officer was reading a local paper, his feet on the desk. He was a short, plump man in store clothes. The hat beside the Eastern shoes was a derby. Its owner's pink cheeks were smooth and soft. Most Western sheriffs had come from the range and showed it, but this one was clearly a politician. His visitor guessed before he had talked with him long that he could sit on a fence adroitly.

"I'm Jerry East," the Texan said. "Mr. Bowdre says you want to see me."

The sheriff removed his feet from the desk and rose. "Quite right. We've got to get to the bottom of this foul murder. Sit down, Mr. East, and tell me your story."

East took the offered chair. "Not much to tell. I stopped at the Baxter ranch and traded horses with the old gentleman. On my way to the Prong I met a fellow driving a wagon loaded with lumber. Must have been Jim Baxter."

"Stop to talk with him?"

"No. I yelled to him it was hot for this time of

74

year. He called back something I didn't make out."

"Where did you meet him?"

"About six miles from here, I should judge."

"When?"

"I don't know exactly. I would guess about four o'clock or a little after."

"Meet anybody else on the road?"

"Soon after I left the Baxter ranch a fellow crossed the road in front of me and rode into the brush. That was about half an hour before I saw the wagon with the lumber."

Yeager showed surprise. "When Chuck Herrick talked with me over the phone he didn't say anything about you having met another man."

"He didn't know I had." The Texan grinned sheepishly. "Fact is, I was so busy trying to convince the gents of Powder Horn I wasn't the killer that I never got down to mentioning it."

"Would you know the man if you saw him again?"

The witness hesitated. He had known he would be asked that question and had given some time to considering what answer he would give.

"I'll be doggoned if I know, Mr. Sheriff," he said. "Maybe I would. Maybe I wouldn't. He was about seventy-five yards away from me when he rode across the road. You know how it is. You see a stranger for about four seconds and never expect to see him again."

"What color horse?"

"Roan—or sorrel. I wouldn't be sure which."

"That's a lot of help," Yeager said, disgusted. "Four-fifths of the horses in this country are roan or sorrel. What about the rider?"

"Why, I dunno. He looked like any fellow you'd meet out on the range."

"Was he wearing chaps?"

"Seems to me—" The Texan rubbed his chin with the palm of a hand to help his memory. "I'll be dawged if I know."

"Big—little? Fat—lean? Tall—short?"

"Well, sir, you got me there. When a man is on horseback, quite a ways off, you don't know how big he is—or how tall."

"You're sure you saw a man at all?"

"Yes, sir, I couldn't of been mistaken about that. He wasn't any mirage."

Yeager frowned disapproval, but he was not sorry this dumb puncher was so vague. There was dynamite in the Baxter killing, and there was an election coming up in the fall. The sheriff did not want his chance of succeeding himself to be blown up in the explosion, as it very well might be if the crime was solved and big men shown to be back of it. His best bet was to be very active, very earnest in trying to find the guilty party, and to wind up with no evidence against anybody. If he could do that he would make no enemies.

"Was this man you saw carrying a rifle?"

"I didn't see one."

"Probably just a cowpuncher riding the line."

Yeager might be right about that. Anyhow, if that was how he felt about it East did not want to disturb his opinion. The Texan knew he was concealing evidence, though what he had not told might have no bearing on the case. He had what seemed to him a good reason for reticence. If he gave the sheriff a more accurate description of the man who had crossed the road the details would be broadcast by word of mouth to every far pocket of the Powder River country. They would give a picture that would fit forty men in a radius of fifty miles. But if the man Jerry East had seen was the killer he would be immediately on guard. He would reason that safety for him lay in destroying the witness who had seen him in the vicinity of the murder spot. From that hour the Texan would be in imminent danger. Since East did not want to have to get out of the country it was better for the present not to talk. His judgment was that if he told all he could Yeager would fumble the clue, if it really was one, and by warning the guilty man do more harm than good. Anyhow the Texan was not sure he would know the man.

East was annoyed at himself for having mentioned having seen the man. He decided to add a picturesque touch that would show the fellow was a harmless range rider. The information he tossed out was invented impromptu.

"I reckon you're right, sheriff," he agreed. "One thing I forgot to tell you. He was singing, 'My Bonny lies over the ocean.' Fellow had a right carrying voice."

"That cinches it," Yeager announced. "If he had been aiming to ambush a man he wouldn't of been shouting his presence around."

The Texan said that sounded reasonable. He had not thought of it that way.

"Might have been Happy Jack you met. He saw Jim soon after you did. Happy is a cheerful cuss and might have been singing."

East slapped his thigh. "Sure. I'll bet it was him I met." His face grew serious. "Say, you don't reckon this Happy Jack—"

The sentence died away unfinished.

Yeager shook his head. "Happy wasn't carrying a rifle. Anyhow he is no killer."

"Seeing as I've been drug into this, I wish you would find the guilty man, Mr. Yeager," the Texan said unhappily. "Folks still look at me like I had something to do with it. Mind if I kinda sashay over the ground at Dry Creek and talk to some of the people who live down that way?"

The sheriff looked his slack caller over rather contemptuously. "Start your detective work soon as you please and let me know when you have found the murderer," he sneered.

"I don't figure on finding him, but I sure would like my name cleared."

The saddlebum smiled apologetically and walked out of the office.

CHAPTER NINE

JERRY EAST WENT to the Ranchers' Corral to rent a horse for a day. A curly-headed blond cowboy in checked cotton trousers, scuffed boots, and a big Stetson with a rattlesnake skin around the band sat on the feedbox kicking his heels against its side. Bowdre introduced him as Happy Jack.

"If he's got another name I never heard it," he said. "Maybe he left it in Nebraska where he says he came from."

Happy Jack said he was pleased to meet Mr. East and as for Tim Bowdre he could go to hell any time he was a mind to. A friendly grin took the sting out of the suggestion.

"You fellows ought to put yore heads together and fix up a story how Jim Baxter died of apoplexy, seeing you were the two last fellows saw him alive," Bowdre advised.

As a humorous thrust this did not go so well.

"I did not see you smile, Tim," Happy Jack warned. "One man saw Jim after I did—the wolf who shot him. I know you mean to be funny, but even so I can't laugh my head off. Jim and I were side-kicks when we worked at the Slash Seventy-Two. I'll feel a hell of a lot better when the murderer is rubbed out."

East did not doubt that Happy Jack was innocent. One look at this open-faced boy was enough to prejudice anybody in his favor. Unless his whole appearance was a lie he was no cold-blooded killer.

"I reckon my foolishness missed fire that time," Bowdre said. "Course you know I wouldn't be talkin' thataway if I had any doubts. You know that."

"Sure I know it," the cowboy replied. "But it hurts me for folks to play like I shot Jim. I feel too bad about it."

The Texan agreed that to be even on the outskirts of an unsolved murder was not pleasant.

In answer to a question Happy Jack told the circumstances about the finding of the body. Everett Baxter, a younger brother, had run across it in the late afternoon while riding in from fixing a fence broken by stock. Happy Jack was at the ranch when Ev drove into the yard with Jim's body on top of the lumber he had been bringing for his house. Three of the ranch hands had ridden to the scene of the crime with Happy Jack and had found beneath a bridge several splashes of tobacco juice evidently made by the murderer while waiting for his victim.

Happy Jack had been at the funeral of Jim Baxter and was now headed for the Sugg ranch where he was employed. East rode with him, and at the Texan's request, he went out of his way to show the Southerner the spot where the tragedy had occurred. There could be no doubt that the assassin had first shot young Baxter with a rifle, then had put a bullet into the back of his head from a revolver.

"If you're aimin' to see old man Baxter I might as well go along and introduce you," Happy Jack said. "Though come to think you've done met."

The Baxter ranch was a small spread, not too well equipped. The house was a long, low structure of log with a wing made of whipsawed lumber. They found Baxter and his son Everett shoeing a horse.

When Happy Jack mentioned the name of his companion the rancher took it sourly. He had already had dealings with the Texan. This stranger had been accused of murdering his son. The alibi offered by him had stood up, but this did not prove he was not a party to the killing.

"What does he want here?" Baxter growled.

East explained gently that he was not satisfied to remain an object of suspicion. He wanted to do anything he could to find the murderer and see him punished.

"I don't know you," Baxter said harshly. "You may have been in this killing of my son up to your neck. You came here and bought a horse from me, and an hour after you left my son was killed. You were packing a rifle and a revolver. Maybe you are innocent. I don't know. If I were sure you weren't I would see you never left here alive. I don't want any truck with you. Get out."

East said, "Sorry. I'd like to talk this over with you, but I can't blame you for turning me down if you have any doubt about me."

As he swung to the saddle a young woman came out of the house. She gave an exclamation of recognition and hurried forward. The girl was Amy Truesdale. East dismounted and waited for her. He realized that after the funeral she must have come here with her lover's people to spend some time with them.

"What are you doing here, Mr. East?" she asked.

"That's what my father asked him," Everett said resentfully. "Unless he is figurin' on getting another of us."

"But he didn't do it," Amy cried. "He couldn't have. He was at Johnson's Prong when it happened."

"He could have been in cahoots with the fellow who did, couldn't he?" the old man demanded.

"He wasn't. I know he wasn't. That's what I thought when I shot him—that he was guilty—and afterward I knew I was wrong."

"When you shot him?" The old man stared astonishment at her.

"Yes. He was at the Slash Seventy-Two—a prisoner. And somebody said Sheriff Herrick was going to turn him loose. Then—I don't know why I went so crazy—I shot at him."

East held up his left hand, smiling. "And cut my middle finger off clean as a whistle."

Though old Baxter had been aware that Amy had an uncertain temper, he was very fond of her. "Goddle-mighty!" he said, goggling at her. "Can't you let the menfolks do the shooting, honey?"

"I—I'm awf'ly ashamed." She flushed to her throat. "But Mr. East was nice as could be about it. He said he didn't need that finger, anyhow." Amy smiled faintly, to mark this as a joke.

Everett looked at Miss Amy with vast respect. He had never shot at a man, and this slip of a girl had just missed killing one.

To old Baxter's mind it was not convincing proof of the stranger's innocence that he had forgiven a girl for making a target of him. "I don't know him. Who is he? What's he doing in this country?" he snapped.

East went over the story he had told several times in the past few days. The ranchman was more than half convinced it was the truth. Happy Jack said, "I think he's a good egg, Rufe."

"Maybe so. How was I to know? He came around bothering me right after I had buried my boy, wanting to make talk about it."

Amy slipped her arm under that of the old-timer. "I know, Uncle Rufe. Naturally you thought Mr. East was in too big a hurry."

"I don't want to let the trail get too cold," the Texan explained. "But I should have waited till tomorrow."

"What is it you want to know?" Baxter asked brusquely.

"Did Jim have any enemies? Do you suspect someone? In your opinion was this a hired killing? If I'm going to find out anything I have to start from somewhere."

"If you're in the clear why are you so hot to find out who did it?" Everett wanted to know.

The Texan's level direct gaze met his. "Because I am an honest man and don't want folks for the rest of my life to think I may be tied in with a cold-blooded murder."

Rufus Baxter said he thought this had been done by a hired assassin. Jim had had no personal enemies, at least none who would stoop to anything as vile as this. Jim had been a good boy. There was nothing in his record to explain any such punishment or vengeance. The only satisfactory explanation was that the land he had taken up along Sun Creek would, if fenced, keep cattle of several big outfits from reaching water without a long trek.

East bluntly asked what outfits.

"If you are one of their spies you can go back and tell your employers I'm not afraid to name the outfits," Baxter said hardily. He ticked them off on his fingers. "Morley's Diamond Tail— Lang's T Anchor—that English company, the JK."

Amy patted the old rancher's gnarled hand. "He's not going back to tell them anything, Uncle Rufe. You can tie to Mr. East."

"You know a lot about it," Baxter grunted amiably. "But you may be right this time. I hope so."

East pressed home questions and learned that Baxter could give him nothing but a suspicion as to the identity of the actual killer. A stock detective named Rod Allen had been very active in recovering stolen stock for the big Association. He had been seen in the neighborhood recently and might have shot Jim, though he and young Baxter had never quarreled.

"Find the man who did it, Mr. East," Amy cried, in a burst of feminine ferocity. "And when you do, treat him the way he did Jim, without giving him a chance."

The Texan shook his head. "I can't do that, Miss Amy." He smiled. "I know a nice young lady who tried that way. Chances are we'll never know who did it, but if we should be lucky the thing to do is drag him into court and find out who is back of him."

"That's right," agreed Happy Jack. "Make him tell who is putting up the dough to murder homesteaders."

"Then bump off the guys hiring the fellow," Everett said angrily.

"Don't get too big for yore pants, son," his father advised. "You're only a kid."

"Back of a gun I'm the same size as John L. Sullivan," the boy retorted.

East said mildly, with a smile, "Mr. Law is bigger than either of you. Let him settle it."

Amy changed sides. "Mr. East is right. My way wasn't the right one."

Happy Jack grinned. "Trouble is, Mr. Law is slower than molasses in January. It has taken him a doggoned long time to reach out and grab this phantom killer."

The Texan was of the opinion that the hired terror must be near the end of his rope. The whole district had its eyes open to spot him.

CHAPTER TEN

AS THE DAYS WORE AWAY Jerry East found the resentment against him dying down. He had an easy, casual manner, friendly and informal, that led men to discount the likelihood of his being a cold-blooded killer. Moreover, he was a stranger in the community, and the phantom murderer must be somebody as familiar with the terrain as one is with the palm of his hand. He must know every gulch and every swell of the wide range, so that he could disappear into the mountain retreats by means of the crooked trails leading into far-flung solitudes where game was plentiful.

Without knowing whether the killer was large or small, dark or fair, East built up a mental picture of his attributes. The fellow must be stealthy as an Indian, as patient as a stalking animal, one who moved catlike up ravines and through the brush taking on the color of his environment like a ptarmigan, a rider who followed the hill folds and never rode the ridges. He must be a man with no sense of the value of human life, completely cold and callous. Yet on the surface he might be a good fellow, an entertaining drinking companion. Possibly he was a small rancher in the hills who held the confidence of those he was destroying. Or he might be a stock detective who had been wary enough to escape without leaving evidence to be picked up later by those who already suspected him because of his occupation.

East tried to fit into the picture he had developed the men he had met since his arrival. Chris Dunn—Cad Withers—Jake Hanson—Dick Stuart—Casey the bartender at the hotel saloon—the loose-lipped cowboy Yorky—Duffield—Steve Sanborn—Daggs—the owners of the Slash 72 or one of their cowboys. Some he discarded at once. Withers was too slack and futile. Casey did not have the opportunity even if he had the will. The Carruthers brothers were not of the stuff of which killers were made. Stuart had a wife and three children, so would have little chance to disappear unnoticed for days at a time.

It was likely the guilty man was somebody he had not yet met. The cattle detective Rod Allen had been mentioned by Baxter. He was said to be a hard, ruthless man, antagonistic toward all the homesteaders taking up water and grass that had been used by the big outfits. East had heard that he was very friendly with Morley of the Diamond Tail, who was the most disliked of all the big ranchers by the little fellows because of his overbearing disregard of others' rights.

Within a week East heard from several men about the man he had seen crossing the road shortly before the killing of Jim Baxter. Sheriff Yeager had evidently talked. The Texan was glad he had not told him more. The reports had passed from mouth to mouth and came to Jerry garbled. One account was that a big fellow with a rifle had waved East around. [When a rustler was caught while illegally branding a calf not his own he waved around the horseman who by chance had interrupted him. He did this in order not to be recognized. The unexpected witness then made a wide detour and went on his way.] Another reported that the saddlebum had heard the shots and met the fellow galloping away. The latter, of course, could not be true, since East was miles away at the time of the killing.

But talk of this kind disturbed East. The assassin would hear it and get to worrying how much he knew. If it troubled him too much he would try to eliminate the witness against him.

One afternoon East sauntered into the hotel saloon and lined up at the bar with two or three others. The room was pretty well filled, and among those present were at least two whom he wanted to convince that he had seen nothing dangerous.

Somebody asked him if he really had seen a man who might be the killer. The question saved East from trying adroitly to introduce the subject himself.

"Funny how a thing gets twisted by the time it has been told two—three times," East said. "I did see a cowboy cross the road a ways ahead of me. He came outa the brush and went into it. I wouldn't know him from Adam if I ever saw him again."

"How far from you was he?" asked Dunn.

"Dogged if I know. Maybe a hundred yards."

"You nearsighted, fellow?" demanded Duffield.

"I see right good, Mr. Duffield," the Texan answered amiably, "but not so well when the sun is in my eyes."

"Always got an answer, haven't you, fellow?" Duffield growled. "I never saw a guy who could alibi everything so slick."

"Maybe you never saw anybody who had less to alibi," East answered, still without rancor.

Dunn rose to leave. "You fellows be on time at the roundup Monday," he reminded the ranchmen present. "We've got to cover a lot of country and we'll need all the riders we can get."

On his way to the door East intercepted the roundup foreman.

"Mind if I ride with you?" he asked. "I'll be wanting a job soon, and I'd like to show I can throw a rope."

Dunn did not answer for a moment. His hard eyes bored into those of the Texan. He was thinking that they could use another hand and that it might be a good idea to have this man under his observation for a time.

"Far as I know nobody needs a rep and I reckon nobody could afford to hire another rider," he said. [Rep is short for representative—a rider sent by a cattleman to look after his interests if he is unable to attend the roundup himself.]

"For a few days I would be willing to work for nothing, so as to show I am worth my salt," East answered.

"All right. At Carson's horse ranch Monday morning early. I'll bring a string of horses you can ride."

The Texan knew that early in the cow country means before dawn. As he arrived riders were drifting in toward the chuck wagon from several directions. With them they brought their strings and threw them into a one-rope corral with the rest of the cavvy.

The morning was crisply cold, but as they rode from the horse ranch to the summit of a hill they could see the sun above the horizon flooding the tops of the land waves with light. Though there had been overstocking, the feed range was still in good condition. In the distance the serrated peaks of the Big Horns rose out of the mists not yet dissolved by the sun rays.

Presently half a dozen riders turned into a draw to comb Wolf Creek and Black Eagle Prong. At the next rise Dunn divided his men again. East found himself in a group of four told to push down the stuff from the headwaters of Cherry Creek. They passed cattle grazing as they moved up the stream but paid no attention to them. On the way down these would be added to the bunch picked up above.

The riders fanned out to sweep down all the stock on this watershed. Once or twice East caught sight of them, far up on the ridges to right and left. He gathered a few cows and calves and pushed them down the creek. Here and there he swept in others, taking care not to push them fast enough to frighten the animals. The banks of the stream were netted here and there with tangles of cherry trees and running cedar holding close to the ground.

Occasionally a steer bolted, and he had to charge through the brush to head it back into the bunch. The country grew more open. A faint "Hi-yi" came to him from the right. He heard the sound of bawling cows. A trickle of them appeared out of a draw. Others he saw dropping over a steep shale bench. Riders showed back of them. Presently his gather merged with the other groups, and they turned up a trough leading to a high mesa. On the way to the roundup ground they combed wooded pockets and prodded cattle out of small hill folds. They could see half a dozen bunches converging toward a common point. The blatting of calves separated from their mothers in the drive and the lowing of cows summoning them filled the air.

Smoke rose in the clear air from a fire of small

logs that had been roped and dragged to the branding-ground. A dozen irons were heating in the red coals. Men lounged in their saddles or squatted on their heels by the fire while the irons heated. A cordon of riders surrounded the gathered herd.

Yorky reported to Dunn that he had caught a glimpse of the stock inspector Rod Allen among the cedars on Paddy Murphy's Prong.

"Sure it was Allen?" Dunn asked sharply.

"Y'betcha. The boys josh me for packing field glasses, but if I hadn't of had them I wouldn't of known it was Allen."

"What was he doing there?"

"Brother, yore guess is as good as mine."

"Spying, like he's always doing," Duffield snarled.

Skillful ropers who knew all the brands rode in and out among the cattle dropping loops over the heads of calves and dragging them to the fire. Duffield came out with a stray calf that had been separated from its mother in the drive.

"KD," he announced, and the tally keeper jotted it down in a little book. KD was Duffield's brand.

A man in leathers went down the rope, caught the squirming calf under the flank and the shoulder, and flung it to the ground. He put his weight on it while another puncher held its hind legs taut. As the red-hot iron burned into the hair and flesh an acrid smoke rose. After the ears were slit the calf was released. It rose, shook itself, and ran bleating to a cow that had pushed its way to the edge of the herd. East noticed that the cow carried a Slash 72 brand. Before them all Duffield had just stolen a calf belonging to the Carruthers brothers. Apparently none of the others had noticed the brand of its mother. Both animals had already disappeared into the herd.

From a place in the ring of riders holding the herd Stuart called a warning. "Look who's coming."

Three riders had emerged from a land dip to the top of a rise and were headed for the roundup grounds. The roping and branding was for the moment forgotten. Men watched the horsemen moving toward them at a road gait. The new arrivals were Rod Allen, Hal Carruthers, and Cash Morley of the Diamond Tail. They pulled up a dozen yards from the fire.

"Aren't you a little previous?" Allen asked with acid sarcasm. "The roundup is set for next week."

"Your roundup, not ours," Dunn told him curtly.

"The only legal one," Morley flung out angrily. He was a short, thickset man, wattled like a turkey cock and as red. Arrogance rode in his manner and speech.

"To hell with that stuff," Duffield cried. "We'll hold a roundup whenever we please. If you don't like it, lump it."

"Take care, Duffield," Morley warned contemptuously. "Or you'll get in trouble."

"Meaning that you'll have yore hired warrior kill me?" Duffield asked, glaring at him.

"I don't hire anybody to kill my snakes for me," the manager of the Diamond Tail retorted boldly, eyes fixed on his challenger.

"Come—come, gentlemen, this won't do," interrupted Carruthers. "We're here to straighten out this business, not to start trouble."

"Call off your wolves then," Dunn advised brusquely. "Order them to lay off our stock and leave our fences alone. Make them quit bullying homesteaders."

"And killing decent folks," added Yorky.

"It hasn't been proved that any of our men do that," Carruthers said. "Let us stick to the present issue. One roundup is enough. Why two?"

"To protect our rights," Dunn told him.

"You would get fair play at the regular roundup. You would all be there to see that."

"We've been there before and we think different," Stuart disagreed. "The big ranches run it and don't give a damn what we think."

Several others concurred in this opinion.

Carruthers made another suggestion. "Since you are interested in your rights you won't object to me protecting mine by having a rep ride with you."

Dunn thought that over. It was a reasonable request, with the undercurrent of a demand. To refuse it would be to break a fundamental rule of all roundups, that any cattle owner in the neighborhood was entitled to participation. "I'll talk that over with the other boys," he said.

The ranchmen of his group drew to one side and discussed the proposal. If they allowed the representative of the Slash 72 to ride with them they could not refuse other outfits the same privilege. Duffield favored refusing permission. That would bring a showdown and they might as well have it now as later. But the wiser heads opposed this. It would be better to have the law on their side before they made a clean break. Dunn urged a compromise, to let the big ranches choose three riders to represent them all. This the others accepted.

Dunn reported to the three outsiders what they had decided. Angrily Morley rejected the offer. He was entitled to have a representative of his own, even if this was a rump roundup without any legal standing. Carruthers was all for consenting to the proffered terms. He said he would get in touch with several of his neighbors and try to bring them to his point of view.

The three men left the roundup ground with Morley still simmering.

CHAPTER ELEVEN

SQUATTED ON THEIR HEELS, in that pre-dawn semidarkness when the first gray rumor of day was streaking the sky, twenty punchers gobbled their breakfasts preparatory to rolling up their sleeping-bags for a camp move. The graveyard shift of wranglers was driving in the cavvy from the feed ground so that riders could select their mounts for the morning circle.

Rod Allen sat a little apart from the others. He was one of the three representatives selected by the big ranches to see they did not get the worst of the calf-branding. That his presence was poison to many of those here he knew. If it disturbed him he gave no sign. His hard, leathery face was expressionless, the watchful eyes in it cold as iced marble. He was a big-bodied muscular man, strong of body and will. To the small stockmen and homesteaders it seemed that he went out of his way to show his insolent scorn of them.

The cook packed his chuck wagon, and the men tossed their rolls into the bed and lashed them down. While they were saddling their horses the cook started for the new campground on North Fork.

"All up?" Dunn asked, his eyes sweeping over the group.

One had just roped his bronc and several were tightening cinches but Dunn did not wait for them. They would join the others presently. The men rode into the day just breaking over the hilltops.

East lined up beside the stock detective. He had noted that nobody spoke to the man except for some brief necessary word.

"You are not exactly popular, Mr. Allen," the Texan said lightly, smiling at him.

Allen slanted a hard, searching look at him. "I'm sure worried about that," he replied.

"You've got a tough job, one that must make you enemies. Don't you feel a little nervous riding with this bunch?"

"Why should I? You haven't noticed any of them treading on my toes."

"No. I reckon that wouldn't be quite safe. I wasn't thinking of your toes."

The lids over the jade eyes narrowed. "You were thinking they might plug me in the back. Have you heard any declared intentions?"

"None. Dunn wouldn't want that. Only some crazy fool would do it."

"But several would like to, if they had the guts. That it?"

"They are some edgy just now on account of the Baxter killing."

"Putting that on me, are they?"

"I wouldn't say so." East laughed ruefully.

"They put it on me to start off. But they are certainly looking for someone to put it on." He added, after a moment, "I wouldn't deny you're way up on their list of suspects."

"Why? What evidence?"

"Not much. There's a rumor you were in the neighborhood when two of these four ranchmen were killed, and I've heard that you had a fight once with Carlton."

"I whopped the stuffing out of him because he called me a liar, if you call that a fight. He's the one would bear a grudge, not me."

"I'm only telling you what I've picked up from talk." East grinned defensively. "I'd say they suspicioned you on account of your disposition. By their way of it you act like they are riffraff you would sweep into the trash dump."

"I never had any use for thieves," Allen said curtly. "They might as well know it."

East lifted his hand in a mild gesture that included the pack of riders in front of them. "Would you say all these homesteaders and small-fry cattle owners are thieves? That would not be my opinion."

Dunn stopped on a knoll and assigned his men to territory for the gather. East with four others was given Twelve Mile Creek to comb. It was rough country with plenty of brush along the stream and hill pockets higher up on the watershed. The riders had to plow through thorny tangles. They were chasing animals that had not been worked since last fall and were wild as deer and almost as fleet. In trying to head a small bunch from the mouth of a gulch East got out of contact with his neighbors. He cut off the stock and headed them downward toward North Fork. His glance picked up half a dozen more grazing on a hillside across a ravine from where he was. As he showed up they took alarm and raced into a draw, tails up and hoofs flying. Into a stony defile he followed them at a gallop, expecting to swing them to the left at the bottom. But it became apparent to him soon that he was in a gorge cutting through the ridge which bounded the watershed his group was working. They were leading him out of his assigned territory. Giving up the chase, he rode back to the mesa above.

The cattle he had left here had drifted and were feeding along the foot of a hogback which ran out as a spur from the rampart above. He crossed the mesa at a jog trot, working close to the ridge along the rock-strewn slope at its foot. He could see that a draw parallel to the hogback and skirted by a thick grove of young aspens led to some sort of dry water-run that in the rainy season probably fed the North Fork.

Uneasy at the sound of his presence, the stock took up the march again to escape his interference. They traveled in single file along the edge of the aspens. He stayed well back of them, to avoid frightening them into a stampede. When he got them out of this hill country to the plain it would be easier to handle them. They would be more used to the sense of a suggested direction.

The crack of a rifle sounded, and a slug thudded against his foot. He flung himself from the saddle on the far side from the rimrock, landed on his feet, and dived into the thick grove of aspens. As he plunged forward his arms and shoulders flung the slender boughs aside. Twice more the rifle boomed. East knew he could not be seen through the screen of leaves about him. The gunman must be firing at the agitation in the foliage. A dip in the ground befriended the target. He dropped into it and followed the trough running parallel to the hogback. Here the aspens were not so dense, and he worked his way down without betraying his movements. The six-shooter in his belt was no long-range match for a rifle, and his urgent desire was to get away from there as quickly and quietly as possible.

The first shot had torn the heel from his boot, and his foot was still numb from the shock of it. His guess was that the killer had not found time to set the scene. He had seen East about to disappear into the ravine that would lead him down to the plains, and he had flung a long shot in the hope of stopping him. East felt that this man stalking him was the phantom assassin who had murdered Jim Baxter and three other homesteaders. The fellow had become alarmed at the rumors he had heard and made up his mind to get rid of the witness who might know too much.

Below the aspen patch the water-run dipped steeply into a rocky ravine. On the edge of the grove his cow pony was quietly grazing fifty yards away. A man afoot in this country was at a great disadvantage. East debated with himself a moment before deciding to make a run for his mount. The gunman might still be on the rimrock watching for another chance at his victim or he might be on his way down to cut him off from escape.

The closely packed young trees protected him for half of the way, but the last twenty yards he had to take in the open. He had snatched up the reins and was vaulting into the saddle when the first shot came. It flung up a spurt of dirt five yards in front of him. His pony swung on its tracks and jumped to a gallop. The crash of the second shot echoed down the hogback just before he reached the shelter of the aspens. They were both long tries at a moving target and neither of them had scored a hit.

The stone-cluttered gully into which he had dropped widened into a small canyon descending straight to the undulating bench below, which from this height looked level as a dance floor. He was in a hurry to reach it, for once out of the hills the fellow back of him could not attack without coming into the open and being recognized. That would not suit the assassin at all. The chances of meeting another rider driving in his gather would be too great. East put more pressure on the cattle in front of him. Whether they stampeded was no longer important to him.

A dozen times he looked back before he reached the mouth of the canyon to make sure he was not being followed by a killer coming fast to destroy him. When he came out on the rolling tableland he breathed freer. A few hundred yards from him a cowboy was topping a rise with a bunch of young stuff in front of him. As the cattle converged East recognized the wearer of the big Stetson with a rattlesnake skin around the band. The man was Happy Jack.

"Thought we'd lost you, Texas," Happy Jack called to him. "The country up there sure stands on its end."

East agreed that the hills were some tangled. He slewed around in the saddle to take another look at the exit of the defile from which he had just come. A rifleman might risk a shot from there and then disappear into the pockets among the crags and buttresses of the range.

"What was all the shooting about?" Happy Jack inquired.

"Fellow after big game," East told him.

"Must have been a grizzly, the way he kept pluggin' at it."

"No. A man."

Happy Jack turned startled eyes on him, and at the same time noticed the heelless boot and a hole in the leather tapadero. "Goddlemighty!" he cried. "Someone taking a crack at you."

"Five cracks," the Texan corrected.

"But—why?" The cowboy goggled at him.

"He thinks I know too much."

"About what?"

"The murder of Jim Baxter." East explained. "There's been fool talk about my seeing the killer. The fellow is afraid it's true."

"What fellow?"

"He was up on the rimrock. I didn't even see him."

A big-boned steer broke up the conversation by starting to bolt. East put his horse to a gallop in pursuit. When he had turned the animal back to the others he stayed on the far flank to guide them. Just now he wanted to be alone with the thoughts that churned furiously up in him.

There were two rifles in camp, and they belonged to Duffield and Dunn. They had been brought along ostensibly to kill game for the use of the camp, since plenty of deer and antelope ranged in the country they were working. Most of the time these weapons lay in the bottom of the chuck wagon, but it would not be difficult for anybody wanting to use one of them to slip it from there unobserved. On the other hand a man riding circle could not take a Winchester with him and escape notice, though it was possible he might get possession of it the night before and hide it where he could lay his hands on it in the hills. But that would be to assume the fellow could know what territory East was covering—and only Dunn could be sure of that in advance.

It was quite likely that the man who had just tried to murder him was not on the roundup at all. The trapper Daggs came to his mind. More than once he had wondered if he was not the phantom killer. The rider he had seen crossing the road shortly before the ambushing of Jim Baxter had been mounted on a roan or a sorrel with white stockings. He had never told that to anybody, nor had he mentioned that the fellow wore a low-crowned black Stetson. The first time he had seen Daggs the trapper was riding a horse and wearing a hat that fitted this description. Moreover, the man's occupation was one that permitted him to range the country at will. East's suspicion was quickened by the evident interest Daggs had shown in his movements. Also there was his habit of squirting tobacco juice at a target.

Yet in the *remuda* on this roundup there were a dozen ponies of a roan or sorrel color with white stockings. Both Duffield and Dunn had one in the string they rode. And half of the cowboys chewed tobacco.

As soon as East reached the campground he went to the chuck wagon, apparently to look for his roll but really to discover if the two rifles were still in the bed. Neither of them was there.

The riders were coming into the branding-ground, two of them dragging small dead trees they had roped for the cook's fire. With each arrival the gathered herd increased, and the dust of their restless hoofs filled the air. The sound of bawling cows and calves was almost constant.

CHAPTER TWELVE

ACROSS THE SADDLE in front of him Dunn had an antelope he had shot. From a remark he dropped, East gathered that he had not been riding circle but had stayed down in the plains to bring back some game. Presently Duffield reached camp. He had no rifle with him.

Happy Jack broke the news of the attempt to kill East. "What do you know, boys? Some guy up in the hills came pretty near bumping off Texas. Shot the heel off his boot."

East became the center of attention. Without appearing to do so, he watched three men to see how they took it. If Dunn and Duffield were not surprised, they put on a good act. Allen's impassive face registered nothing.

He said, with a thin smile, "Two of us unpopular, I reckon."

The Texan met directly his blank eyes. "Seems I warned the wrong man."

"Why would anybody want to kill you?" Duffield demanded suspiciously. "You fixed up an alibi, didn't you?"

"I had one, if that's what you mean. No fixing up was needed."

"Something funny about this," Dunn commented.

"Yes," East answered dryly. "I nearly laughed my head off."

"Looks like someone wants you dead—*if* you were shot at."

"I heard a lot of shots," Happy Jack volunteered.

"Same here," Stuart said.

Dunn's hard gaze raked East. "Question is, who fired them?"

"That's right," the Texan agreed blandly. "I probably shot at myself while I was asleep."

"The bullet tore through the tap after it hit his boot," Happy Jack explained. He added, a chip on his shoulder, "What's the idea in claiming Texas did it himself?"

"I didn't say so," Dunn retorted. "Let's have a look at the stirrup."

Happy Jack brought the saddle, and Dunn examined it. "Could be that one bullet took off the heel and went through the edge of the tap," he said, and pointed a question at East.

"Any reason you know of why somebody is hell-bent on collecting you?"

"I can guess." The Texan looked steadily at the foreman of the roundup. "He's the fellow who crossed the road in front of me just before Jim Baxter was killed, and he has a crazy idea I saw more than I did."

"And you figure he's with us here on the roundup?"

"I don't know who or where he is. But I can tell you where he was an hour ago—up on the rimrock trying to pick me off with long shots."

"By yore say-so," Duffield jeered. "Look here, fellow. There are only two rifles with this outfit. Dunn went hunting with one and got him a buck. The other belongs to me, and it's lying in the chuck wagon right now."

"Sure of that, are you?" East asked.

"Course I am." Duffield walked to the wagon, rummaged among some sacks, and turned a startled face to those he had just left. "It ain't here."

There was a long pregnant silence. Someone murmured, "Not there?"

Duffield called to the cook. "Doc, you move my rifle?"

The cook shook his head. "Haven't touched it."

The big man lumbered back, the head on his heavy rounded shoulders thrust forward. "I'll skin the hide off'n the fellow who took it," he threatened angrily. "Or anybody who claims I had it today."

"I rode beside you when we left this mo'ning, Duffield," Yorky spoke up. "You didn't have it with you then."

"Not then or any time since I laid it in the wagon." Duffield's face was dark with rage. "Some of you know where that rifle is. I want it." His fury broke on East. "You're at the bottom of this. It's a play to get me in bad because I was for stringing you up. I've a mind to whale the stuffing outa you right damn now."

The Texan's cool eyes rested on the man's brutal face. "I ought to tell you, Mr. Duffield, that I don't whale easy," he said gently.

Duffield was an outrageous bully who loved to beat up smaller opponents. His knotted fist swung at the Texan, whose head moved lightly to one side and let it pass over his shoulder. East turned quickly, his back to the bully, caught the hairy wrist in both hands, and leaned forward with a lunge. The man went over his head, body whirling like a wheel, and struck the ground heavily on his back. He lay there motionless for a moment, the breath knocked out of him, then scrambled awkwardly to his feet. He was still dazed, still shaken by the fall, but his outraged pride would not brook any delay. Like a wild bull, he charged at the Texan.

East sidestepped, caught the blow on his forearm, and drove a hard right to the man's neck as he passed. Duffield came in again, a savage snarl rumbling in his throat. He was a notorious rough-and-tumble fighter, and he meant to beat this Fancy Dan into insensibility as soon as he could. His fists were flailing like the blades of a windmill, crashing in with a pile-driving force that might have felled a two-year-old steer. Most of the blows East ducked or deflected, taking them on his arms and shoulders when he could not avoid them entirely. His foe was flatfooted and slow, and he telegraphed his punches before they started. But even so the face of the Texan was bruised and bleeding, though he ended the flurry of fists by pumping two damaging lefts into the belly of the ranchman that sent him back grunting.

Duffield sucked in a deep breath and attacked again. But East had found the Achilles heel of the fellow, and he kept slamming swift jolts into the fat belly. He was a trained boxer, with long, smooth muscles swiftly responsive. His footwork was something to see, and the movements of the arms and long slim body were rhythmic as well-oiled machinery. Though his opponent outweighed him fifty pounds and was far stronger, he did not know how to utilize the advantage. The Texan smothered his blows, danced out of range, blocked wild swings, and hammered fists that hurt into the midriff that had grown soft from years of heavy drinking.

The big man puffed like a porpoise. He kept plowing in, hoping to end the fight with one lethal blow. Until now he had always won his battles by savage slogging, by hammering his foe until he could no longer stand and take it. What bewildered him was that he could not land on a vulnerable spot. This saddlebum was too fast on his feet, and the fellow's sharp clean-cut counters tore into his stomach and kidneys so fast that he could not parry them. Waves of nausea swept through him. His arms were so heavy he could hardly raise them, and his legs dragged as if they were weighted with lead. His breath came raggedly. He realized with a sense of shock that unless he could close with the Texan and get him to the ground by sheer physical force he was beaten.

Duffield heavy-footed forward, arms low to protect the body. A right and a left slashed at his face. He grunted, trying to crowd close. East stopped him with a smash to the cheek that rocked his head. The big man glared murderously at his enemy and shuffled to the attack again, head bent low and arms outstretched. East whipped an uppercut beneath the jaw, then slipped past the reaching fingers.

"Come in and fight, blast you," Duffield gasped.

He stood, feet spread wide, panting heavily, the big fists hanging helplessly at his sides. *Time for the knockout,* East thought, and set himself for the blow. He drove it to the chin, all the force of his weight back of it. The big man swayed, tried desperately to steady himself, tottered, and went down like a tree that has been felled. He lay where he struck, lax and inert.

The Texan looked down on him, then with surprise at the blood-soaked bandage on his own finger. The wound he had torn open was throbbing painfully. He had been too busy to notice it.

Happy Jack spoke first, a wide grin on his face. "I never expected to see this joyful day and be right on the spot in a grandstand seat." He let out a whoop of delight. "I'm sure loving to see Mr. Beat-'em-up Duffield get his comeuppance after he's been askin' for it so long."

Allen said, his cold eyes narrowed, "You're quite a John L. Sullivan with your fists, Mr. East, but Duffield isn't going to like this and soon as he is able he is liable to stagger to his roll for a gun." He added pointedly, "If I was in your shoes I'd hop a bronc and light out for a while—say about twenty years—unless you are as handy with a six-shooter as with your dukes."

"He didn't give me any option," East said quietly.

"Maybe not," Dunn snapped. "But I won't have a killing on this roundup. Fork yore bronc and beat it, East."

The Texan thought this was a good idea, even though the invitation for him to go had not been given in quite a friendly spirit. He roped his pony, saddled, and waved a good-by to Happy Jack.

His finger was hurting a good deal, and at the first brook he stopped to bathe it in the cold running water. For a bandage he used a strip of the bandanna he had been wearing around his neck.

Ruefully he smiled at his reflection in the pool. "Jerry East, you're the doggonedest guy for getting into trouble. Here's another bunch of it unloaded on yore lap. This fellow Duffield will be plenty sore."

He remounted and rode to Powder Horn.

CHAPTER THIRTEEN

JERRY EAST COULD BE STUBBORN, but not to the point of folly. He did not in the least mind running away when the odds were too great for him or when reason dictated a retreat. This was not his roundup, anyhow. Why stay and be forced into a gun fight in which either he or Duffield would be killed? Moreover, there was another danger it would be folly to incur. An unknown enemy was anxious to get rid of him and would have succeeded if he had caught him at closer range. It was not likely he would give up with only one try. In this rough country of open range his chances of success were too good. Jerry had come here for one definite purpose and he did not intend to have it defeated because he was too obstinate to use good sense. At Powder Horn, if he was careful, it would not be easy to assassinate him without detection.

East tied at the rack in front of the hotel, then strolled down to Jake Parsons's store for a sack of smoking. Nell Herrick was there buying groceries. She gave him a smiling nod, and he rolled a cigarette and smoked it while she finished getting what she wanted. Her basket was heavy with supplies. He picked it from the counter when she was ready to go. As they

116

came out to the sidewalk two men rode up and dismounted. Each of them had a deer tied to his saddle. They had evidently just come back from hunting. The men were Daggs and Sanborn.

The remittance man came forward and stepped to the sidewalk with the indolent grace of a cat, but East noticed that his eyes had grown quick with life and that red spots burned in the woman's cheeks that had not been there a minute before.

"Journeys end," Sanborn said lightly, and let his steady gaze carry to Nell Herrick the rest of the quotation.

East read in her eyes, disdainful and a little defiant, that she was telling the man this one was not ending in lovers meeting.

"You got a deer," East commented.

"A good hunter usually brings home game," Sanborn said, but the Texan was aware that the underdrift of the words was a challenge to the woman.

Her low-pitched, husky voice mocked him. "A deer is a poor, defenseless creature," she replied, "but you have to carry a powerful rifle to destroy its free and happy life."

"When a man goes out to hunt he uses the weapons he has. All's fair in—war." His bland smile was confident.

The Texan guessed that under this double talk was an edge of conflict based on a strong attraction. Beneath Nell Herrick's anger ran a wild current of emotion. She turned on him hot, tawny eyes sparked with tiny gold flecks.

"If you are ready, Mr. East," she said.

He nodded, but before he moved had another word to say. "Dunn got an antelope today on the North Fork," he mentioned. "Where were you hunting?"

"In the hills back of the North Fork valley."

Sanborn's casual answer had come with no instant of hesitation, but the thought was strong in the Texan's mind that these men had been quartering over the district where he had been riding circle a few hours earlier. It would have been possible for one of them unknown to the other to have fired the shots at him.

Nell Herrick walked beside him down the street with rhythmic ease, as if merely living was a joy. He was conscious of her tall and slenderly full body, so electric with vitality, even while his mind was speculating about Sanborn's place in the picture.

It was plain that his grace, his good looks, and a certain sardonic indifference would attract women. He was the kind that would take what they had to offer and lightly let them go. But any nonchalance he might affect toward Nell Herrick was a pretext only. He was drawn as strongly to her as she was to him, though it might be only a temporary infatuation. It would not hurt his conscience to wreck the Herrick home.

But East felt the man did not fit into the role of a superficial hunter of women spurred by cheap vanity. There was more to him than that. He had the leashed strength of a coiled spring. But whether the force in him was good or dark and sinister he did not know. Nor could he tell whether there was a weak link in him.

Mrs. Herrick broke a long silence. "I thought you were at the roundup."

"Dunn sent me back. I had a little trouble."

"With Mr. Dunn?"

"No." He smiled wryly at her. "Fact is, I had two spots of it."

"You've been in a fight." She glanced again at his battered face. "Or have you been in two?"

"Just one today. I ran away from the other, if you could call it a fight."

"Better tell me about it," she said. "I might as well know now as later."

He told her the story of the day's adventures, ascribing his victory over Duffield to luck.

She let her eyes drift over his well-packed shoulders and the poised co-ordinated power of his lean body. It occurred to her that luck might not be the word to explain Duffield's defeat.

"Good gracious! For one who looks so gentle you certainly do have a knack of getting into trouble," she told him. "And of course you know you are not out of this. Duffield is mean. You have hurt his pride. He won't rest till he gets even. I think you had better go back to Idaho, Mr. East—or maybe Texas. That is farther."

"I'll have to risk Mr. Duffield's annoyance," he replied cheerfully. "I want to find out who is so anxious to collect me."

"And why, I suppose?"

"I think I know why." He gave her what he thought was the reason back of the attack on him.

She nodded assent. "That must be it. Of course you are mad if you stay here. There is no defense against a dry-gulcher."

"I'll be careful," he promised, and added, "Man is born unto trouble, as the sparks fly upward."

"You are a very lighthearted, foolish Job," she said. "How can you be careful when you don't know who your enemy is—the other one, not Duffield? Or do you?"

"No. I have several possibles in mind. Would one of these do? Duffield—Dunn—the stock inspector Allen—Daggs—Sanborn."

She instantly eliminated Sanborn's name from the list. "He isn't that kind of man. If he wanted to kill you he would do it openly—pick a quarrel with you before everybody." Color beat into her face. "I know him very well. He simply could not have murdered these settlers. It just isn't in him."

"I'm glad to hear it," he answered. "There is something likable about him, though he is wild and lawless. He is a dangerous man, but he does not look evil."

"Who isn't dangerous in this Western country, if he is worth anything?" she asked impatiently. "You are. My husband is, even if you wouldn't think so to look at his quiet tolerance. I wouldn't be interested in a man who isn't."

He could believe that. It gave him a new light on her marriage to Herrick. She had found in him some quality that had struck a spark to her imagination, something more exciting than the solid integrity of a good middle-aged citizen.

East was full of a live curiosity about this woman. She had character. But was there a quicksilver in her blood that made her too restless to tie her life permanently to that of one man? He was of opinion that Steve Sanborn had been at some time a factor in her past and he felt sure the pressing desire was in him to dominate her future.

They passed through the gate and down the path between the rows of jonquils to the Herrick house. The sheriff had just come in from a duty call into the country and was unsaddling at the barn. He joined them on the porch.

Nell asked her husband if his trip had been successful. He told her the trouble was of no importance. Spud Clancy had imbibed too much tanglefoot and made himself obnoxious with a six-shooter but he was now repentant at his folly.

"This Texas man has been getting himself into another jam," she said, and told Herrick what had occurred.

He was distressed and added his voice to those who thought East ought to be on his way.

"He won't go," Nell responded. "Of course there is a reason we don't know. He came to Powder Horn for some private purpose and he is just mule enough to stay and get killed."

In that country one did not probe into the reasons why a man came or went. It was up to him to tell as much or as little as he pleased.

"Mr. East must do as he thinks best, Nell," her husband said gently. "All we can do is point out the danger in staying."

"At least he ought to let us know to whom we ought to send word of his death after it happens," Nell said. "It would save us some trouble."

East smiled at the sheriff's wife. "It won't be that way, Mrs. Herrick, but since you have smoked me out I might as well come clean. I'm here to find out who killed my brother, Henry Carlton."

After a moment the sheriff spoke. "Then your name isn't East."

"Yes, my name is East. His name wasn't Carlton. At Yampa he got in a jam with the law and had to light out. Or thought he did. Leaving was a mistake. He beat up a deputy sheriff who came to replevin a horse he had bought without knowing it was stolen. So he came here and changed his name."

"And became a victim of the phantom killer," Nell murmured.

"Yes," East answered grimly. "I've asked several about his local reputation. If he rustled stock nobody seems to know of it. The reason generally given for his murder is that he had homesteaded a claim on a creek where the Diamond Tail cattle grazed and watered."

In the sheriff's reply there was caution. "I didn't know your brother, but I never heard of any harm in him."

The eyes turned on the sheriff by the Texan had cold lights in them. "You know Cash Morley. Ever hear any harm of him?"

Herrick responded stiffly, with obvious reserve. "Morley is not well liked by the smaller ranchmen. They claim he is overbearing."

"Is that all they claim? The first night I reached this town at least two men practically accused Morley of hiring killers." East's voice was even and low but it held an edge of ice.

"That hasn't been proved," the sheriff said.

"No. All we know is that all of the men who were dry-gulched lived close to the boundaries of his range and were in his way."

"That might be said of other big cattlemen."

"I've seen Morley. His manner is arrogant, his face smug, and his blue eyes would freeze a Christmas party. I'll put my money on him."

"And what will you do about it?" Mrs. Herrick asked.

"I'd like to get a job working for his outfit.

Maybe I can find out something if I'm around the Diamond Tail." East's chilly smile was for the benefit of the sheriff. "I'm not going to take the law into my own hands, if that is what you are afraid of."

"Glad to hear that," Herrick answered. "If that's a promise—"

Nell finished for him the uncompleted sentence. "Neither Charles nor I will breathe a word to anybody of what you have told us."

This time the Texan's smile was warm. "I didn't think you would."

The woman looked directly at her husband. "He thinks maybe Steve Sanborn is the phantom killer."

Herrick met her eyes and held them for a long moment. He shook his head. "What makes him think that?"

"Just that he has a rifle and sometimes goes out hunting. If Mr. East has any other reason he didn't give it to me."

The sheriff said gravely, "You can put that notion out of your head, East. He is not cold-blooded enough for that and he cares nothing about money. Sanborn is his own man."

East agreed that they were probably right.

"Are you packing a six-shooter?" the sheriff asked.

"Not right now," the Texan drawled. "I have one in my roll."

"Get it out," Herrick advised. "I don't believe in gun-toting and rarely carry one myself. But if you are going to stick around here—"

"With an open season on you," his wife interrupted.

"And Duffield in particular out for my scalp," East added.

"Unless you are bulletproof," Nell scoffed, "and have a special arrangement with God to look after you." She was annoyed at his insouciance. His intention of staying troubled her. She had come to like him, his whimsical smile, the reserve back of his easy friendliness, and she did not care to think of his warmth and supple strength forever gone.

"If I have I'll never forget that I'm His deputy appointed to do the job," he assured her.

Walking back to the hotel, East's thoughts were of the two he had just left. Herrick was a man who would do to ride the river with, strong and patient and understanding. His wife might be a rebel against conventions, but the Texan had never known a woman in whom life flowed more abundantly nor one more likely to let the current of her emotions sweep her against the rocks. They had been good to him. He wished there was something he could do for them in return.

CHAPTER FOURTEEN

A FRINGED SURREY WAS TIED at the hitchrack in front of the hotel. The near horse carried a Slash 72 brand. Amy Truesdale came out to the porch. She was dressed in a flowered-print dress and wore a straw sailor hat with two ribbons down the back. At sight of East her dark eyes brightened.

"What's the matter with you?" she asked after catching sight of his face.

"I ran against a door."

"You've been fighting."

"How did you guess it?" he drawled.

"With that sore finger. You ought to know better."

"Yes," he agreed, and added, "It was the other fellow who didn't know better. He forgot about my finger."

"Who was it?"

He shook his head. "Let's talk about you."

She brushed that aside. "Father and Mr. Hal Carruthers were coming to town. I want to buy some things, so I came along." The girl hesitated an instant before plunging on with what was really in her mind. "If you were to ask Father for a job with the Slash Seventy-Two I think he would take you."

He laughed. "You've softened him up for the

126

saddlebum, have you? Did you tell him I was riding with the small fry's roundup?"

"No. Were you?"

"Until they kicked me out."

Carruthers and his foreman came out of the hotel. Truesdale looked the cattleman in every crease of his dusty corduroys and calfskin vest. He had the settled spread of middle age and had gathered weight without fat on his bulky frame. Crisscross wrinkles furrowed the back of his coffee-tanned neck.

"This is Mr. East, Father," Amy said. "Mr. Carruthers has already met him."

"Several times," Hal Carruthers said. "On two of the occasions Mr. East was the innocent villain."

Amy flushed. "I was the villain once, but Mr. East has forgiven me."

Her father looked the Texan over with no approval. "I must apologize for my daughter's folly. She is a badly brought-up brat."

"A little impetuous," East corrected genially. "But her unhappiness ought to be considered in mitigation."

"I don't understand you," Truesdale told him bluntly. "The scalawags of this district put a rope around your neck. A week or two later you are riding with them on an illegal roundup."

"We are taught to forgive our enemies," East explained in bland mockery.

"A man is judged by the company he keeps," the foreman said dourly. He was put out because he had come to town prepared to offer this man a job and had just learned East was riding with the opposite faction.

"They drove him away from the roundup," Amy pointed out. She had asked her father to employ the Texan and she did not like the way the situation was working out.

"What for?" demanded Truesdale.

East lifted a hand in a gesture of indifference. He did not care for the foreman's manner and in any case he did not want to work for the Slash 72, since he had other plans. "It's a long story. I don't reckon we'll go into it now."

"If you want it that way." The foreman spoke to his daughter. "We'll be pulling out for the ranch in about twenty minutes. Any shopping you've got to do you had better hop to."

He turned his back on East and walked away. Carruthers hesitated, shrugged his shoulders, and followed.

Amy was disappointed. "You and Father both acted like boys with chips on your shoulders. Don't you want to work?"

"Not for a man who starts by bullying me." He smiled, to take the sting out of his refusal. "Maybe I'm a little too choosy. No reflections on your father."

Amy sighed. It was difficult to make plans for

other people who did not know what was best for them. "Dad *is* bossy," she admitted. "I'm awf'ly sorry. I thought—Oh, well, I can't make you come."

Her mobile face reflected every change of mood in the girl. East guessed she had set her heart on getting him a job at the Slash 72. It would have been, in her own mind at least, a sort of compensation for what she had done to him. That he had struck the bright and shining eagerness from the girl's face disturbed him.

He said, gently, "I'm sorry, too. It was good of you to try."

She answered wistfully, "Like Father, I don't understand you."

It came to him again, as it had when he had first seen her in an attractive dress at the sheriff's house, that she was going to blossom out into a beautiful woman. When he had first seen her lean, lithe body in the soiled, rough clothes of a range rider, her face distorted with grief, she had seemed to him an ugly little thing. The uncertainty of youth still hampered her, but the bone structure of her face was fine in composition and the eyes lovely.

"You are going to be beautiful some day," he told her.

His words surprised himself. He was not given to easy compliments. Perhaps he had felt her young pride needed some buttress against defeat.

Astonishment held her silent. She stared at him, lips parted and breath suspended. Color beat into the planes of her cheeks.

"What's the use of saying that?" Her voice was sharp with resentment. "I've always been an ugly duckling. Anyone with eyes can see that."

"I had no right to say it," he admitted. "But it's true. Ask Mrs. Herrick."

"I don't need to ask her. I have a looking-glass."

"You are not pretty. Beauty is something deeper. Women don't have it until they have lived. It sort of glows from inside."

She searched his eyes. There was none of the sardonic mockery she had more than once read in them. He meant it. That was the amazing thing. The warmth of a new hope flooded her face and justified his prophecy.

"It glows there now," he said.

The pink in her cheeks deepened, ran to the roots of her hair. She slipped quickly past him and ran into the hotel, shy as a wild fawn.

CHAPTER FIFTEEN

EAST WENT TO HIS ROOM and loaded the Winchester he had left in a corner. He mentioned to the clerk in the lobby, for the benefit of anybody who might be listening, that he was going out to have a look for game since he had seen three men bring in meat that day. Forking his horse, he rode out of the south end of town at a road gait, but before he had traveled a mile he cut sharply into a draw leading into a country of low rolling hills. He kept away from the benches when possible and followed ravines where he would be most likely to escape observation.

He carried Amy in his mind. A girl so young would soon get over her grief for Jim Baxter and in this land of few women would inevitably marry. Some women could choose for a husband any decent man and be contented with him. But not Amy. She was like a spirited young filly and must be handled gently but firmly. No man could make her happy unless she deeply loved and respected him. If she found such a man Jerry believed she had a capacity for a rich life.

His thoughts drifted to another woman. He was not sure that Nell Herrick's nature would allow her to be satisfied with any man permanently. There was a current of unrest in her, a longing for something she had not yet found. That she would not find it if she went to Sanborn the Texan was convinced.

These reflections did not interfere with alert watchfulness. His gaze searched closely the scrub on the hillsides, scanned every wash and hollow carefully. It was his opinion that safety for him depended on a never ceasing wariness. He came to a brushy scarp dotted with box elders and decided not to ride the defile below it, but made instead a wide detour through dry gullies that brought him to a tableland he had to take. His mount clambered up, and he saw a wide bench well-grassed. In the distance there were cattle on it. Two men were driving them toward a line cabin near which was a corral. He returned the greeting they waved him. No need to be afraid of men he met in the open, not with a rifle within reach.

From the far end of the bench he could see the distant pocket that sheltered the buildings of the Diamond Tail. He let the pony pick its way along the sharp rocky drop to the valley below. A gate opened into a ten-mile pasture, and for an hour he rode across its uneven floor. The sun was sliding into a crotch between two peaks. Presently a pattern of gold and scarlet and purple slashed the sky back of the sierras. Soon it would be dusk.

As he topped the last rise he saw pinpricks of light in the still faraway ranch house. They guided him on the final stretch of his long ride. Before entering the lane leading to the yard he made sure his six-shooter lay free in its holster. He was not expecting trouble, but it might jump up at him.

A man came out of the bunkhouse and bow-legged across the yard toward the big house. He caught sight of the rider and flung out a question.

"How come you are late for chuck first time in yore life?" he asked. When East rode into the fan-shaped triangle of light from the house the cowboy added, "Thought you were Bill Roper."

"I came to see Mr. Morley," East said.

"Better light and tie. He's probably at supper now. I'll let him know you are here. Any name?"

"Jerry East. Tell him not to hurry. I'll wait."

The Diamond Tail man looked at the stranger more intently. He had heard a good deal about him of late. Seemed he was the kind of guy who stirred things up when he was around.

"Sure. Make yoreself at home."

East tied the bridle to the rack, strolled to the porch, and sat down in a big armchair. He rolled a cigarette and relaxed.

Half an hour later a short, plump man strutted out to the porch. He was smoking a cigar. "Want to see me?" he demanded.

"That's right, Mr. Morley," the Texan said. "I heard you could use another man during the roundup and for a while after."

He had risen and he topped the manager of the Diamond Tail by six inches, but the latter's arrogance made him feel taller.

"I don't hire men who have been riding in this bastard roundup."

East drawled, "Then I reckon that lets me out."

Morley had expected some apology or protest. He was not ready to have the man eliminate himself so promptly. His representative had ridden in a few minutes ago from the roundup with an unusual story involving this stranger.

"You had a fight today with Duffield, I've been told," the manager said.

"You've heard correctly," the Texan answered in his soft Southern voice.

"And there's some fairy tale about you being shot at in the hills."

"News to me."

"You weren't shot at?"

"I didn't say so. I said I hadn't heard the fairy tale."

"Well, were you or weren't you?" Morley barked. "You'll find it doesn't pay to get funny with me, my man."

East was nobody's man but his own. However, he did not raise the point, since he had not come here to quarrel with this little spitfire.

"Somebody took a few cracks at me," he replied.

"Why?"

"I did not wait to find out. I lit out pronto."

"But there must have been a reason. You've got a guess what it is?"

"Sure. I was around an hour or so before Jim Baxter was killed. A cowboy crossed the road in front of me. At quite some distance. I would not know him from Adam. But some crazy stories were started about me knowing who he is. They are all bunk. I haven't a ghost of an idea."

"You think he was trying to get rid of a witness?"

"Nobody knows me here. I have no enemies. It's the only reason I can figure out."

"Dunn kicked you out of the roundup today."

"After my fracas with Duffield. He didn't want any difficulty in camp."

"So you come to me for a job. Why?"

"I told you why, Mr. Morley. A fellow in town told me you needed a rider."

Morley's cold blue eyes searched him. "I don't need a troublemaker. Any fighting my men do is at my orders."

"Fair enough," East agreed. "If you'll inquire you will find out that Duffield jumped me. I had to defend myself."

"Have you had supper?"

"No, I haven't."

"Go to the bunkhouse and tell Solly Moore to see you get some. Stay there tonight. I'll think this over and let you know in the morning."

After supper East returned to the bunkhouse. He discovered that though the men were shy about questioning him they wanted full details of the fight. They were delighted that Duffield had at last walked into the thrashing he had long been inviting. The stranger in their midst told a very dull story. He reckoned he had been kinda lucky in jarring the wind out of Duffield by flinging him over his head sort of unexpected. That probably took the pep out of the big fellow. Soon as Duffield was down, East had lit out. He had been mighty glad to escape.

It was disappointing to hear this poor-spirited tale after the story the ranch rep had told of the thorough thrashing Duffield had received. The ranch hands had wanted to welcome a hero, and the fellow would not give them a chance.

"Must be some mistake," Solly said in disgust. "This guy couldn't of whopped Duffield unless someone had roped the big fellow's fists to his sides."

In the morning Morley sent for the Texan.

"What's the idea in your sticking around with someone gunning for you?" he asked. "Why don't you light a shuck for parts unknown?"

"I'm some stubborn," East replied. "I don't like to be kicked around. When I'm good and ready I'll leave."

They had moved into the office of the manager.

Morley seated himself back of the desk and waved the other man to a chair.

East thought, *He wants something and he is going to proposition me.*

The cold blue eyes of the Diamond Tail man rested for a long time on this lank, lounging stranger. "I need a man," he said at last, "but that doesn't mean you will fill the bill."

"If you want one like me I'll do fine," East said.

The ranchman ignored this pleasantry. "He's got to have sand in his craw, be plenty tough, plenty smart."

"This territory is supposed to be a country with the bark on," Jerry suggested. "There ought to be men like that around."

"I hadn't finished," Morley snapped. "He has to be my man one hundred percent—take orders and ask no questions." Solly Moore passed the window on his way to the corral. "If I told him to beat up Solly with a two-by-four I would expect him to do it."

"Sounds like a nice job. I can see the fellow who took it would be popular."

"I'm just using Solly's name as an example. He is one of my best men. The point is, I'm not hiring somebody to debate with me but to do as I say. The pay would be liberal."

"Including doctor's bills, in case I was the one got busted up."

Morley lifted a hand in an impatient gesture. "I'm not expecting to use you as a bruiser. What I'm telling you is that I want a man wholly loyal. Are you good with a six-shooter?"

"I'm supposed to be." East asked with cool insolence, "Do you want someone killed?"

The eyes of the men met, hard and probing, and held fast.

"No," Morley replied. "Nothing like that. But war is coming to this country, the way things look. Where would you stand if it does?"

The Texan said promptly, "I wouldn't be in it— unless someone made it worth my while."

The cowman nodded, pleased that he had read this drifter aright. "So I thought." He studied the Texan with blue icy eyes. "It might be worth your while—if you are tough enough and not too squeamish."

"Maybe you had better talk some more about that, Mr. Morley." East leaned forward, an elbow on the desk. The Diamond Tail man read the glitter of greed in his eyes.

The ranch manager talked, his voice almost a murmur. He chose words carefully, to hint at a good deal not said. The time was coming when a man had to be on one side or other. It might be necessary to hire a few good men to keep the thieves from stealing the big ranches poor. The pay would be good and the risk small.

138

"How good?" East demanded. "I wouldn't work for peanuts."

"Well, that would depend." Morley's voice was suavely businesslike. "This thing may not come to a head for two—three months. Until then I couldn't pay more than fifty a month—unless there was a special job, in which case the pay might be big—run into the hundreds."

"How come you picked on me?" the Texan wanted to know.

"On account of what my rep at the roundup, Rod Allen, told me about your fight with Duffield, who is a hard man to handle. I am convinced the fellow is a rustler. Since you have quarreled with him and he will be ugly as a bear with a sore paw until he has stopped your clock, you can't throw in with his crowd. You will be safer with us. I thought you might see it that way, too."

The Texan's laugh was sarcastic. "You are taking me on as a favor to protect me. Listen, Mr. Morley. I've been around quite some. When the time comes for me to do the special job I'll set the price."

"We'll cross that bridge later. For the present you will have an easy time. Go back to Powder Horn and don't let anybody know you are working for me. Hang around the saloons and mix with the nesters and homesteaders. Keep your ears open. Don't come out here unless I send for you. Once a week Solly Moore will be in town. Report to him what they say or plan to do. Talk like you hate the big outfits and are in sympathy with the rustlers. If you can spot any of the fellows who are branding our calves that will be good."

"I don't get you," East answered offensively. "A minute ago I couldn't play with Duffield's crowd for fear he would get my scalp, now I'm to sleep three in a bed with them. It can't be both ways."

"Stick close to town and there can't be any dry-gulching. When Duffield is around you can lie low if you are afraid of him." Morley added callously, "A man who can't protect himself from Duffield in the open isn't any use to me."

East said almost in a whisper, his eyes narrowed, "Might be a good idea to bump him off from an alley some night when he is in town."

The ranch manager raised a plump protesting hand. "Don't ask me how to take care of him. I'm not interested. He's your problem. I haven't a thing to do with it, even if he is a no-good scalawag."

Rod Allen walked into the room. His hard eyes shuttled from Morley to East and back again. He said insolently to the little man back of the desk, "So you and this saddlebum are side-kicks now."

Morley's face flushed almost purple with anger. "Somebody appointed you manager of this ranch, Allen?" he asked.

"I'm only a cattle inspector," Allen jeered. "Naturally I'm some surprised to see the boss of the Diamond Tail hobnobbing with a fellow who has just quit riding on the rustlers' roundup."

"If it's any of your affair, I've just been telling East that for the very reason you have given I can't employ him on this ranch."

"I see. And you bring him into your office to tell him that nice and private."

Jerry East could see that this was not a tiff that had flared up over a momentary irritation. There was some hostility between them much deeper than annoyance. This surprised him, for he had heard repeatedly of the close association binding them. More than once he had listened to a hint suggesting Allen as Morley's killer.

"I bring him into my office because I choose to do so."

"Perhaps you don't choose for me to be here," Allen retorted.

Morley glared at the inspector and with difficulty choked down a furious retort. "You're acting foolish, Rod," he said thickly. "I don't want any trouble with you. Stay here. This fellow is getting out."

East backed his new employer's play. He said mildly to Allen, "I been trying to tell Mr. Morley that I'm not tied up with any rustlers, but I can't get him to see it that-away."

He walked out of the office and to the corral. On the chance that he might hear something more he saddled leisurely. But Allen was still in the office with Morley when he left. On his way to town he again made use of the ravines and gulches that crisscrossed the terrain.

That he was making progress he felt sure. All the difficulties which had harassed him were working to his advantage. But for them Morley would not have hired him. The threat of lynching, the suspicions of the small settlers against him, the fight with Duffield, were assurances to the manager of the Diamond Tail that he did not belong to the opposite faction. The action of Dunn in dismissing him from the roundup confirmed this.

That Morley was implicated in the death of his brother he was now more convinced. The man had not said directly that he wanted to use him as a killer, but the thought had been in his mind. No man needed two assassins. It began to look to East as if he intended to get rid of the killer he already had. Was that killer Rod Allen? The man was bold, ruthless, and wary. In a wild and careless community such as this he was remarkable in that he had no minor vices. He did not gamble, drink, or use tobacco. This did not fit in with the evidence against the killer, who seemed to chew tobacco copiously. But that might be a herring across the trail.

Jerry East did not like what he was doing. It left a bad taste in his mouth. He would have preferred to play his hand openly, but it was only by deception that he could bring to justice those who were guilty. It relieved his conscience to know that the path he was treading was a perilous one.

CHAPTER SIXTEEN

JERRY EAST DID NOT INTEND to throw down on himself. Even in town he took precautions against being ambushed or taken by surprise. If he sat in a game of poker his back was to the wall with the window and door facing him. When he went into a store or a saloon it was by a side entrance. At night he did not sit in a lighted room unless the curtains were drawn. Yet he was careful not to let these safety devices be noticeable. Nobody watching his casual ease could have told he was under a strain.

He saw Nell Herrick one morning stepping from her husband's office. She waited for him to cross the street.

"I caught a mess of trout yesterday," she said. "Will you join us at supper tonight?"

He said that would please him very much.

Nell tilted her head at the door through which she had just come.

"Charles is inside," she told him in a low voice. "He has something to say to you."

She walked down the street, and he turned into the sheriff's office.

Herrick was making out an expense account with the stub of a pencil. He slewed his head around to see who had come into the room.

"I been lookin' for you," the officer began.

East threw up his hands. "Don't shoot, sheriff. I surrender."

"Dick Stuart just left. He was in from the roundup to buy some supplies. He was talking about your rookus with Duffield. Afraid that is unfinished business, Jerry. The old blister left camp soon after you did as full of p'ison as a rattler. Swears it's going to be you or him, one."

"He's taking it too hard. Somebody was bound to lick him eventually. Anyhow, he crowded me into the fight."

"He's full of swollen pride, and he can't take it," the sheriff remarked. "Are you heeled?"

"Yes."

Herrick's face set to a worried frown. "I don't like this at all. But what can I do?"

"Not a thing. It's in my lap."

East was right. The sheriff could not lift a hand to stop Duffield. If he killed the Texan in a fair fight it would do no good to arrest him. Public opinion would demand his release. The unwritten law of the frontier was that a man must protect himself. The .45 strapped to his side was both judge and jury.

"I can get word to him that if he starts any gun play it must be on the level."

"That would suit me." East added grimly, "Though it won't stop him."

"It might stop him from killing without warning."

"Yes. He would not like to be strangled for murdering me."

"Stay under cover till I get word to him. No use being foolhardy. If I hear he is in town I'll notify you."

Though East did not go into hiding, he was careful not to expose himself unduly. When he went around corners he took the middle of the street. Duffield always tied at the hitchrack in front of Gann's when he came to town. The Texan checked the ponies there before he walked out of the hotel.

Instead of taking the road to reach Herrick's he went by way of the riverbank and up through the pasture. Nell was rolling biscuit dough. She said through the open window, "Come sit in the kitchen till Charles gets home."

"This is the sort of thing that makes a bachelor feel he is missing life," he told her after he had seated himself where he could keep an eye on both window and door.

"If bachelors went into kitchens oftener and got the rich odor of good cooking there would not be as many," she assured him.

"You would make men materialists," he charged. "I was thinking of the cook and not her products."

She slid a derisive look at him. "You are becoming very aware of women—going around telling girls how beautiful they are."

He shook his head. "Can't be me. You have the wrong man."

"And sending them around to me to agree that it is true."

"Amy Truesdale," he said. "So she came to you."

"Blushing and hesitating, to ask me if it wasn't ridiculous."

"And you told her?"

She cut the biscuits out and put them in the pan before answering.

"What did you expect me to tell her?"

"Amy was unhappy because she could not convince her father and me that I ought to work for the Slash Seventy-Two. So I gave her something else to think about."

"You certainly did. She has always been considered an ugly little brat."

"As a kid she probably was. She is still a little stringy. I was looking ahead a year or two. Amy is going to be a fine-looking woman."

"You couldn't get a popular vote to endorse that opinion," Nell said dryly.

"No. Most of us are blind to all but obvious beauty. But you are not." He added, after a moment, "Well, what did you tell her?"

She heard her husband coming up the porch steps and put the biscuits in the oven. "I told her not to think you a Columbus because you had discovered what everybody would see in a year or two, that if she learned to dress she would be the loveliest girl in the county."

"Who is this that is going to be the loveliest girl in the county?" Herrick asked, coming into the kitchen.

"Amy Truesdale."

"Hmp! Maybe—if you don't count married women." The sheriff's eyes rested on his wife. They told her that no woman in the world could touch her for looks.

The color in Nell's face did not deepen, but her eyes shone with pleasure. There was a dash of flour on one of the bare forearms she put around her husband's neck. "That's worth a kiss, my man," she told him gaily.

It was a good, clinging kiss, warm and soft, with a touch of passion in it. To see it made Jerry East feel better. Somehow the picture of Steve Sanborn was pushed into the background.

Before they sat down to dinner Herrick drew all the curtains close. "Somebody might want to look in on our happy family," he said lightly.

Not until they had finished eating did he give East a bit of news. Nell had gone into the kitchen with some of the dishes. The sheriff did not want her to hear it.

"Duffield is in town," he whispered.

East said, after a ponderable moment, "Where is he?"

"At Gann's, drinking. I saw him tie and presently dropped into the saloon. I wasn't in time to hear the question he asked Casey, but I caught the answer. Casey said, 'I don't know where he's at.' Duffield noticed me, and the subject was dropped. But if a look could talk Casey's look at me did."

"What did it say?"

"It said, 'For God's sake, keep East away from this man.'"

The Texan drummed on the table with his fingertips. He was making up his mind what to do.

Nell came back from the kitchen and was at once aware of a significance in the atmosphere. She looked from one to the other. "Well, gentlemen, let's have it," she said.

East came back to the party with a forced smile. "Like I was saying, Charles, if Nell has a sister can cook like her I want the address."

"Liar," Nell said evenly.

"Might as well tell her, Jerry," Herrick advised. "She won't rest till she finds out."

"I'll guess," Nell volunteered. "Duffield is in town looking for Jerry."

"He is in town," the sheriff corrected.

"What are you going to do?" Nell asked East quickly.

"In a little while I'm going home to bed," he replied.

"You won't go looking for him?"

"No. I don't want to see him."

"But if he sees you?"

"There won't be any trouble unless Duffield starts it," East said.

"Why go up town at all? You can stay here. I can make up a bed."

East looked at his host for help. Certain obligations of men were hard to explain to a woman. "No. I'll go back to the hotel the river way and slip in the back door. I'll avoid him if I can—but I won't hide."

"That's just your silly boy pride. Do you have to let a drunken ruffian bully you into being killed?"

"I don't intend to be killed." He appealed to Herrick again. "Explain to Nell how it is, Charles."

"I didn't want you to hear about this," the sheriff said to his wife gently. "But since you know, I'd better tell you how it stands. Duffield has come to town to kill Jerry. That's public knowledge. He has boasted of his intention to half a dozen men. Jerry can do his best to keep out of the fellow's way in the hope that he will cool off. But he can't crawl into a hole. And when they meet, if Duffield lays it on the line, Jerry has no option but to fight."

Nell gave up. A man on the frontier had to live by the code of his fellows. It did not matter what a woman thought. She did not count when his masculine pride was involved.

She sighed, letting out the breath slowly from her lungs. "If you must, you must," she submitted.

"I'll walk uptown with Jerry," the sheriff remarked. "Want to close up the office."

Both of the others knew that what he wanted was to make sure of fair play.

Nell said to her husband, "Come home soon."

He nodded, smiling at her. "I hear my boss." He knew what her appeal meant, that he was to come home and tell her there had been no trouble.

CHAPTER SEVENTEEN

THE SHERIFF AND HIS GUEST walked back to the hotel by way of the river path. It was a soft velvet night of moon and stars. A pattern of light and shadow sifted through the branches of the cottonwoods above their heads and silvered the rippling river. East's thoughts were somber. There was no urge in his heart to kill Duffield. He had no feeling against the man. A current stronger than himself was driving him to an issue he could not avoid. Men were put into a beautiful world and made of it a hell. To his mind flashed a snatch of hymn he used to sing at Sunday School in a little town on the Brazos. *Though every prospect pleases, and only man is vile.*

Herrick said, "If it comes to a showdown, watch his every move and beat him to the draw."

Like most well-meant advice this had no value. Of course East would be watching Duffield with intense concentration, reading his mind, muscles and nerves keyed to swift action—if the fellow's shot did not come as a blast of surprise.

They left the riverbank and walked past a mound of cans and empty bottles to the rear of the hotel. A man came out of the back of the saloon and recognized them.

"Well, look who's here," he cried. The man was the cowboy Yorky.

"Shut your trap," the sheriff ordered. "East isn't looking for trouble."

"He's gonna find it, anyhow," Yorky retorted, a note of jubilance in his voice.

They went past him into the hotel. East took the back stairway to his room, and Herrick followed the corridor to the lobby. Two or three loungers sat in the chairs. The sheriff gave them a casual nod and passed by the side door into the saloon. The games were going, and there was a small group at the bar. Most of the latter were cronies of Duffield.

Through the back door Yorky came hurriedly and joined them. He said, with quick excitement, "The guy you're lookin' for sneaked in the back way just now."

Duffield swung round and demanded harshly, "Where's he at?"

"I dunno. In the lobby, maybe." Yorky's glance picked up the sheriff. "Ask Herrick. He was with him."

The drunken bully snarled at the officer. "Where's he hidin'?"

"Take it easy," Herrick suggested evenly. "Maybe this can be fixed up. East will be reasonable. Sleep on it. Tomorrow—"

"We'll settle this right damn now," Duffield interrupted. He pushed through the door into the lobby. "Where's that fellow East?" he yelped.

Gann broke the heavy silence that followed. "I haven't seen him since before supper," he told the angry ruffian.

"That don't go. Yorky saw him come in by the back door."

"He must of gone up to his room by the other stairs," Yorky volunteered.

"What room?" Duffield snapped. The question was a command. He stood over the hotel owner huge and explosive.

"Twenty-one," Gann replied. "I'll send word—"

The big rancher brushed past him and headed down the corridor, half a dozen others at his heels. They were taking the back stairway. Herrick went up the main one three steps at a time. He ran along the hall and pounded on the door of room twenty-one.

"Duffield is on his way up," he called.

East flung open the door. Already he had come to swift decision. "I won't be here," he answered. "Tell him I'll walk down River Street tomorrow morning at ten o'clock."

He slammed the door shut and went out of the open window. Beneath it was a lean-to shed. The Texan's feet found the clapboards. He slid down and dropped off.

Keeping close to the house, he ran around it, raced down the alley, and vanished into the night.

Duffield and his cohorts found Herrick standing in front of room twenty-one. "Get outa my way," the ranchman ordered.

The sheriff stood aside. "He isn't here."

Duffield slammed into the room waving his revolver.

"He's lit out." The man's voice was hoarse with the rage he had worked up. His fury expended itself in puerile destruction. He flung a bullet through the cheap-looking glass over the bureau, then pushed the .45 back into its holster. Snatching up a chair, he broke it into pieces against the foot of the bed. A shirt lying on a pillow he ripped to shreds. A tintype of a middle-aged woman he trampled into bits beneath his feet. The Texan's roll he tossed out of the window.

Not until the man's mad anger was spent did Herrick give the message left by his friend.

"East told me to tell you he would walk down River Street tomorrow at ten o'clock in the morning." The officer spoke with grim, hard finality. "He does not want any trouble, but he will pack a six-shooter. If you have a lick of sense you will go home tonight and stay there, Duffield. But if you are fool enough to go on, remember one thing. This will be a fair fight in the open. If one of you forgets that I'll help hang him to a telegraph pole."

"I don't need any shenanigan to get this

fellow," Duffield boasted. "But he's flown the coop. Scared stiff. He won't show up."

"Don't bank on that," Herrick warned. "He'll be on River Street, like he says he will. You've been letting liquor talk for you. Cool off and forget the whole thing."

"I'll see him fry in hell first."

Duffield clumped out of the room and went back downstairs to the saloon, where he lined up at the bar again with those who abetted him and bolstered his confidence.

"Texas will be fifty miles from here before mo'ning," Yorky predicted. "Headin' back for Idaho. Well, that's one way to stay alive."

Casey gave them a refill and polished the bar. He was of a different opinion but he did not say so. This was strictly none of his business. His thoughts, however, were another matter. One of them was that if he were in Duffield's place he would not spend the night drinking. East would be on hand as he had said, and he was no man to face in a gun fight when one was carrying a hang-over and had jangled nerves.

Bowlegged Jody of the Slash 72 peered into his glass before downing its contents and found there philosophic wisdom. "A man is like a watermelon. You cain't tell whether it's good till you thump it. Take a guy. He thinks he's got it—figures he can stand up and take what's coming. Texas put up a good bluff, even with

156

himself, till you crowded him. Then at the last minute he got panicky and lit out. You never can tell."

At two o'clock Casey said, "Last drink, gents. We're closing."

CHAPTER EIGHTEEN

TO NELL it seemed hours before she heard her husband open the gate and come down the walk. She ran down the porch steps to meet him.

"I heard a shot," she cried. "What happened?"

"They haven't met. Duffield went after Jerry, but he had ducked out."

Nell was surprised. "Jerry ran away?"

"For tonight. He left word that he would walk down River Street tomorrow morning."

"A challenge?"

"I wouldn't call it that." Herrick explained. "He left to give Duffield a chance to change his mind. But the fellow won't do that. His idea is—and it is shared by those drinking with him—that Jerry has shown a yellow streak and will not be seen in these parts again. They are wrong. It would save trouble if they had him pegged right. But he'll be here."

"There will be a gun fight?"

"Sure as the sun rises tomorrow. After the bragging he has done Duffield can't back down, and he wouldn't if he could."

She had him tell her just what had occurred. He gave her one promise. There would be no sniping from ambush. He had made it clear to

Duffield that any foul play would meet with swift retribution.

"Where did Jerry go?" Nell asked.

Her husband smiled. "He was in a hurry and didn't leave an address. My guess is he is sleeping in the open. I went down to the corral. He had stopped to get his horse."

Womanlike, she was concerned about a detail. "He won't have any breakfast."

Herrick had made a good guess. East camped four miles down the river in a clump of cottonwoods. He sat before the fire for a long time, his mind occupied by the situation which confronted him. It was none of his choosing, though it had sprung out of his purpose to bring to justice if possible the murderer of his brother. It was strange how a man could become such a victim of circumstances. His memory dragged out of the past a snatch of verse. A schoolteacher from New Hampshire had come to their little town on the Brazos, a girl with a head full of poetry she was always reciting to them. *So free we seem, so fettered fast we are.* It was true. All he had to do was to saddle his picketed horse and ride out of this mess he was in, but he could not do it any more than if Herrick had him ironed hand and foot. He had to stay and see this out.

The standing of Duffield in this situation was not clear to him. He was a notorious bully, always eager to show his prowess, a savage who took pleasure in inflicting pain and humiliation on those weaker than himself, and in addition he was a fellow of ungovernable temper. That was enough to explain his attack on East at the roundup camp and his determination to have revenge for his defeat. But there might be a deeper motive. The man might be the unknown killer. He was a rustler openly in the camp of those fighting the big ranches. But Morley was a plotter. It would be a shrewd trick to employ one of the hostile group to destroy his own associates.

Morley had shown no desire to protect Duffield but rather the reverse. There might be a reason for that. Since the rustler was a ruffian of uncontrollable rages, he might no longer be a safe tool for the manager of the Diamond Tail to employ. East might have been sent back to town from the ranch in the hope that he would be forced to kill Duffield. That was a question only later developments could answer.

The Texan fell asleep at last and woke with the warm sun beating on his face. There was no hurry. It would be well not to reach town until the time he had set. To stand around waiting for his foe to appear would do the nerves of the big rancher no good. In his impatience he might resort to Casey's bar for stimulation.

East stripped and bathed in the cold water of the river fresh from the snowbanks of the mountains.

The shock of the plunge sent a tingle of well-being through his blood. He lay in the pleasant warmth of the sun and let thoughts happen. There was no use dwelling on the ordeal ahead of him. He could make no plan to set the scene. At some point as he walked up River Street he would meet Duffield. The ranchman would hardly dare to shoot him down from cover, not with the eyes of all the town on him. He would have to take his fighting hazard.

But though East forced himself to think of other things, the moment his will released its clutch a picture of the duel projected itself before his mind. He must not get nervous or jumpy, nor at the last instant let himself get in too much of a hurry. No use firing panicky shots from too great a distance. His job was to kill a man, not because of any hatred but to save his own life.

He brought in his horse, saddled, and headed for Powder Horn. The pony he held to a road gait. From a thicket in front of him a deer broke with a great crackling of brush. His startled mount did some crow-hopping.

"Steady, Cap," East said, gentling the animal. "Nobody is gunning for *you*."

As he drew into the outskirts of the town he glanced at his watch. It was eight minutes to ten. Soon now it would be over one way or the other.

In the pleasant sunshine Powder Horn looked

peaceful as old age. A woman was hanging washing on a line back of a log cabin. Three little girls were playing hopscotch.

At the corral he turned in and tied his horse in a stall. The owner of the wagon lot was not there. A sardonic smile twisted the lips of the Texan. Karl had gone uptown to see the killing.

While still in the stall East made sure his .45 lay lightly in the holster. It was now three minutes to ten. He had timed his arrival just right. Across a vacant lot he followed a path to River Street. His senses were extraordinarily alert. A scent of honeysuckle drifted to his nostrils. Back of a store a boy's piping voice was singing, "Good-by, my lover, good-by." Except for one man standing in front of Buck Swanson's saloon the street seemed empty of life.

The man was the cowboy Yorky. With the sun in his eyes he had to shade them to make sure that the person sauntering up the street was the Texan. Swiftly he vanished into the saloon. Evidently he had gone to report to Duffield, who must be in Swanson's place waiting for his scout. Unless it was a trick to catch East off guard.

A dog came out of an alley, stretched itself, and lay down comfortably in the middle of the road. From the alley walked a barefoot boy whittling a stick. A figure appeared in the entrance of Parsons's store and yelled to the boy to get off the street. The boy stopped, startled, then scuttled back into the alley. The dog put its head down on its paws.

As East moved up into the business section he saw that there were heads in every window and men posted on the roofs. His arms hung by his sides, the .45 still in its holster. From the sheriff's office Herrick stepped.

"Duffield is at The Good Cheer," he warned. "Careful he doesn't catch you with the sun in your eyes."

An awning shaded the sidewalk in front of the office. Rillings's saloon was half a block down.

"I'll wait here," East decided. His eyes would be shaded, and the enemy could not get at him from the rear.

The swing doors at Rillings's were pushed open, and Duffield came out. He had been drinking ever since he came to town but he was not now drunk. At sight of the Texan he gave a yelp of triumph.

"I've got you where you can't get away, you damned saddlebum," he cried. His six-shooter was in his hand, half raised.

The distance was too great for accurate shooting. East's arm still hung by his side. "I'm not looking for trouble, Duffield," he answered in a clear voice. "You're forcing it on me."

"You bet I am." The ranchman flat-footed heavily forward. His weapon swept up, and the gun roared.

East's .45 came out marvelously fast, but he held his fire and let the big man get closer. A bullet ripped through his coat.

The sound of the ranchman's third shot was echoing through the street canyon when East's finger touched the trigger. Duffield let out a groan, and his left hand clutched at his stomach. He swayed on his feet, then staggered forward, still firing, to meet a second blast from the Texan's revolver, this time in the heart. The big body of the man stiffened, seemed to hesitate a moment before the knees buckled and let Duffield, already dead, plunge into the dust.

From a dozen buildings excited men poured out to the street.

Herrick got in the first word. "Self-defense," he pronounced loudly. "East tried to talk him out of it. He let him have the first shots. And he had to kill the fool to save himself."

"That's sure right," Cad Withers agreed, swimming with the current as usual. "Duffield was a mighty hard man to get along with. I'm plumb easygoing, but two—three times he came pretty near jumping me."

Half of those present had at one time or another faced the same experience. One old-timer summed up the general opinion curtly with the judgment, "No regrets."

The sheriff took East with him into his office and closed the door.

"I reckon you don't want that mob fussin' around you," he said.

East put the revolver back into its holster. He was not happy over what he had been forced to do. "It is a silly, bad business," he told Herrick dejectedly. "There was no need of it, if he had used any sense. I don't see how I could have avoided it—except by running away."

His friend put a hand on the Texan's shoulder. "I know how you feel, son, for I had to do it once. I felt mighty bad. He was a worthless, no-'count horse thief, but he was a human being. If it's any comfort, Duffield was a bad egg with very little good in him. And nobody can say he didn't crowd you into it."

He took East home with him for dinner, and Nell exerted herself to feed the guest well and to keep the conversation light. She was greatly relieved the danger was past. What Jerry East had done left no crosscurrents of doubt in her mind. She liked and admired him. He was intensely masculine, and his strength was on the side of good. Duffield had stood for evil. He was better dead.

CHAPTER NINETEEN

JERRY EAST HAD PLAYED the part of a drifting saddlebum both because the role explained his presence in the district and because tongues would loosen to freer gossip in the presence of so aimless and amiable a character. But he had become involved in a tangle of circumstances that made it impossible for him to maintain the impersonation.

The duel with Duffield had made him a marked man. In the minds of those he met he was now a killer, though the reputation of a dangerous gunman was one he did not at all want. When he walked into Gann's saloon he was treated not only with respect but with a certain caution. Nobody slapped him on the back or made him the object of any pleasant foolery. Half a dozen settlers in the neighborhood had committed homicide, but none of them on a stage set deliberately before the whole town. A hundred eyes had seen the Texan saunter coolly up the street, let his raging foe pour shots at him, then destroy the aggressor with deadly efficiency. It was a story that would be told by some of the witnesses for forty years.

In front of the barbershop he met Solly Moore one morning.

"At the wagon yard in half an hour," he murmured without stopping.

Presently he drifted down to the corral ostensibly to make sure Karl had fed his horse. The owner of the yard was greasing a wagon. East sat on the tongue and chatted with him until he saw Moore riding down the street. The Texan reckoned he must be going and timed his departure to meet the Diamond Tail man just outside the gate.

"Tell Morley I'm not doing him any good here," he said. "I haven't a thing to report."

"Someone was telling me Duffield got bumped off," Moore said dryly. "Maybe you haven't heard it."

"He got hell in the neck and drank himself into a coffin. Does that interest Morley?"

"I wouldn't know. I'm just a hired hand. Fellow, you sure go to town."

"Nothing to that. I had to save my bacon. The point is, folks kinda walk around me now. They button up their lips. If there is anything going on they don't tell me."

"All right. I'll let the old man know how it is. Maybe he'll want you out at the ranch. Be seeing you."

Moore rode into the wagon yard, and East strolled back uptown. If in killing Duffield he had already done the special job for which Morley had employed him the chances were that he would be discharged now, but if the victim Morley had in mind was somebody else it would be likely that he would be recalled to the ranch. His deductions were based on the surmise that the manager of the Diamond Tail was back of the dry-gulching of the four settlers. Granted that this was true, it followed that he did not need two assassins. The use of a second would increase the danger of detection—unless the purpose of hiring him was to get rid of the first. This was sheer guesswork, East realized, but he had a strong hunch that it was near the truth.

He passed between the sheriff's office and the poolroom adjoining the river and sat down on the bank. It did not disturb him that he had plenty of time on his hands, and he watched the water fling up foam against the boulders in the bed of the stream.

A voice hailed him. Herrick was standing at the back door of his office. "How about siding me on a ride? I've got a call into the country."

"Why not?" East answered. "I'm not doing a thing but watching the grass grow. Soon as I can slap a saddle on my bronc I'll be with you."

They jogged out of town at a road gait.

"Where we headed for?" Jerry asked.

"To Dunn's place. He sent in word by Stuart that someone had set fire to one of his haystacks early this morning."

"Could it have been an accident?"

"Dunn says not." The sheriff added a worried comment of his own. "Funny thing. Maybe just a coincidence, but a few days before each of these mysterious dry-gulchings some property of the man later killed was destroyed and an ace of spades left on the spot. Chapin found one of his steers dead with a bullet through its forehead not a hundred yards from his house. In your brother's case it was a colt shot in his pasture. Radway had a windmill blown up and Jim Baxter a wagon load of lumber burned. Looks like the killer was giving them a chance to light out of the country before he rubbed them out."

"You think somebody is serving notice on Dunn that he is next."

"I hope not. But Dunn is a leader of his faction. He was wagon boss of the roundup just finished. That hasn't made him popular with some folks."

From a bench they dropped into a valley where Dunn's ranch house was. He had a pretty good-looking spread. The house and adjoining buildings had been painted. They had an air of prosperity. There was still some smoke rising from the ashes of what had been a haystack.

Dunn stood in the doorway of his house and watched them ride into the yard. His hard gaze rested on East suspiciously.

"Got any idea who did this, Chris?" the sheriff asked.

"You mean who lit the match?"

"Well, yes."

"No evidence. If I guessed I might be wrong." Dunn pulled a hand out of his trousers pocket and showed an ace of spades. "But he left me this souvenir to let me know my number is up."

Herrick's face was very serious. "Be careful, Chris. Don't give him a chance."

"Fine. Who shall I be careful of?" His bleak eyes turned on East. "I hear you killed Duffield."

Jerry gave as answer the monosyllable "Yes." He let Herrick explain that he had been forced into it.

Dunn's sneer was offensive. "That so? The way it came to me Duffield had been boozing for twenty-four hours before you knocked him off. He was in no condition for a gun fight."

The sheriff intervened again. "Duffield spread the word all over that he meant to kill Jerry on sight. Whose fault was it that he filled up with liquor? He wasn't drunk at the time of the fight. You're barking up the wrong tree, Chris. Jerry did his best to avoid trouble."

"Queer that one so peaceable is always around where trouble is." Dunn flung a question at East. "Where were you this morning—say about four o'clock?"

"In bed asleep."

"Can you prove that?"

"No. Do you think I fired your stack?"

"Somebody hired by the big outfits did it. After

I kicked you out of the roundup you went to the Diamond Tail and had a powwow with Morley." His ice-cold steady eyes searched the Texan's face.

East drew a tobacco sack from his breast pocket, shook the makings carefully into a paper, rolled and lit his smoke. When he spoke it was gently, the words falling in a slow drawl.

"Mr. Dunn, I'm 'most grown up. I go where I like, when I like, with no nurse along. Don't get worried about me getting lost. Or being corrupted by bad company. Just take it easy."

Dunn was no Duffield. Unless his judgment approved, he did not let his temper explode. He had a reason to be sore this morning. But there would be no profit in going out of his way to pick a quarrel with this cool-eyed, brown-faced Texan. After all he had driven the man from the roundup. He could not complain if the fellow was friendly with the enemy.

"So it's not my business," he answered. "Maybe you are right. We'll find that out later." Abruptly he turned to the sheriff. "Do I sit here and wait till this phantom killer bumps me off?"

The sheriff had no ready answer for that, at least not one the rancher was likely to accept. "Why not leave your place with one of the hands in charge for two—three weeks until this business clears up? You been talking about visiting your sister in Cheyenne."

Dunn scowled, and his face set. His mouth became a thin, tight slit. "Where did you get the idea, Chuck, that I would let some damned brush wolf drive me from my ranch?" he asked.

"The county doesn't allow me much money for extras, but I could put a deputy on your place for a little while," the sheriff suggested.

"No," Dunn declined. "He couldn't do a thing. I'll look after my own hide. Spread the word that if I see anybody skulkin' around I'll pump lead into him and ask questions later."

The sheriff and his companion climbed the bench back of Dunn's place and struck across country for the wagon road. They descended into the plain, which from above had appeared to be flat as a billiard table but was on nearer approach wrinkled as a piece of stiff brown paper crushed in the hand. The floor was like a washboard road a thousand times enlarged, a series of gentle ridges and easy descents stretching far as the eye could see.

Between two of these ridges the wagon road ran and presently dived into a miniature gulch which dropped by way of red sandstone foothills to the valley below. Rounding a sharp bend, they pulled up abruptly.

In a deep cut below them was the stage from the north. One of the horses had been shot. Old Hank Wolff, the driver, was bathing the head of the shotgun messenger, who lay on the ground barely conscious.

Wolff looked up when they rode forward. "Holdup," he announced.

"Ferrill been shot?" Herrick asked.

"No, they whammed him over the head with the barrel of a Winchester."

"How many of them?"

"Just two."

"No passengers?"

"Sure." Hank looked around. "Where's he at?"

They found a man behind a huge boulder. He was an immensely fat man, a drummer, and his big dish face was splotchy with fright. He came out from cover, teeth still chattering, and wanted to know if they were sure the bandits would not return.

"Why would they come back?" Hank asked. "They got the gold shipment. You oughtn't to travel without yore mammy, Fat."

"Recognize them, Hank?" the sheriff asked.

"They looked like cowboys," the stage driver answered. "Both of 'em wore bandannas over their faces. The big one had on chaps, the other striped pants. They were waiting for us behind rocks, the big guy back of that boulder Fat here homesteaded later on. First thing, he shot my off leader. Course they had the deadwood on us. Ferrill couldn't do a thing but drop his Winchester when they hollered to him."

The shotgun messenger was coming back to the world. Hammers were beating in his head, and the ground was tilting up to the sky. He put a hand to his wet sticky scalp and looked at the blood with surprise.

"Holy smoke!" he said. "Jumbo pistol-whipped me."

"He slammed a rifle barrel against yore nut," Hank corrected.

The sheriff and East quartered over the ground carefully. They found where two horses had been tied. Since the spot was a rock cut the hoofprints were blurred. One was better defined than the others. It showed the track of a shoe worn thin along the outer edge.

Back of the boulder where the drummer had later taken refuge was a great splash of tobacco on a flat rock. To East's mind jumped a detail that Happy Jack had mentioned in describing the place where Jim Baxter's body had been found, brown smears of tobacco juice not yet dried squirted against the timbering of the bridge under which the assassin had waited for his victim.

"You chew tobacco?" East asked the drummer.

"No, sir, I smoke cigars." He added, his voice tremulous in spite of his wish to make it hard, "If I'd had a gun—"

"Too bad I didn't know you were a fighting man," Ferrill jeered. "You might of had mine for all the good it did me."

"Which way did they go?" Herrick asked.

"They took off for the hills," Hank said. "Hole-in-the-Wall gang."

"Likely," the sheriff agreed. "You carrying much gold?"

"Considerable, I reckon. The box was some heavy."

"You check on their mounts, Hank?"

"Never even saw the horses till they were quite a ways off."

"Did you say you wouldn't know either of the holdups again, Hank?"

The driver looked at Herrick out of hard, wary eyes. "How would I know two masked guys, seeing I didn't get a look at their faces?" He offered information for what it was worth. "One of the birds was big as all getout, the other kinda medium."

"Stetson hats?"

"Yeah—black ones. Boots kinda scuffed." Hank referred this description to the shotgun messenger. "That how you sized them up, Ferrill? I was busy with the horses. They were acting up some account of one of them being shot."

The shotgun messenger grinned wryly. "I reckon. They both looked about eight foot to me and their six-guns cannons. But probably Hank is right."

"How come you got slammed on the head?" the sheriff asked.

"My error. I dropped my sawed-off when they first covered us, and after I hopped to the ground I reached for my forty-five to hand it to the guy standing nearest. He mistook my intentions and cracked me on the noodle with his gun barrel. I can't rightways blame him."

The sheriff pressed for more accurate descriptions of the bandits, but did not get any information that would differentiate them from a hundred others. The smaller fellow, Wolff mentioned again, was wearing striped pants and a blue-and-white-checked flannel shirt. He did not talk much, and when he did it was to give an order that carried authority.

They dragged away the dead horse, unhitched its neighbor, and put the still groggy messenger inside the stage. The two wheelers dragged the coach back to town, where the news of the robbery created a mild sensation, one that would have been much greater if the stage had not already been held up three times within a year. Powder Horn was on the route from the gold fields to the railroad, and the bullion shipments were tempting to the semi-outlaws in the hills who found it lucrative to turn road agent occasionally.

Herrick organized a posse of five to take up the hunt for the bandits. Among the special deputies were Sanborn and East. The sheriff did not expect to capture the guilty men. Their horses' hoofprints, if the posse picked them up at all, would thin down to a vanishing-point long before the riders disappeared in the Hole-in-the-Wall, a refuge of ranges with a hundred defiles, innumerable pockets, and lonely creeks inhabited only by those who had broken the law and flitted to and fro in these hiding-places unknown to honest men.

"It's one of those needle-in-a-haystack propositions," Sanborn told the Texan. "If we follow them into the Hole it will be filled with absentees. In a week we might not see a soul. In case we did he would be innocent as Mary's little lamb and couldn't tell us a thing. But Herrick has to make a bluff, and someone has to ride with him. So we're elected."

Twenty-four hours later East was ready to agree with Sanborn. This was a country torn and twisted by upheavals of nature many centuries ago. They had ridden into gorges, climbed the shoulders of steep ranges, and crossed rocky divides without catching sight of any of the skulking nomads who infested this no man's land.

"Looks like we're the first explorers ever dropped into this neck of the woods," East suggested.

"Quite a few wanted gents hole up here," Sanborn differed. "They know this lonesome region as a schoolmarm does her A B C's. Right now some of them may be looking down on us from the rimrock of that hogback. If so, I hope they haven't got itching fingers. We wouldn't have a chance."

This had occurred to East several times. He could not help admiring Herrick, who had been a good sheriff for three terms and had driven into this outlaws' paradise several scoundrels who would like nothing better than to get a safe shot at him. He led the way, in and out of steep canyons and up boulder-strewn scarps, with a cool and resolute disregard of danger.

On the morning of the third day he decided to give up the hunt. Whatever slight chance of catching the road agents they might have had was gone now. Long ago the fellows had cached the gold and changed the clothes they had been wearing. To identify them would be impossible. There had been a faint hope in Herrick's mind of picking up one or two of the other bad men who had found refuge here when the law had been too hot on their heels. But that no longer seemed likely.

They were eating breakfast in a thin, fine drizzle with no promise of sunshine in the heavy sky. Two ways led down to the entrance of the Hole. One offered a fairly easy descent. The sheriff asked Sanborn with two others of the posse to take the pack horses and follow this route. He and East would travel by Dead

Man's Pass, a trail about which he had always been curious. It had a sinister reputation. He knew of nobody who had ever gone over it except the bad men who nested in this unknown district.

Herrick was not sure he could find among so many defiles the one that would bring him to this outlaws' path. He had been told that it dropped to the foothills from a park known as Smith's Retreat, a spread of level land well watered and grassed, named for a fugitive who had long since vanished from the scene.

"We'd better wait for you outside the gateway," Sanborn said. "To make sure some of these wolves haven't eaten you up."

"No. Go on to town. We'll be along later." The sheriff grinned at East. "Before any wolves eat us Jerry and I will give them considerable indigestion."

They packed the camp outfit, saddled, and mounted.

"Be seeing you—maybe," Sanborn called back to Herrick and East as the parties separated.

CHAPTER TWENTY

THE RIDERS DREW UP on the rim of the small park through which ran a little mountain stream. It was a charming spot, the floor strewn with wild flowers lending color to a background of lush grass. Among the cottonwoods at the far corner was a log cabin. Herrick judged the owner was not at home, since the time was noon and no smoke issued from the chimney. Nonetheless he did not take this for granted. When he and East circled the rim to get back of the one-room house rifles in their hands rested across the saddles.

They tied their mounts and slipped down on foot to the rear of the cabin. Through a four-pane window Herrick peered into the room. There was nobody in it, though there was evidence of possession. On the walls hung bridles, slickers, overalls, and chaps. The floor was littered with boots, old newspapers, socks, and soiled clothes. Provisions were packed on three shelves close to the stove. Four bunks had been built against one wall, two of them above the others, and on three of them bedding was tossed back carelessly just as each occupant had left it when he rose.

The door was not fastened, and they walked into the room. In the stove there were still some live embers. The fry pan was greasy and the dishes unwashed. On a shelf were some packs of dirty cards, poker chips, pipes, a plug of chewing-tobacco, and a half-empty sack of smoking. East found in the table drawer some old letters. There was also an empty envelope addressed to David Daggs on the back of which had been penciled what was evidently the scores of a pitch game. This Jerry put in his pocket.

He and the sheriff were not in the cabin more than five minutes. The outlaws might return in force at any time. A trail worn by many horse hoofs led to a gulch which in turn brought them after devious windings to a ragged wall rising several hundred feet above the surrounding terrain. Ages ago some convulsion had cracked this, leaving a passage through it so narrow that at times they could almost touch the smooth rock face with their outstretched hands. So deep were they buried that the sky above was a narrow ribbon of gray. The slope was sharp, but toward the bottom it became more gentle. The passage widened, with patches of grass here and there, and the walls were lower and less perpendicular. An angle deflected the path sharply to the right, and as the sheriff and his deputy rode around this elbow they came face to face with three horsemen.

The one in the middle was a huge hulk of a man, with heavy rounded shoulders, thick hairy wrists, a face red, coarse-featured, brutal, sullen.

The sheriff knew him—Anse Walden, very much wanted for murder. On his right rode Nick Fox, sometimes known as Half-Pint on account of his size. Meanness was written on his weazened face and in his sly and furtive look. The third member of this choice trio was a tall man, lank as a shad, loose-jointed, with small pig eyes set in a bony face stamped with vice and selfishness. Long ago Sink Curry had given hostages to the devil. His was a lost soul which believed in nothing good. They had one thing in common—these three scoundrels. Evil was branded deep on them.

They sat motionless, stunned by surprise, each of them assured that the sheriff had come for him.

"What in hell you doing here?" demanded Walden heavily.

"Heading for home," Herrick answered evenly. "Like to have you ride along with me, Anse. There's a charge against you."

"I got business here," Walden jeered.

"Ain't you out of yore bailiwick, sheriff?" Curry asked. "The law ain't supposed to pass the deadline at the gateway."

His horse did some dancing toward the canyon wall.

"Stay where you're at, Sink," Herrick ordered curtly. "And don't let your hand stray."

All of them knew that guns would flash very soon, but none of them were ready to start the battle. The outlaws were hoping to maneuver for position, the officer to induce two of the bad men to desert their leader.

"Drag it, Herrick," snapped Curry. "Beat it while yore hide is whole."

"Keep out of this, Curry," the sheriff said. "I don't want you just now. Anse will be all for today."

Fox did not like this setup. He was notably gun-shy, and Herrick had a reputation as a game man who would carry through.

"Now, be reasonable, sheriff," he whined. "We ain't lookin' for trouble. Like you say, I'm not in this. But you hadn't ought to take Anse when he's so busy with his stock. It ain't neighborly."

A crimson blotch of anger darkened the ugly face of Walden. "He's not taking me anywhere," the big man growled. "And you're in this clear up to the top of yore yellow spine. You'd like to run out on me. Try it, and I'll pour lead in you."

"Who's this guy with you, Herrick?" demanded Curry.

"A deputy," the sheriff answered. "Mr. East— from Texas. The man who had to rub Duffield out."

The story of the duel had already reached the Hole-in-the-Wall. Curry looked at the brown, lean Texan and he did not like what he saw. The outlaw was a gun fighter, but he preferred to choose the time, place, and opponent. It would be foolish to force a fight with these two men. A lie might help. "We're giving you a chance to drag it—you and yore friend both, Herrick. You got no chance to arrest Anse. Three other fellows are coming up the pass behind us. They'll be here in three—four minutes. Be smart."

The officer hesitated. These fellows were bad *hombres*, hard and dangerous men expert with weapons. He did not relish a battle with them, nor did he want to involve Jerry in such a desperate encounter. But he was sheriff of the county, and he had to live with himself. If he let this murderer go the obligation would lie on him to resign. An out suggested itself.

"I have to arrest Anse, and I am going to do it," he said quietly. "But Mr. East is a stranger. Why bring him into this? Let him ride down the pass and back to Powder Horn."

"That's fine," Fox agreed quickly. "I can ride along and make sure—"

"I'm staying," East cut in quietly.

This preliminary sparring got on the nerves of Walden. He never sidestepped a fight, but he lacked the cool courage that could wait patiently for the right moment. An irritable urge was in him to get it over with as soon as possible.

"Cut the gab," he snarled. "If you want me, Herrick, come and get me."

The sheriff did not reach for his gun. He said, his voice low and even, "You are under arrest, Anse."

Walden's sullen rage broke bounds. He whipped out his .45 and fired at the sheriff. Startled by the explosion, his young horse rocketed into the air. As it came down Walden jerked the reins savagely, and the horse crashed into Curry's mount. The two animals, excited by the deafening reports of the heavy six-shooters, began to buck wildly. Fox had bolted for the shelter of a large boulder close to the rock wall, but the other outlaws, even while they tried to steady their pitching ponies, answered the fire of the officers.

The roar of guns filled the canyon. Bullets stabbed across intersecting lanes of fire. Smoke rose in thin shreds and floated into other white gossamer ribbons. Through the film tense distorted faces showed, vanished, appeared again. Furious oaths ripped out. Shifting hoofs scraped the gravel. A horse screamed with pain.

From the throat of a man a moaning sob broke. His head slumped, and the fingers of his left hand fastened on the saddle horn. As his huge body plunged to the ground a bullet from his weapon plowed into the dirt.

Sink Curry had had enough. He swung his horse around, drove in the spur, and tore down the pass at a gallop. The head of Fox showed back of a boulder.

"I give up," he cried. "I give up. Goddlemighty, why did Anse start this?"

"Drop your pistol and come out," East ordered.

Fox relaxed his shaking fingers, and the weapon fell, a thin trickle of smoke rising from the barrel. "I was drug into this," he pleaded. "You know I was, sheriff. I said for him to go with you. I offered to take Mr. East safe outa the pass."

East picked up the six-shooter and broke it. "And then fired three shots at us," he said.

"I—I shot at Anse," the outlaw lied.

Herrick looked down at the fallen bandit, the weapon still ready in his hand. The fingers of Walden twitched and were still. In the hairy throat there was a strangling sound, after which the lungs emptied, and the big body collapsed.

"He's dead," East said.

The sheriff nodded. "Anse played his hand badly when he scared his horse and Curry's. That was a big break for us. Hadn't been that their mounts were crow-hoppin' all the time they would have got one of us, sure."

"If there's anything I can do, gents, count on me," Fox said virtuously. "Anse sure had it coming."

Herrick said coldly, "I'm taking you to town."

"That don't seem necessary," the little man protested weakly. "I jest happened to be with those birds. Haven't seen either of them before for a month."

The sheriff did not argue the point, though he

186

had in his pocket two letters to Fox he had found in the cabin.

"You have several things to explain," he said. "One of them is why you are riding a Diamond Tail horse with a blotched brand."

"I bought it. I swear I did."

"You'll have a chance to tell that to Morley. Sit over against that wall till we're ready to go."

Walden's horse had stopped a hundred yards down the canyon and was grazing. East roped the animal, and they tied the body of its master to the saddle.

"Sink's horse was wounded," the sheriff said. "I don't know how bad, but if Sink is set afoot he may be waiting at the mouth of the pass to get us from the rocks. Not likely, I reckon. He seemed plumb anxious to be on his way. But on the off chance he's figurin' on collecting us and a mount to get away on we'll let Br'er Fox lead the procession till we're out of the gulch."

They saw nothing of Curry. Evidently he had pressing business elsewhere. Unmolested, they rode out of the gorge to the bench below.

East turned in his saddle and looked back at the cleft from which they had just emerged. "If it never had the right to be called Dead Man's Pass before today it has now," he said.

They crossed the bench and descended from it on a long slope of decomposed granite to the flat floor of the plain. In the far distance the Wind

River range swept its saw-toothed edge on the horizon line.

The shadow of night was beginning to fall before they drew into the town. Cad Withers was standing on the sidewalk when the small cavalcade stopped in front of the sheriff's office.

"Holy smoke!" yelled the fat man. "Come a-running, boys, and see what the sheriff has done brought home with him."

From stores and saloons men answered the call. In an amazingly short time the street was jammed with packed men crowding close. Those in the outskirts did not know what they were trying to see.

Later they all had a chance to file through the coroner's office and look at the two holes in the dead man's body, one close to the heart and the other in the throat. Herrick and his deputy had each scored one hit.

There had been talk of grooming another candidate for sheriff at the coming election on the ground that Herrick was too kindly for the job. The sponsors of the change gave up the idea that night. Herrick had made himself solid for election.

CHAPTER TWENTY-ONE

CLIFF TRUESDALE WALKED into the office of the sheriff and found that officer punching a hole in a stirrup leather for a rivet. He settled himself in a vacant chair comfortably.

"I hear, old-timer, that you did a good job in Dead Man's Pass," he said. "Anse Walden was a curly wolf of the worst kind."

Herrick slipped the rivet into the hole. "Maybe it was a good job. I don't know." The eyes that looked into those of the foreman were troubled. "I can't sleep after I kill a man, Cliff, no matter how bad he was. I get to wondering what right I have to take the life of a human being made by God."

"Not the way to look at it, Chuck," the foreman differed. "You didn't kill him. He did that himself long ago when he went bad. Walden made his choice and he knew that his doom was waiting for him. It just happens that your finger was on the trigger of the gun that destroyed him."

"That's what I tell myself." The sheriff hammered down the end of the rivet. "I wanted to bring him in alive, but he wouldn't have it that way. Lucky for me a good man was siding me. His bullet hit Walden before mine did."

"I want to ask you about that fellow East,"

Truesdale said, frowning. "I can't put my finger on him. He hops around worse than a flea. First off, the nesters start to hang him. Pretty soon he's riding on the roundup with them. Then he gets into a jam with them, and they kick him out, the way it came to me. He kills Duffield, and that is a good riddance, after which he is on your posse and helps get rid of about the worst bad man in the district, which is saying plenty. Will you tell me what side he is on, if any?"

Amy Truesdale stepped into the office. After exchanging greetings with the sheriff she explained to her father that she had seen him go in and that she needed five dollars more for her shopping.

"What's got into you that you have gone clothes-crazy?" Cliff asked. "You never used to care what you wore."

The eyes of the girl sparkled. "Isn't that just like a man, Mr. Herrick? For years he nags at me to stop being a tomboy and act like a lady. Being an obedient girl, I obey him, and then he thinks I would look better in any old scuff clothes. Perhaps I had better go back to jeans."

Herrick smiled. He had a soft spot in his heart for this young lady. "If this is a family row I'm not in it. I'll only say that Cliff might as well yield now as later."

"I've already given up," Cliff answered. He gave his daughter a ten-dollar gold piece. "You may want some doodads with that dress, honey."

Amy kissed her father impulsively and turned to go. But before she reached the door Cliff's words to the sheriff stopped her.

"You haven't answered my question about East, Chuck."

"I don't think he is on either side," Herrick replied. "Why should he be? He is a stranger here. But I'll say this, Cliff. He will do to ride the river with. I know him pretty well. He is clean and straight clear through. Sink Curry gave him a chance to duck the fight in the pass. Jerry would not have it that way."

Amy felt a warm glow of pride in her friend. She did not need the praise of others to reinforce her trust in him, but she was glad that Herrick was just as sure.

"He is not a gunman," the sheriff continued. "Don't get that idea because he has been dragged into these difficulties. In this office right after he had shot Duffield Jerry was almost sick about what he had done. He had tried his best to avoid it, but there was no way out unless he ran away. He couldn't do that. My opinion is that no finer man ever came up the trail."

"I am glad to hear that," the foreman said. "I reckon I have done him an injustice, but I still don't know why he is hanging around here."

"You'll know some day. He is no fugitive from justice, if you have been thinking that. His reason for being here is creditable. I can't tell you any more."

Amy stepped out of the office and before she had walked a dozen steps met Jerry East.

"Are your ears burning, sir?" she asked.

"So Herrick has been defending my good name," he said.

"How do you know? By the census there are eight hundred and forty-three souls in this town. Is Mr. Herrick your only friend?"

"No. There is Nell Herrick—and I think one other."

Her eyes held fast to his, but she blushed to her hair. "I *know* of one other," she said bravely.

"I hold her friendship dear," he said, smiling at her. "But I think this time Herrick did most of the defending. Your father went into his office a few minutes ago. He does not know what to make of me since I ride with both the hares and the hounds. My guess is that Charles tried to clear his mind."

"Your guess is one-hundred-percent correct, Mr. East."

"Jerry," he corrected.

"Jerry," she substituted.

He fell into step beside her. "I haven't seen you since the last time we met," he told her with a grin. "That time I embarrassed you, and you ran away from me. Later, after you have been told fifty times what I prophesied in my feeble way, you will no longer blush at the most outrageous compliments. By the way, did you go to Nell and get her opinion as I advised?"

She stopped walking, to look reproachfully at him. "Mr. East, you are trying again—"

"Jerry," he interrupted.

"All right—Jerry. You are making fun of me. It is very amusing to you, I am sure, but—" She broke off to fling a question at him. "Is this what they call flirting?"

The Texan laughed, but she felt the friendliness of his mirth. "I don't think so. Flirting is to trifle without meaning it. But you see I am a sort of older brother to you, and it is good for a girl to be teased. It gives her poise, and usually she likes it even when she pretends she doesn't. Cross your heart, Amy. Would you rather I hadn't told you that you aren't an ugly duckling?"

The wild-rose color was in her cheeks. "You have no right to ask such questions," she announced severely. "It's too—too familiar."

"Do you think I'm a forward jackanapes, Amy?" he inquired.

"No—no, I don't. I think—" The sentence died away, since she did not quite know what she thought. "Is it nice to embarrass me?"

He threw up his hands. "I'll quit—till next time. Look at it this way, Amy. You are a young lady, now. You must learn to hit back and attack without feeling that you would like to run away. This has been lesson number one. Think up something good to put me in my place next time."

"Does there have to be a next time?" she demanded. "How do you know I want lessons, even from such an experienced teacher?"

He clapped his hands softly. "That's the way to talk. You are doing better already. But it is my duty as an older brother to help you."

"Who made you my older brother?"

"Oh, that. I just adopted you. Here comes your father. Don't bother about thanking me for the lesson. It was a pleasure."

There was something else in her mind and she unburdened it quickly. "Did you have to go with Mr. Herrick into the Hole-in-the-Wall? Must you get into every single bit of trouble in the county?"

"I'm ducking it from now on, but I owed the Herricks a lot so I sided him on that trip. A man has to pay his debts, you know."

"Yes," she agreed reluctantly. "And now you have a lot more enemies—all the bad men in the Hole-in-the-Wall. You know how they feel. That's their refuge, and law officers aren't expected to come in there."

"What outlaws think and want isn't important," her father said. "They are like a nest of rattle-snakes in the back yard and have to be cleaned out. You and Herrick made a good start, East. I don't know what your plans are for the future, but there is a place for you at the Slash Seventy-Two. There's a chance it might work into something good. I expect to go into business for myself soon. My place will have to be filled. Mind, I don't promise anything. Maybe you are not the man we want for foreman. But I don't mind telling you that Mr. Hal Carruthers got interested in you and wrote to Buck Rollins about you and he came back with a strong recommendation. If you start riding for our outfit you will have to show us how good you are."

"Make that offer of a job to me in a few weeks and I'll be mighty glad to take it, Mr. Truesdale," East told him. "I can't say yes right now. My time is tied up, but I don't think it will be for long."

The foreman was annoyed. This was the second time he had practically offered East a job and the fellow was stalling just as he had before. Maybe he was just plumb lazy and did not want to work. What had he to do that was so important? From what Truesdale could learn he spent a good deal of his time playing poker or bellying up to the bar with loafers. In spite of what Rollins and Herrick thought of him he might be nothing but a saddlebum.

"If the job is open then I'll let you know," the foreman said curtly.

The Texan understood the Slash 72 man's

resentment. He had been offered a chance that a good many riders worked a lifetime without getting and he had deliberately closed the door on it. Truesdale would not ask him again.

CHAPTER TWENTY-TWO

IN FRONT OF THE GOOD CHEER, Solly Moore stopped East. He glanced up and down the street before he spoke.

"Morley says for you to come out to the ranch," he said. "You are doing him no good here."

"That's right," the Texan agreed. "Nobody tells me anything he wouldn't say before the whole world."

"He'll be looking for you this evening," Solly murmured and passed into the saloon.

After dinner at the hotel East walked down to the corral and saddled Cap. Steve Sanborn was in the wagon yard talking with Karl. He was sitting on a feedbox drumming his heels against its sides. Indolently he watched the Texan. His muscles were relaxed, but his mind was alert. The man from the Brazos interested him more than most people did. There was not even a touch of swagger about Jerry East. He had the easy-go-lucky manner and the casual drawl of the Lone Star State cowpuncher but his reactions were as swift as a released coiled spring. The whimsical ironic smile masked a dangerous force. Back of it were patience, a capacity for silence, a steely will. Sanborn would have given a good deal to know what the man thought of him, how much

197

he suspected and knew. None of East's actions were hurried, and none of them suggested concern. But he must know he was treading a dangerous trail. The fellow was here on some undeclared business. What was it?

Sanborn said, with a thin flavor of raillery, "After Mr. East rides there is always news—bad news for some."

"I can't always be a stormy petrel," Jerry answered. "My luck is bound to change. A peaceable guy can't keep getting into these doggoned jams forever."

"I don't know where you are riding," Sanborn continued. "It's none of my affair. I hope you won't think I am intruding when I mention that quite a few gents would like to collect the peaceable guy's scalp."

"I'm much obliged for your interest," East replied. "I'll try to hang on to it."

Riding toward the Diamond Tail, Jerry considered Sanborn and what he had said. His words had been a warning rather than a threat. They might have been based on private information or merely on a size-up of the situation. While he did not approve of Sanborn, he felt a reluctant liking for the man and he thought it likely that this was reciprocated.

The afternoon sun was still high in the sky when he reached the Diamond Tail. All the men were still at work, and the place had a deserted appearance. As he tied in front of the bunkhouse he caught sight of the colored cook taking a ham from the smokehouse to his kitchen. He hailed the man, who waited for him to move closer.

"Mr. Morley at home?" Jerry asked.

"No, sah, he ain't. Is you Mr. East?" After the Texan had told him he was, the cook gave him a message. "Mr. Morley he say for you to put yore roll in the bunkhouse and git Solly Moore to fix you up after he comes home."

East unsaddled Cap and turned the horse into the corral. He carried his war bag into the men's quarters, rummaged around in the box of books until he found one that suited him, then lay down on a bunk to read.

He was still reading when the men rode in, dismounted, and dribbled into the bunkhouse. They were surprised to see him even after Solly Moore told them he had joined the ranch as a rider.

"I heard Morley tell you that he wouldn't have you account of you riding on that roundup," one of them commented.

"Mebbe he changed his mind because of his being in that fight with Herrick when they killed Anse Walden," Moore suggested.

"I'm not right sure I've got a job here," East told them. "All I know is Mr. Morley sent me word he'd like to talk with me."

After supper he played seven-up by the light of

a lantern for an hour, then turned in on the bunk Moore assigned him. Not until the other men had started to work next morning did Morley send for him.

They walked out to the corral where Morley was sure they could not be heard.

The manager put a forearm on the top rail of the fence and looked at his hired hand a long time without speaking. East endured the scrutiny with an inner amusement. He rolled and lit a cigarette in leisurely silence. It was Morley's move and he could take his time about making it.

"For a saddlebum you throw a long shadow," he said.

The Texan made no comment. It was still Morley's play.

"I'm not sure you'll suit me," the little man continued. "I'm not paying you to plow your own field with my oxen. Duffield and Walden didn't mean a thing to me."

East drawled, "Thought you would like me to demonstrate. You wanted to know if I was tough and good with a six-shooter."

"That didn't mean I want a fellow who makes trouble all over the place. You're spotted now as a killer. If you made any move now you would be suspected. I don't like that."

"What you want, Mr. Morley, is a Sunday School teacher who is an A-one bad man on the side," East jeered. "The only one I ever heard of was John Wesley Hardin. You can't get him. He is in the Texas penitentiary right now."

"I'm looking for a dependable man," Morley corrected stiffly. "I am for law and order, but the conditions in this country are such that we have to fight for it. There are key men who lead the rustlers and the riffraff. There are scoundrels like this phantom killer. As the law is administered now it will not lift a hand against them. It may be necessary to use other means."

The Texan slid in a suggestion. "Men like Walden."

"Yes. Only worse. I'm not complaining because you helped Herrick get rid of him. My point is that one who undertakes the public service I have in mind must avoid publicity. He has to keep his mouth clamped. And be inconspicuous. You can't take a step without being noticed."

"I've hunted big game all my life," East said. "You can't do that without knowing how to keep under cover."

"Will you take orders?" The manager's red wattled face showed a flare of anger. "You act to me like a fellow who wants to play his own hand instead of working for the outfit that pays you."

Greed glittered in the Texan's eyes. "I'm out for the dough, Mr. Morley, and for a lot of it. I can take orders all right from a man who is paying me enough."

Moved by a rage that surged up from inside him for some unknown reason, Morley slammed a fist on the top rail. "I've had men working for me that got too big for their breeches. Don't do that, East. I'm top dog on this ranch."

"I don't aim to forget who my boss is," the Texan said mildly. "I can be polite as all get-out when the price is right."

"Remember that and we'll get along fine," Morley told him. "I'll have some special job for you soon, I think. Until then trail with the other riders and don't let them get any idea that you are on a different footing from them. Solly is in charge of the routine work on the ranch. He'll fit you out with a string and tell you what to do."

Jerry watched the little man strut back to the house, arrogance even in the set of his shoulders, so completely satisfied with himself that he did not doubt he had bought another ruffian body and soul. The Texan rolled and smoked two more cigarettes before he left the corral. He was busy reconstructing the talk with Morley. Phrases and sentences the man had used stuck out like a white cow in a herd of red ones. *It may be necessary to use other means.* And later, *I've had men working for me who got too big for their breeches.* Morley had said this last in a sudden burst of anger. The sore was not a dead but a very live one. He still had somebody working for him whom he could not tolerate much longer, a man who knew too much to be given his time and discharged. He had mentioned the phantom killer as a menace. Jerry believed he was very near to the heart of his problem.

CHAPTER TWENTY-THREE

HERRICK TREATED HIS PRISONER Nick Fox better than the law required. He gave him books to read, tobacco to smoke, and occasionally brought from home an apple pie or some fried chicken to add to his usual fare. Sometimes while the Hole-in-the-Wall man ate his meals the sheriff would stay and chat with him. The officer was not moved solely by kindness. There was evidence enough to send the captured man to the penitentiary on at least two counts. But Fox was small fry. If he would tell what he knew about the more desperate villains with whom he had companioned it would pay to let him go. Herrick dangled before him a choice, to serve a term in prison or to give information leading to the arrest and conviction of others more wanted by the law.

Fox had no insurmountable scruples about betraying his companions. The trouble was that if he did the matter would not end there. He had treasure buried in the country where the robbers roosted, his share of one train and two stage holdups, but if he went back to dig it up after double-crossing his associates he would probably not live to bring it out.

He took refuge in protestations of ignorance.

He lived a sort of hermit life—knew the nomadic refugees in the Hole just well enough to pass the time of day but didn't have any truck with them. If he had ever done anything against the law it was because he had been kind of pushed into it. Crowded by the sheriff, he admitted that he had spent a couple of days with Walden and Curry preparatory to going on a bear hunt with them. No sir, if Dave Daggs had ever been up in the Hole he had never heard of it. About the latest stage robbery—he did not even know of it till Herrick brought him to town. Nobody ever told him anything, account of his not being one of the boys, as you might say.

Herrick was building a lattice on the porch for rose bushes. "He's as slippery as an eel," he told East the next time he saw the Texan. "Acts as if he is really eager to help me but just doesn't know a thing. What scares him the most is the fear that I will take him into the Hole as a guide."

"How about putting one over on him that there is talk of breaking into the jail and stringing him up?" Jerry asked. "That would loosen his tongue."

Herrick considered that. "Seems like that would be playing it low on him. A kind of legal blackmail. I don't like it."

"I don't like several things I am doing," East answered dryly. "Fox is pulling plenty of weasel talk on you. Turn about is fair play."

"Yeah, but I'm sheriff. I like to play it straight with my prisoners."

"Let me have a talk with him," East suggested.

Herrick grinned at him. "Maybe I will. I'll think of it and let you know."

Nell came out to the porch with a pitcher of lemonade for them.

"How do you like it at the Diamond Tail?" she asked their guest.

"I didn't expect to like it—and I don't," he told her. "But I think that is where I am most likely to find out what I want to know."

"Amy feels badly that you did not accept her father's offer of a job at the Slash Seventy-Two," she said.

"So do I. It's just the opening I would have liked if there hadn't been a prior option on my time."

"She is recovering nicely from the death of Jim Baxter," Nell mentioned innocently. "I don't think she ever was in love with him. She just thought so."

"Amy is a fine girl," Jerry said. "Look after her, Nell, and see she doesn't marry just anybody."

"You can take care of that better than I can, Jerry," she replied, mischief in her eyes.

East looked at the sheriff gravely. "Nothing you can do about it, Chuck. They are born that way. Soon as a woman gets married she starts in trying to fix things up for her friends."

"You might do worse, Jerry," Herrick told him. "Personally I like being bossed."

"You poor henpecked man." Nell patted her husband's shoulder and smiled at East. "I can boss him about little things but I couldn't budge him an inch about important ones."

The sheriff's surprised eyes rested on his wife a moment. A matter she did not yet know of, one that might turn out to be very important, was just now occupying his mind.

On the way uptown Herrick spoke of it to East. "A fellow came to me this morning with a tip on the stage robbery. Half an hour after the holdup, while he was riding line for the KZ, he saw a man riding across country toward town. Jim yelled at the guy and started over to borrow the makings, but the horseman waved him around, then cut into a gully and disappeared. Being some curious, Jim watched from a wooded bluff till the man came out the lower end of the draw and headed for the river."

"Did he recognize the man?" East asked.

"No. Too far away. His mount was a buckskin."

"You think he may have been one of the stage robbers," East said.

Herrick nodded. "They might have separated right after the holdup. I figured if this fellow was one of them he would come into town from the south. So I asked Karl if he had noticed any rider passing the corral on his way in to town.

He hadn't, but he happened to mention that Steve Sanborn had brought his buckskin in about that time. Steve keeps it at the corral. Told Karl he had been hunting."

"Bring any game in with him?"

"No, and that was queer. He always does when he hunts."

"He sometimes goes hunting with Daggs," Jerry suggested.

"That's right. Steve has been running with Daggs lately."

"I wouldn't put it past Daggs to hold up a stage, but Sanborn is a horse of a different color. I'm surprised."

"Steve is a reckless man. He likes excitement, and lately he has been drinking a good deal." Herrick summed up his opinion of the man in a sentence. "He might hold up a stage just for the hell of it."

"He might," East agreed. "I hope not. There's something likable about him."

"Yes." Herrick's face showed worry. "I'd hate to have him in this. It would worry me a lot."

East thought he knew why. Steve Sanborn was or had been Nell's friend. Her husband did not want to take any action that might look vindictive or that might distress his wife.

"If he is guilty he is certainly a cool customer," the Texan said. "Think of him riding with us on the posse and laughing up his sleeve at us."

"He's cool enough, all right," the sheriff admitted gloomily.

Already he had done some checking up and he would have to do more. He did not at all like the idea. His normal instinct was to play his cards openly but one gathering evidence cannot do that.

"Karl tell you how Sanborn was dressed when he reached the corral?" East inquired.

"Sanborn was wearing striped trousers. I took a look at the buckskin. Pretended I thought it was a little lame. The horse had been reshod the day after the holdup."

"Careful man—Steve," the Texan commented dryly. "Taking no chances of having identified any track the horse left."

"I dropped in to see Hertzog the blacksmith. Thought he might be able to point out the shoes he took off the buckskin. No luck. In the shop there is a pile of shoes two feet high. He couldn't even make a guess. I played I had a bet on it."

"Daggs chews tobacco," East reflected aloud.

"So do forty other men I know."

"Including the phantom killer."

"Right." The sheriff snapped a question at him. "You think Daggs may be both the killer and the holdup?"

"I'm just guessing." East pointed out that Daggs had more opportunity than most men. "He is foot-loose and can be any place at any time."

The sheriff rubbed his bristly cheek. "Think

I'll talk with Hank Wolff again. He knows or guesses something he didn't tell us."

"You don't think—"

"Hank is honest as they come," Herrick interrupted. "But he has learned to button his lip. The stage is robbed two—three times a year. He figures it is up to the law to get the road agents. If he suspects anybody and blabs names the bandits would likely not be convicted, but they would be sore at Hank and next time they might rub him out."

From the stage driver Herrick got no additional information, but he took pains to talk with the fat drummer, Green, who had been on the stage at the time of the holdup. The man was staying overnight at the hotel on his way back to Sheridan after having covered the towns in the lower half of the territory.

They sat in a corner of the lobby smoking cigars. Green was quite willing to talk. Herrick could see that the tale of this adventure was going to be one of the stock stories the drummer would tell for the rest of his life. He had a good listener now and he made the most of it. The officer interrupted two or three times to put pertinent questions. He was asking one when Sanborn sauntered into the room.

"Yes, sir," the salesman answered. "The big fellow made one slip. He called his partner Steve."

An imp of reckless deviltry danced in Sanborn's eye. He strolled across the lobby and drew up a chair beside the commercial traveler. After lighting a cigar he tilted his chair back comfortably.

"We have the best sheriff in the territory, Mr. Green," he said. "Busy as a bee all the time. With a man like him around crime certainly doesn't pay."

"My record hasn't been too good so far, but I hope to improve," Herrick replied. "Mr. Green, this is Mr. Steve Sanborn. I don't know whether you have met him before."

The traveling man offered Sanborn his fat hand. "Glad to meet you, Mr.—er—I didn't quite get the name."

Sanborn shook the hand warmly. "Call me Steve," he said. "You can remember that easier. It's a common name in this part of the country."

Green's mouth opened, but no words came out of it. He stared at Sanborn uncertainly. The manner of the local men had been friendly, their voices even and pleasant, yet the traveling man had become aware of double talk, of a certain challenge beneath the give-and-take. And the name Steve. A small flutter of alarm stirred in his stomach.

"Queer about names," the sheriff said. "You won't hear one for months, then you'll run into it several times. There aren't so many called Steve around here. You might call this a coincidence."

"So you might." Sanborn turned his smiling face on Green. "What did this bandit Steve look like?"

The salesman thought, *This can't be the man. He wouldn't stand there with that mocking grin defying me.* Yet he had an unhappy conviction that it was. He said, "A big fellow—rough and mean—make two of you—maybe it wasn't Steve the other robber called him—something like that."

"It looks as if I won't have to arrest you after all, Sanborn," the sheriff said. "You can't have shrunk to half-size in a week or two."

Sanborn laughed. "You had me scared for a minute." His voice was as cool and easy as the sheriff's had been. "Well, if you are sure you don't want me I'll drop in next door and try my luck at poker."

He nodded amiably at the salesman and walked through the side doorway into the saloon.

The startled eyes of Green fastened on the sheriff. "He isn't—he can't be—"

"Why, no. How can he be, since your friend the outlaw is twice as big as Sanborn? And anyhow maybe it was John Henry the other holdup called him and not Steve."

The traveling man did not like the touch of contempt in the officer's voice. "I'd hate to get the wrong man into trouble," he said resentfully.

"Sure," Herrick agreed blandly. "But you would worry more if you picked the right one."

There was the sting of a small whiplash in that remark, but Green decided not to make anything of it. He was beginning to feel a pleasant thrill of excitement. This was going to help his story when he told it in the smoking-rooms of Pullman cars. The facts would have to be twisted a little, but that did not matter. He could put it that he had practically pointed out one of the bandits to the sheriff, who had been afraid to arrest him, and that the outlaw had backed out of the room, flung himself on the nearest horse, and galloped away.

CHAPTER TWENTY-FOUR

HERRICK SAT WITH THE WEEKLY PAPER before his eyes, but his wife became aware he was not reading it.

"Something troubling you, big boy?" she asked, needle poised above the sock she was darning.

"It's about this stage robbery," he said, lowering the paper. "Begins to look as if Steve Sanborn was in it."

The shock of what Charles had said drove the blood from her cheeks. She stared at him silently, thoughts churning through her mind. If Steve was implicated and her husband found evidence of it the house of cards she had built would come tumbling down. For Steve might try to use what he knew about her to protect himself. He could be ruthless.

"What makes you think so?" she asked at last.

Nell wondered if her voice was as quavery as she felt.

He told her what he had found out. It was not convincing proof, but she had no doubt whatever of Steve's guilt. This was just the sort of thing he would do. He would love the excitement and the risk, as well as the inner mirth he would get from riding with the posse to arrest himself.

"Are you going to arrest him?"

"Not yet," he answered. "I haven't enough on him. But I may have soon." He added, "I wish I didn't have to do it, honey."

She knew his inflexible integrity. There would be no use making an appeal to him, even if he knew how terribly much it meant to her. He would follow the straight, hard line of duty. She said in a low small voice, "If you must you must."

"Yes," he agreed.

"You have never asked me about my past life," she continued. "You took me on faith."

"I still do," he broke in. "You don't need to tell me more than you have. What is past does not belong to me."

"When I was desperately unhappy Steve helped me very much. He gave me strength and courage." She lifted a hand in a gesture of distress. "I know he is wild and reckless—doesn't care anything about the law. But he isn't a bad man, not like that man you killed, Anse Walden. He's just—not grown up."

"That's the trouble with most of these young cowboys who go bad. There may be a lot of good in them, but they take the wrong turn. The law has to judge them by what they do. Sanborn ought to know better. He is educated, and he has let himself slip into bad ways. You and I are not responsible for that. I hope I won't find enough to take action against him, but I have to keep on looking for evidence."

"If he would go away," she cried. "But he won't."

Except on rare occasions he was an undemonstrative man. Now he put a hand on her shoulder and looked gravely into her eyes. "I want more than anything in the world to make you happy, dear. It's hard luck that I have to work against your friend. But I'm sheriff. It's my job. I can't lie down on it."

"You will do what you think right," she said. In her low throaty voice was the forewarning of the tragedy she felt sure was going to overwhelm her. "I have been happier here than for a long, long time. Maybe I don't deserve that. I guess—"

She rose with a swift fluid movement and walked into the bedroom, closing the door behind her. Herrick looked at the closed door. A tight cold wave froze him. What he must do would shut him out of her life. Already he had quenched the gay joy it had been such a pleasure for him to watch in her. If he continued he would bring her grief and distress. Yet there was nothing else he could do. She had come into his life and was going out of it again. Sunshine in the spring. A light in the window at night that meant home. Something fine and bright that had changed his life. It was strange that the lift of a woman's voice, the sparkle in her eye, the warmth of her smile could mean so much to a man, that the lithe grace of her body when she moved was beauty not to be found elsewhere on earth.

He was better informed as to her past life than he had ever let her know. Just before their marriage an anonymous friend or foe had sent him several clippings from a Springfield, Illinois, paper. They told the story of her trial for the murder of a man whom the prosecution alleged had been her lover and was about to marry another woman. There had been a touch of mystery about the case. Nell had made no defense except that the victim had threatened her with a revolver and when she pushed the weapon aside his own finger had accidentally pulled the trigger which sent a bullet crashing into his throat. On the stand she had refused to answer all questions bearing upon their past relations. To the surprise of everybody she had been acquitted. Herrick thought he could guess the reason for the verdict. In the stories of the reporters there had been an underlying sympathy for the defendant, an admiration for the self-contained integrity of this young woman who had taken the law into her own hands. The jury must have felt that society would not suffer with her at large.

The newspaper accounts had been full of lacunae. Except for one shadowy sister in the background Nell had no family. Once since their marriage she had made a reference to the death of Jeanie, who must have passed away soon after the trial. Herrick had a feeling that during the trial Nell had deliberately by-passed all the little devices that might have stirred the feeling of the jury on her side. She had been hiding something she was afraid might be dragged out.

Charles Herrick had been so much in love with her, so sure of her innate decency, that he had burned the clippings and never mentioned them to her. If she ever wanted him to know about her past she would tell him. No doubt Steve Sanborn had come into her life in the friendless days when she felt herself alone in a hostile world. He probably knew her story and in his reckless, generous way had been more deeply interested in her because of it. How much the man meant to her now Herrick could not tell, but he could understand that she felt she must do anything for him that she could. It was one of life's little ironies that her husband not only could not help her but must stand in opposition to her wishes.

CHAPTER TWENTY-FIVE

BEFORE JERRY EAST LEFT TOWN Dick Stuart arrived with word that Chris Dunn had been shot at and missed. The killer had been lying back of a cottonwood and had fired at him when he first came out of the house in the morning. He had escaped because at that instant he had stooped to pick up some kindling piled on the porch. Before a second shot could be fired he had dived inside and slammed the door shut. The bullet had torn through the jamb about waist-high at the very spot where Dunn had been standing.

Jerry pondered this on the way out to the Diamond Tail. Either the phantom killer was at work again or Dunn was taking pains to make it appear he had been chosen as the next victim. If the latter was true the scene had been set to make the story convincing. According to Stuart there was a half-ring of tobacco splashes back of the cottonwood and deeper in the small grove had been found evidence of a horse tied there.

As soon as Jerry reached the Diamond Tail he made cautious inquiries whether Allen had spent the night at the ranch as he occasionally did. None of the men had seen him. That he was not there proved nothing, since it was Allen's business as a stock inspector to be all over the district. All it did was to fail to clear the man by giving him an alibi.

To Solly Moore the Texan murmured a word. "Like to talk with Morley tonight." The foreman gave no sign that he had heard, but an hour later he stuck his head in the bunkhouse.

"You—Texas. The boss wants to see you about that keg of nails you were to order. Says you got the wrong size."

East grunted that he had ordered tenpennies like he was told, but he rose from the cot where he had been lounging and walked up to the house.

Morley was in the room he used as an office. At sight of the Texan he snapped, "Shut the door."

"Sure," East replied. "We might get our death of pneumonia this wintry night."

"I told you not to get funny with me," the manager said sourly. "If you have anything important to report let's have it."

East noticed that in spite of Morley's impatience he lowered his voice almost to a whisper.

"I don't know how important it is to you, but it is right important to Chris Dunn." Jerry moved forward to the desk, brushed some papers aside, and sat on the corner of it with one leg dangling. "He was shot at this morning."

"What!" Morley's body stiffened. "Who shot at him?"

"He would like to know that," East drawled.

"Looks like this phantom killer again. He took a crack at Dunn first thing when he came out of the house. Missed. Dunn dived for cover without waiting to talk it over. They found the place where the guy lay back of a cottonwood and chewed tobacco. I reckon he lit out pronto soon as he could hit the saddle."

"Funny he missed if he had a clean shot at Dunn," Morley said.

"The way it came to me Dunn stooped right then to pick some kindling off the porch." East laughed softly. "This bird will lose his reputation if he ain't careful. Must have buck fever. He takes four—five cracks at me and one at Dunn and gets nothing but one boot heel."

Morley lit a cigar and puffed it. "I wonder who this killer is?" he asked reflectively.

"Same question I was going to put to you," East said.

The words were innocent, but the look that went with them held scarcely veiled insolence.

"Don't talk to me like that," Morley stormed. "I won't have it."

"Now what did I say that was out of order?" the Texan wanted to know humbly. "All I mentioned was—"

"I heard what you said," the manager interrupted angrily. "I didn't hire you to devil me, you damned saddlebum."

"I'm beginning to mull over why you did hire

me," East replied. "There was talk of a special job with big pay."

"Let me handle that," Morley said sharply. "I'll tell you what I want you to do and when."

"And if I decide to take it on I'll tell you how much it will cost you," East added.

A darker color flushed the manager's face. "I don't know why I put up with your rotten impudence," he snarled. "You're nothing but a two-bit puncher I picked up on the chuck line."

The Texan was amused. The little man's choleric face made him resemble more than ever an irate turkey cock. He might begin to gobble any moment.

"Just a saddlebum," East agreed. "But when I hire out my gun it isn't a two-bit proposition."

"You are eaten up with a greed for money," Morley exploded.

"I like the dinero," admitted East. "Let's put it that I am a businessman on the make." He enjoyed needling his employer, but he realized it would not be wise to let his impish humor carry him too far. "No use getting sore at me, Mr. Morley. I aim to be reasonable—and efficient. After all, you're paying the freight."

The ranch manager was mollified. "Then don't rile me up, East. I'm not a patient man. I want things done my way."

"That's all right. We'll get along fine. I'll be here when you want me."

East rose to go, but Morley stopped him with a gesture. "I'm disturbed about this Dunn business. No community can stand having a killer going around shooting anybody he pleases. It can't wait to catch him red-handed. There's only one thing to do with a villain like that."

"Soon as we know for sure who he is," East tossed in casually.

"That's it exactly." Morley leaned across the desk and lowered his voice. "I have a suspicion, but of course I haven't proof. I'm working on it and may get evidence soon."

The Texan did not ask him whom he suspected. He felt that Morley was debating in his mind whether to tell him now or wait. Any question might push off the information by stirring up doubt. Better let it come voluntarily.

"We can limit the field," Morley continued. "He has to be a man not tied down by a job, one who has the opportunity to move about freely. Can you think of such a one?"

"I can think of too blamed many to be of any help," East said. "All the rustlers roosting in the hills—the guys up in the Hole-in-the-Wall—half a dozen loafers around Powder Horn—some warrior that may be hired by one of the big ranches."

"Consider the motive, too. This fellow must know all the men he has killed. And he must hate them enough to go to a good deal of trouble."

"Unless he finds it profitable," East said. "I'm not trying to get you mad, Mr. Morley, but you know what all the little fellows say—that it is part of a campaign by the big ranches to drive out homesteaders."

"Nothing to that—nothing at all. If there was anything like that on foot I would know of it. One of these days I will tell you who I think is the guilty man. But I want to be sure and not get the wrong one."

Morley had made up his mind he had said enough at present. East did not try to rush him. He left the manager with a reasonable assurance that when the word was given his tool would be ready to obey orders. At least Jerry hoped he had. It had been necessary to convince his employer that he was a tough and callous scoundrel. But one might overdo the part. If he seemed too hard and self-willed Morley might decide he had better stay with his present killer rather than take on another.

East was pretty sure he knew who the assassin was, and he was more than ever convinced that Morley stood back of him.

CHAPTER TWENTY-SIX

NELL WAS ON THE BACK PORCH churning when she heard footsteps and looked up to see Steve Sanborn.

"What a model housewife Sheriff Herrick's bride turned out to be," he said, a smile of friendly derision on his face. "It shows you can't ever tell. When I first knew her——" He let the sentence die in the air. She could finish it to suit herself.

"You oughtn't to be here, Steve," she said. "But I'm glad you came. I want to talk with you."

"That makes it mutual. Shall we talk about the advantages of San Francisco as a home town for you and me?"

"Don't be that way, Steve," she begged. "I'm married to the man I want and I'm afraid I am going to lose him."

He took the churn dasher from her and kept it moving. "Why not learn the truth about him now? Some time he is bound to find out about your past. If he is such a prig as to let it make any difference you ought not to want him."

"I ought to have told him before we married," she said bitterly. "But I was too big a coward. I was afraid he wouldn't want me, and I thought it need never come out. It's too late now to tell him."

"It would have been too late to tell him anytime. Chuck is a good man, but he isn't your kind. He is a stuffy, stodgy citizen filled with false ideas about women. Men of his sort think women are good or they are bad, that there is a sharp dividing line and they have to be on one side of it or the other. By his standard Nell Herrick isn't a respectable woman."

"He isn't like that at all," she denied indignantly. "Charles isn't the least bit stodgy."

"If you are so sure of that why don't you tell him?" he asked.

"Maybe I'll have to, before he finds out," she said despondently. "Unless you go away, Steve."

He shook his head. "That's out. I won't run under fire."

Abruptly she flung a question at him. "Did you help rob the stage?"

He laughed. "Before I answer that I would like to know whether my Nell or the sheriff's wife is asking."

"You know that Charles is gathering evidence?"

"All over the lot. He is going to arrest me soon."

"You won't—make any trouble?"

"You mean a gun play. Oh no! I'm a law-abiding citizen. I'll be gentle as Mary's little lamb."

"There is another way you could make trouble— by trying to bargain with him. It wouldn't do any good, no matter what you said about me!"

"He would sacrifice you. That's the point I've been making."

"Only because he would think it his duty."

"Duty." He spat the word out scornfully. "I know a man would go through fire and water for you if you loved him."

"Yes, I think you would," she agreed gently. "Maybe you will anyhow."

"Why?" he demanded brusquely. "So that you may continue living in a fool's paradise a little while longer before the explosion?"

"I think the butter has come," she told him and took the dasher from him.

He watched her take the butter from the churn and squeeze the buttermilk from it. "The setup is wrong, Nell," he went on. "You can't ever be happy with a sword of what's-his-name hanging over you."

"Damocles," she supplied. "I'll have to tell Charles."

"It would be pleasanter just to leave him a note—save wear and tear on the nerves all round."

"Except that I'm not going away."

He shrugged his shoulders. "That makes two of us who are not going, then."

"If you held up the stage—and I am sure now you did—isn't it silly to stay here and go to the penitentiary?"

"I haven't any intention of going to the penitentiary," he said cheerfully. "Herrick can't put it over. He may gather evidence enough to have me tried but not enough to get a conviction."

"How can you be sure?"

"Even if I were found guilty I wouldn't go. I would break jail. But I'd rather not have it come to that." He grinned at her. "You don't need to worry about me. I'll land on my feet. Thought I would give you another chance to change your mind. But if you won't you won't."

Sanborn met Herrick at the gate. "How are you getting along with the case against me, sheriff?" he asked airily.

"I think you robbed the stage, Steve," Herrick said gravely.

"Opinions don't count. Can you prove it?"

"I wish I didn't have to, Steve."

Herrick walked down the path to the house.

Nell said, "You must have met Steve Sanborn as he was leaving."

"Yes. At the gate." He did not ask her what Sanborn had been doing here.

Her eyes met his directly. "He wants me to go away with him."

"And you told him?"

"That I am married to you and want to live with you as long as you wish it."

"That will be as long as I live," he answered.

228

"I don't know." Nell decided to learn her fate now. "I haven't played fair with you, Charles. I—I married you on false pretenses."

"Did you tell me any lies?" he asked. "I don't recall any."

"Isn't it a lie to conceal the truth?"

"No. Not when I told you it wasn't necessary to go into that. If it worries you, tell me now. I suppose what you mean is that you were tried for killing Henry Fallon."

She stared at him, amazed. "You know about that?"

"I knew it before we were married."

"And you never spoke of it."

"Why should I? You would tell me if you wanted me to know."

"How did you find out?"

"Some anonymous kind friend sent me clippings from a Springfield paper about the trial."

Inside she was a flood of happy tears. Never had she loved him so much. "And you married me even though I was a—a—"

"Don't use that word," he broke in sharply. "I married you because I knew a brave true woman when I met her."

"How can you say that, even if there was nothing else against me—and there is?"

"I knew that, too, at least I suspected it, though I didn't know the man was Sanborn."

"You seem to know everything about me, Charles," she said.

Her wistful, emotion-twisted smile touched him.

"You put up so poor a defense I'm surprised you were acquitted," Herrick told her.

"Yes, I should have been sent to prison."

"Oh, no! The jury knew, as I did when I read the newspaper account, that the true story hadn't been brought out. You were protecting somebody else."

Her startled eyes were an admission he had guessed the truth. "I don't know what you mean."

"You know just what I mean. Henry Fallon had been your sister's lover, not yours. She let you take the blame."

"No. Jeanie never knew of the trouble I had got myself into, Charles. She was ill in a Chicago hospital, and when the baby was born a month later they both died. You can't excuse me that way. I was wild with despair and anger. She was innocent and lovely, and Henry Fallon had wrecked her life. He was nearly fifteen years older than she. It was shown at the trial that I took a pistol when I went to see him. I didn't mean to kill him. I was a fool and thought I could frighten him into marrying her. He tried to take the gun from me, and it went off."

"You did wrong, and you suffered for it. Who am I to judge your guilt? Only the other day I, too, killed a man. If you love, you look at the truth behind the facts." He spoke with quiet certainty.

"I had better finish my story," she said. "Jeanie and I had no near relatives. I was a teacher, supporting her and myself with what I made. When I was arrested I had saved nothing. Steve Sanborn had gone to school with me and we had always been friends. He was married, but his wife had run away with a traveling actor. Before my trial he came to me in prison and told me he would take care of Jeanie's expenses without letting her know. He paid the hospital bills and the funeral ones. Of course I had been discharged by the school board. When I went to Chicago to find work he lent me money. Nobody except Steve stood by me. My employer found out about my record and I lost my place. Steve came to Chicago. He wanted me to go away with him. We went to Denver and afterward to Cheyenne. But I couldn't go on with it and I left him."

"Do you still love him?" Herrick asked.

"If I loved him I would be with him now." She added after a moment, "You ought to know who I love, Charles."

He took her in his arms. "There's been a barrier between us," he said. "It has gone forever."

While they were eating dinner half an hour later Herrick recurred to the problem that still existed.

"Steve did so much for you. If I had to send him to the penitentiary I would feel like a coyote. Maybe the best out is for me to resign."

"Put it up to Steve," she suggested. "Offer to quit if he would like to have you. He will understand that if you stay sheriff you will have to do your job."

Her husband smiled. "That's a new one on me, but maybe there is something to it. I'll have a talk with him. At least it will clear the situation up. I would rather finish my term, but I have been feeling lately that I do not want another. I'm not hard enough to be a gun fighter. I still have bad moments over killing Anse Walden."

"I wish you wouldn't run again," Nell said. "I worry for fear you will get hurt. That job as foreman of the KZ is still open for you."

Later in the afternoon Herrick dropped into Gann's saloon and drifted back to the poker table. They were playing stud. He stood behind Sanborn until the hand was finished and then touched his shoulder.

"Like to see you a minute, Steve," he said.

A smile lit Sanborn's reckless eyes. "How official is this, sheriff? Had I better cash my stack or will I be coming back?"

"Leave your chips. I won't keep you but a minute." They walked together out of the building and along the sidewalk to a vacant lot.

"So you didn't bring your handcuffs with you," Sanborn said.

"I hope I never shall for you," Herrick answered. "Fact is, Nell and I have laid our cards on the table. She didn't tell me anything I didn't know or had not guessed, except your very great kindness to her when she was in trouble. She is unhappy about this stagecoach business."

"Tell her she needn't be. I'm not worrying." Sanborn reverted to an angle not yet clear in his mind. Nell might have held back a good deal. He did not want to give away anything her husband had not been told. "I helped her when she was in trouble, did I?"

"After she had killed Henry Fallon. You were the only friend who stood by her."

"She doesn't owe me a thing," Sanborn replied. "Nell gave me more than I gave her. The slate is clean."

"She does not feel that way and neither do I. You have a claim on us."

"No claim on you." Sanborn's hard eyes held steadily to those of the sheriff. "You don't come into anything that may be between me and Nell."

"That may have been between you," Herrick corrected. "I'm making you a proposition, Steve. If I stay sheriff I must gather what evidence I can about the stage holdup. I'm not going to run again next fall. Say the word and I'll resign today. Would you rather take a chance with a new man in office?"

Sanborn chuckled. Herrick was in a jam. He wanted to stand well both with his conscience and with his wife. "Looks like you have your tail in a crack, sheriff, and you would like to duck your responsibility."

"Perhaps. But I'll go through if you want it that way."

"It's not half such a sporting offer as it sounds. But I'm tempted. Maybe I could get myself appointed in your place. I'd have to turn over a new leaf if I did."

"My offer isn't a joke, Steve. Take it or leave it."

"I'll leave it." Mirth bubbled in Sanborn's eyes. "We have an A-one sheriff. He ought to stay and finish his job—clean up this stage robbery and other outrages. As a good citizen he mustn't let anything come before his duty."

"I'll see that he doesn't," Herrick said quietly.

"Besides, I'm playing a little game that interests me, one of those best-man-wins contests. I'll bet you a hundred dollars that I come out on top, sheriff."

"I hope you do, but I'm going to try my best to see you don't," Herrick said.

"Fair enough. I'll give you two to one that none of the three men on the stage the day of the holdup will get up on the stand and swear I was one of the bandits."

"The stage company is more interested in getting the gold back than in punishing the thieves," Herrick mentioned. "If this was returned voluntarily it might be arranged to drop the matter."

"I can see how the company might feel that way, but after the road agents have taken so much trouble they will probably look at it differently. But if I meet either of them I'll speak to him about it."

They separated, the sheriff to go to his office and Sanborn to return to his stud game.

CHAPTER TWENTY-SEVEN

JERRY EAST LAID THE DINNER TRAY on the cot beside Fox. "Come and get it, fellow," he said, imitating the summons of a roundup cook.

"What's the matter with Herrick?" the prisoner inquired.

"He's busy today. A little excitement in town. Don't let it worry you. Likely won't amount to anything. He made me a kind of special deputy." The Texan let his glance wander over the room. "Brings back memories. The sheriff had me in this same room, the time Duffield was fixing to hang me to a telegraph pole."

"What do you mean—excitement? And why should I worry?" There was an anxious look on the sly and weazened face of the outlaw.

"No reason at all. It does no good. And like I said, the trouble will probably blow over."

"What trouble? Spit it out."

"The phantom killer took a crack at Dunn yesterday. You know how unreasonable folks get. They don't know who he is. But right now they are all worked up about crime. Want a cleanup pronto. They figure you are protecting outlaws and are one yourself. So naturally, seeing that you are the only one they can get at handy—"

The color faded from the face of Fox and left

it a greenish yellow. "Goddlemighty! You don't mean—"

"Keep a stiff upper lip. They won't get you unless your number is up. Every time liquor talks it doesn't mean there is going to be trouble." East pushed the tray toward him. "Eat your dinner while it's hot. Forget what I told you."

"Forget it! How can I forget it? Get me outa here before—before—"

The panic in the little man was lifting his voice to a scream.

"If you had been more helpful the boys would feel different," East told him. "But with you being so stubborn about talking—"

"I'll tell anything they want. Go tell 'em that— quick."

"No hurry. They wouldn't do anything before night anyhow. My advice would be to spill all you know."

Fox did not lose any time. He talked volubly of the outlaws who infested the retreat where he lived. They did not have fixed habitats but shifted quarters from one mountain park or pocket to another. Few of them spent are entire year there. When the law was close on their heels they fled to the Hole and stayed there till the heat of the pursuit was past, leaving it again after a time to resume their nefarious pursuits. He mentioned names, men with whom East had no concern. Neither he nor Herrick had any expectation of rounding up all the criminals who found a refuge in the tangled mountain gulches.

The Texan suggested others—Dunn, Allen, Sanborn, Daggs. None of them were habitués of this outlaws' paradise except Daggs. He sometimes came into the Hole ringing a pack horse loaded with supplies for his friends and stayed a few weeks to trap, Fox said. After the latest stage holdup it had been rumored that Daggs was one of the road agents. He had ridden to Anse Walden's cabin immediately after the robbery.

Only one bit of information of positive value to him did East get out of the little man. If he was telling the truth Daggs could not have been the killer of Jim Baxter. On that day he had been with Walden and Curry at their cabin in the park above Dead Man's Pass. East believed what Fox told him as to the date, since the man had no idea why he had been pinned down to a definite time, though it was possible he was lying by reason of long habit.

To the sheriff East reported what Fox had told him. None of it was of much use to Herrick. He already knew the nomadic customs of the bad men in the Hole and the names of some hidden in its fastnesses. The crimes of most of them had been committed outside the county, and he felt no obligation to kill other officers' snakes, as he put it. He did not have the man power to do it nor the money to organize a hunt. Nor did he give much weight to the alibi Fox had given Daggs, who in his opinion was the likeliest man he knew to be the phantom killer.

"Nick Fox is such a doggoned liar he hates to tell the truth even when it will do him more good," the sheriff diagnosed. "Looks to me sometimes he doesn't know himself when he's lying."

East shook his head. "Don't think he was lying this time, Charles. I had Fox plumb frightened. He was talking turkey. The way he was sure of the time was that it was his birthday when he saw Daggs at the cabin." He watched smoke from his cigarette rise in lazy fat rings before he continued. "Unless I'm way off I've got this killer pegged. The name is Rod Allen. Morley is back of the whole thing. He is getting afraid of Allen and wants me to bump him off. So far he hasn't used Allen's name to me, but he will soon."

Herrick agreed it might be Allen. The man was cold, ruthless, and had no regard for the rights of small settlers. It was known that during the Indian troubles a decade or more ago he had held the view that the only good Indian was a dead one. He had acted on that principle.

As East jogged out to the Diamond Tail it was strong in his mind that the crisis was close. Granted that Allen was the killer, he would be aware of this, too. Since the man was no fool, his suspicions must have been aroused by the employment of East as a ranch hand. No doubt he and Morley had discussed it. The manager's explanation probably was that he wanted the Texan near where they could watch him, but the stock detective, to whom wariness had become second nature, would be very doubtful.

CHAPTER TWENTY-EIGHT

THE TWO MEN GLARED at each other across the table, anger in their eyes.

"I told you to leave Dunn alone," Morley said, his voice cold and venomous. "With all this feeling worked up this is no time to set it boiling again. Anybody but a fool would know that. But you have to go ahead and play your own hand, just because you don't like Dunn."

"You've been tellin' me for months Dunn had to go," Allen snarled. "I've got to get these scalawags when the chance comes. Easy for you to sit here and play God Almighty while I take the risk. I won't have it. Don't try to ride me. I've had about enough of you. It makes my belly sick to work for a double-crossing skunk no man alive could count on."

Morley scowled at his killer. "I won't stand for talk like that. You are paid well for what you do. I'll give the orders. You carry them out."

"I'll take no more orders from you. I wouldn't trust you any farther than I could throw a two-year-old bull by the tail. Think I'm a fool and don't know you are getting ready to use this Texas gunman?"

The heady blood that blotched Allen's face

was a warning to his employer. Morley changed his tone.

"I've explained that to you half a dozen times," he said irritably. "Where could he be safer than right under our eyes? I don't believe he saw a thing the day young Baxter was killed. But if so we've got him here to keep check on. I'm protecting you, and instead of thanking me you storm around like a blockhead."

"Yeah, I'm sure you would go a long way to protect me," Allen jeered. "I don't believe a word of it. You've got him here to take my place. What I'm wondering is, *Who is he to kill first?*" The last words fell softly, cold as ice, and the hard, narrowed eyes of the stock detective searched the face of the ranch manager.

A cold wind blew through Morley. A .44 lay in the opened drawer touching his stomach. He felt sure he was in imminent danger, but he did not dare risk reaching for the weapon not four inches from his fingers. Allen was chain lightning on the draw and even if badly wounded would slam bullets into him.

"Sometimes I think you are a fool, Rod," he said mildly. "You and I are tied together so fast that neither one of us can break away. We have to trust each other because plain common sense makes it necessary that we do. We have been through too much side by side as partners in this cleanup business. It's foolish for us to get mad because we become a little annoyed at each other."

"Dear pals fighting side by side," Allen mocked. "You in your office here and me taking a big chance of getting shot or hanged."

"Not if you are careful, Rod. I never saw your match. You can move as silently as your own shadow. You can go anywhere without being seen."

"Don't soft-soap me, Morley. I'm on to you." The killer put his left forefinger on the edge of the table and let it keep time with the words that slid out between his closed teeth. "It would be safer for you to go to sleep in a nest of rattlesnakes than to try to throw me down, Morley. Keep that in yore mind from the minute you wake each day till you go to sleep."

The color washed out of Morley's full-blooded face. "What's come over you, Rod?" he said, a sound in his throat that was almost a groan. "I don't want to quarrel with you. It's worse than senseless. It would be insane. A split-up might destroy us both. Can't you see that? You don't have to go haywire just because I got a little peeved."

Allen rose, smiling down at his employer, a dreadful threat in the fixed sinister smile. "First off, get rid of this Texan. After that—we'll see."

"I'll fire him tonight if you feel that way, Rod,"

the ranch manager promised. "Though I think you are being foolish. He is harmless."

"Was he harmless to Duffield and Walden?" the killer asked.

"The way I size him up he is as gentle as a lamb. Duffield and Walden both forced him to fight to save his own skin. He happened to be lucky."

"We'll follow my size-up and not yours," Allen decided bluntly. "My judgment is that he is one of the coolest sure-shot killers I ever laid eyes on. That's the way we'll play it. When he comes in tonight you'll tie a can to his tail. Understand?"

Morley said that he did, that maybe his idea in hiring East had been a mistake though he had meant it for the best.

At the door Allen turned. "Don't forget I've got my eyes on you, fellow. I'm top dog now, and I aim to stay that. Make one misstep and I'll blast you to kingdom come."

Morley said, appeasement in his voice, "That's a crazy way to talk, Rod, to one who has always been your good friend." The thought in his mind back of the thin smile was, *You have signed your own death warrant, you fool.*

The stock detective walked to the corral to get his horse. A man came out of the bunkhouse and they stopped for a few words. What they said was spoken so low that they had to stand close to hear.

"I've had a row with Morley about that Texan, Bill," Allen said. "He says he'll give East his time, but I don't trust him. If he sends for East make out to be under the window back of his office. Report to me back of Twin Buttes tomorrow morning. Maybe they'll talk in whispers and you won't hear anything. That would mean they are plotting against me. Two minutes will be all the time it takes for him to fire the fellow if he is on the level with me."

"Okay with me, Rod," the cowboy murmured. "I'll do what I can."

CHAPTER TWENTY-NINE

JERRY EAST RODE IN as darkness was beginning to cover the land. He was still eating supper when a summons came from Morley. After finishing the meal he sauntered up to the big house. A few minutes later Bill Roper wandered out into the night from the men's sleeping-quarters.

Morley looked up as Jerry East came into the room. Ever since Allen had left he had been nervous, and with the coming of night his worry had increased. The killer might sneak back and shoot him from the darkness. He had drawn the blinds but did not find that helped much. The sight of the cool easygoing Texan's strong face was a relief, but it was like him to express this in a petulant complaint.

"You took your time coming," he snapped.

"Didn't know there was a fire," East answered. "You Yankees are always in such a doggoned hurry to get somewhere so as to put yore feet on a table and loaf."

"Well, you're here at last." Morley leaned forward in his chair and dropped his voice to a whisper. "I've found out who the killer is."

East showed no sign of the excitement that pounded through his veins. "Seeing that nobody else has, that takes you to the head of the class," he said evenly.

"I've been suspicious of this man a long time," the ranch manager continued. "He had all the opportunity in the world, and he is a cold-blooded villain. In at least two of these murders he was seen around that part of the country an hour or two later."

"That's pretty slim evidence so far," the Texan mentioned, and added with a grin, "I was in the vicinity of one, and some folks claim I am a bad lot, too."

"I've had this fellow in mind for some time. So I did some checking up. A few days after each killing he went to Cheyenne. I had a hunch that he might be banking his money, and I wrote to a friend, the president of the Cattleman's National Bank. Yesterday I got an answer. Here it is." Morley tossed a letter across the table to East.

In his letter the banker explained that it was against the rule for the Cattleman's to disclose information about its depositors, but in this case he would strain a point. Mr. Rodney Allen had deposited $475 on April 25 of the preceding year, $390 on October 7, $450 December 10, and on May 25 of the current year $350.

Jerry let the paper drop from his fingers to the table. "So you think it is Allen," he said.

"I know it. Two hours ago I had a talk with him and I called the turn. The way he took it proved I was right. He threatened that if I exposed him I would be the next on his list." Morley picked up another paper in front of him. "I have here the dates when Radway, Carlton, Chapin, and Baxter were killed. Within ten days after each murder one of these deposits was made. Where did Allen get that money?"

"He must have got it from the man who paid him for the jobs," East replied. "Now I wonder who he could be?"

Morley brushed that aside. "We may never know. What we do know is that Allen is the killer and that he is on the prowl again. I'm next—and after me, you." The man's face was haggard. "I'm not fooling you. He'll get us, unless—"

The eyes of the two men met and held. "What do you aim to do, Mr. Morley?" East asked gently.

"There's only one thing to do. The law can't touch him. We haven't enough proof. But he's guilty as hell." Morley tried to smile and did not make a success of it. "I don't need to tell you what we must do, East."

"And afterward I reckon I'll be puttin' money in the Cattleman's bank," the Texan murmured.

"Not if you have any sense. You'll keep it hidden."

"Sounds reasonable. And how much will I keep hidden each time somebody gets rubbed out? You didn't mention that, Mr. Morley."

"You're doing this job for yourself as much as for me. Naturally the price will be cut accordingly."

"Will it?" East smiled slyly. "Tell you what. We'll shake dice to see which of us does it."

"I'm not a gun fighter, East," Morley explained. "It will have to be you."

"Me? At half price? Oh, no, Mr. Morley. Think again."

Morley mentioned that two hundred and fifty dollars was a lot of money. East reminded him that it was just half of five hundred. They dickered like horse traders and compromised on four hundred.

After that they talked for some time about the best way to do the job. Morley was urgent about one point, that it be done quickly. They could not afford to wait or Allen might beat them to the trigger, for he had served notice that he was out to get them both. Dealing with a man of his record, it would not do to discount the danger. They had to strike first. The manager's voice, though still low, grew shrill as the fear mounted in him.

"Allen might be right outside of this room this very minute ready to murder us," he said.

"I wouldn't think so," East replied, comfort in his voice. "He has all outdoors to pick some lonesome spot. Why would he come where you have a dozen men within call?"

The Texan stepped to the window and raised the blind, intending to show Morley that his fears were foolish. A figure beneath the window crouched low and darted away.

East pulled down the blind. The men in the room looked at each other.

"Was it Allen?" Morley asked shakily. The cold feet of mice ran up and down his spine. His trembling hand had gripped the revolver in the drawer, and the color ebbed from his pink face. There was no arrogance in it now.

"I don't know," East answered. "Couldn't see his face. But somebody wanted to know mighty bad what we were talking about. Might be one of your men in cahoots with him. We had better go to the bunkhouse and check up."

"No. I'm not leaving this room till I'm sure he has gone. It was Allen. Go out and get him now."

East shook his head. "And have him plug me as I walk out of the room? That's not the way I work. The idea is for me to have a bead on him, not for me to be the target. I don't think this man was Allen, but he might be. Chances are he has lit out. Or gone back to the bunkhouse. We'll give him two—three minutes before we move." The Texan's derisive eyes rested on Morley. "Take it easy. Allen isn't going to come busting into the room when he knows we are prepared for him."

The men stood close to the wall, out of the probable line of fire in case a bullet was sent through the door or window. Presently East moved to the door, opened it a few inches, and shot into the air.

Four or five men dribbled out of the bunkhouse.

Others, half dressed, followed them. Morley called to them to come to the house. Solly Moore and Bill Roper were among the first group. East stayed in the background and let the ranch manager ask the questions. Solly did most of the talking for the men. Three or four of the hands had been out during the past quarter of an hour. That did not mean a thing, he explained. Before bedding down all of them went out every night for a few minutes. None of those who had stepped from the bunkhouse recently had seen a stranger or had himself been near the big house.

When Morley's questions had been all answered he knew exactly as much as when he started the investigation.

"What do you figure this snooper wanted?" Bill Roper asked. "Think maybe he was one of a gang trying to run off some of the remuda?"

"Might be that," East agreed. "Anyhow he's lit out like the heel flies were after him. He won't try any rustling tonight."

Morley backed this false lead. "Have one of the boys throw a saddle on a bronc, Solly, and ride down to the pasture and take a look." He flung an order sourly at the Texan. "Want to see you a minute, East."

With East at his heels he walked back into the office.

CHAPTER THIRTY

JERRY EAST SLANTED an inquiring look at Morley. "Did Allen happen to mention where he was headed for from here?"

"For town, he said. That was before we had the kick-up."

"Nothing in that to change his mind," Jerry reflected aloud. "Think I'll mosey in, too."

The ranch manager's gaze searched his face, then fell away. The thought in both of their minds was something not to be dragged out into the open too often. Put into plain words murder has an ugly sound.

"Might be a good idea to check on him," Morley agreed. "You want to be careful. He's dangerous."

"I'll be careful," East promised.

"A killer like he is doesn't deserve a break. He wouldn't give you one. Play it sure."

The Texan's grin was sourly contemptuous. "It would be too bad if he got me and then came out after you."

Morley flushed resentfully. "I was thinking about you, not myself. I wouldn't want to be responsible for anything happening to you."

"I know who you were thinking about." East nodded. "You would feel real bad if my toes were turned up to the daisies. I'll try to see it is not that way. I'd hate to bring you grief."

The night was three hours older when the Texan tied in front of the hotel. A man was seated in a chair close to the wall.

"Hello, Steve," East said. "No poker game tonight?"

"I'm a little fed up with poker." Sanborn yawned. "Time you were stirring up some more entertainment, Texas. This town has gone to sleep."

"It would be nice if some of the ladies would get up a church social." Jerry's gaze rested on a claybank horse tied to the rack beside his own. He thought he had seen it before. "That bronc looks familiar. Whose brand does it carry?"

"I don't know about the brand," Sanborn answered. "Rod Allen owns it now."

On East's face was an expression of shocked surprise. "Don't tell me Allen is sitting in the poker game instead of you."

"Nothing like that," Sanborn replied gravely. "He is probably upstairs in his room enjoying the sweet sleep of the virtuous. Allen has no vices. He is one-hundred-percent pure."

"So I've heard. He doesn't even chew that filthy weed tobacco."

"Heaven forbid. Nor smoke. Nor drink. Nor let his feet wander from the narrow path of righteousness. He does pack a gun. For rattlesnakes, I reckon."

"Quite a few infest this country," East mentioned dryly.

Sanborn watched him walk lightly down the street. He still felt a mild curiosity about this stranger who had been dubbed a saddlebum and had turned out to be surprisingly different.

East reached the end of the sidewalk and continued down the road to the Herrick place. There was still a light in the window. As he took the path from the gate he called, "Hello the house!" Since the sheriff had made his visit to the Hole-in-the-Wall he might be a little apprehensive about a knock on the door so late at night. Sink Curry and some of his friends might be returning his call.

The door opened, and Herrick stood framed in the light from the lamp. "Come on in, Jerry," he called.

Nell walked in from the other room and gave their visitor her friendly quizzical smile. It was strange, Jerry thought, that this quiet reserved woman made men instantly as aware of her as if she had been announced with trumpets.

The Herricks knew that an important reason had brought him here. Otherwise he would not be dropping in at this time of night. But they waited for him to broach the subject. Charles pushed a chair toward East.

"There's a smell of rain in the air," he said. "This country needs a good downpour."

"Get your handcuffs ready, sheriff," East advised. "For me. I've been hired to kill a man—price four hundred dollars."

Nell stared at him. "Who?" she asked.

Jerry gave her a Yankee answer, a return question. "Do you mean who hired me or who I'm to kill?"

"Both."

"I'm to shoot the phantom killer, in the back if I can."

Nell's eyes were bright with excitement. "Do you know who he is?"

"My employer feels sure he does—and I think he is right. He ought to know, since he has paid for all the killings."

"He didn't tell you he had," the sheriff hazarded.

"No. I guessed that. He gave me other evidence."

"I don't understand why if he had those poor homesteaders murdered he wants his gunman killed," Nell said.

"The gunman knows too much, and he is afraid of him. His hired hand feels the same way about him. So one of them is going to die soon."

"If this is a guessing game," the sheriff suggested, "my first choice for the hirer is Morley."

"Right. And the other scoundrel is Allen."

Herrick was not greatly surprised. He had

always thought Allen a cold-blooded fellow with no regard for the rights of others.

East told them in detail the story of his relation with Morley. He admitted that the evidence against Allen was not conclusive, though he was quite convinced that the cattle detective was the killer. His plan was to get Herrick to appoint him a deputy, after which they would together arrest Allen and later Morley. By playing one against the other he was convinced that Morley would weaken and make some sort of confession to save himself. There was a chance, of course, that Morley would deny having ever discussed the matter with East.

In Herrick's opinion that last was almost a certainty. He thought it would be better for him to approach Morley and make sure he would stand by the story he had told East. If he was enough afraid of Allen he would be glad to have him put behind bars, since the plot to murder the man had miscarried. At the same time he would have to protect himself against the chance of being tried with Allen for the crimes committed. The manager of the Diamond Tail was in a ticklish position. The evidence he gave might backfire against him and put him in the dock.

"Wouldn't as wily a plotter as Mr. Morley have protected himself against that?" Nell asked. "He would see that no link could be discovered that connected him with these killings. All of

256

us might feel sure he instigated them and yet be unable to prove it."

"The trouble with your whole case, Jerry, is that with the exception of the deposits in the Cattleman's National it rests wholly on Morley's word," the sheriff said. "If he denied that he had told you anything we couldn't get to first base. We've got the right man. There's no doubt of that in my mind. But proving it is something else."

"I think Charles is right," Nell agreed. "Mr. Morley is our chief witness. How tough is he? Will he stand out against the pressure you put on him?"

"He is desperately afraid of Allen," the Texan answered. "His only thought will be to save himself. If he thinks he can testify against his killer and do that, he won't hesitate a minute."

"How would this do?" Nell suggested. "Let Charles tell him that you had weakened about killing Allen and had put the responsibility of saving Morley on the law. Of course Charles must not let out even a hint that either of you think he had anything to do with the murders, but that you are both trying to work out a way to save him and yet convict Allen. He might co-operate as the best way out of the situation."

"That way we don't get Morley at all," East objected.

"We might," Herrick differed. "Evidence will pop up here and there. Morley's bank withdrawals might tell something. Witnesses may come forward who recall incriminating facts they had not given any weight to. Morley didn't put up all this money alone, but the other contributors may not have known it was to be used to pay for assassinations. If trouble looms they may come forward and tell what they know."

"Allen was at the hotel when I reached town," East said. "My idea was to go up to his room and arrest him, but we'll have to postpone that."

"Better you shouldn't meet him till we are ready to take him into custody," the sheriff decided. "You can stay here tonight."

His wife approved that heartily. She had a spare room where he could sleep. Jerry made only a perfunctory protest.

CHAPTER THIRTY-ONE

ALLEN PICKETED THE CLAYBANK back of Twin Buttes and waited for the arrival of Bill Roper. He lounged beneath a cottonwood, not at all impatient. Bill was dependable, but it might be several hours before he could slip away from whatever job had been assigned him. The cattle inspector was in no hurry. His business was one in which you could not make haste. One spent weeks in apparent idleness on the range, then stumbled on a calf carrying a different brand from the one stamped on the cow it was following.

He was not quite comfortable where he lay. Something in his hip pocket prodded into his flesh. It turned out to be a plug of chewing-tobacco. A cynical smile broke the lines of his hard, leathery face without warming the icy eyes at all. He never chewed except for business reasons, to leave evidence that the phantom killer was addicted to the habit.

A callous man, not given to jumpy nerves, he was a little disturbed this morning. He knew that he and Morley had come to the end of the trail they had been traveling together. The point about which he was not sure was how Morley would react to the break. His judgment was that he had better get rid of the man. But there was a risk in that. You could not continue killing without running into trouble sometime. If it was not necessary he would prefer not to rub Morley out.

He watched a distant rider top a rise, disappear into a swale, and reappear. With his right hand he drew the rifle at his side closer. This was probably Roper or a chance cowboy. But the price of life for him was vigilance, and he never relaxed when in doubt. His field glasses picked the approaching horseman up while still several hundred yards away. The rider was Roper.

The cowboy changed his weight in the saddle. "I can't stop, Rod," he said. "I'm supposed to be riding the line down by the Willow Sinks. I listened in back of the office when Texas and the boss held their powwow. They spoke too low for me to hear what they were saying, but I heard yore name mentioned. It was something about you having money in a bank. The window blind was down, but one of them let it up. I doubled over and scooted, beat it back to the bunkhouse. Soon the Texan fired a shot, and we all piled out. Morley asked forty-two questions. Who had been outa the bunkhouse? Had we noticed any stranger? He looked to me shaky as a scared rabbit. Finally he and the gent from Texas went back into his office."

"No mention of my name?" Allen asked.

"No. East made a crack it was probably some-body trying to run off some horses from the pasture. I kinda gave him that idea and he jumped at it."

Allen warned Roper not to tell anybody that he had seen him. He knew now what he must do, though he did not say so to the cowpuncher. If Morley knew he had money in the bank he must have been gathering evidence against him. Either he was going to betray him to the law or he was going to have the Texan dry-gulch him. The thing to do was move fast.

He lay that afternoon on a butte overlooking the Diamond Tail, his glasses trained on the house and yard, watching those who came and went. About three o'clock a small cloud of dust on the road caught his eye. A buggy was moving toward the ranch. As it turned into the yard he recognized the driver, Charles Herrick. If he had known any doubts before, they were banished now. Morley must have sent for the sheriff to get him to arrest Allen.

The guess of the stock detective was entirely wrong. Morley was not only surprised but uneasy at seeing the sheriff, though he could not give a definite reason for being worried. He put a good face on his inner doubts.

"What brings you out to this neck of the woods, Chuck?" he asked with professional heartiness. "Don't tell me that anybody on the Diamond Tail has been hurrahing the town."

"Something more serious," Herrick said. "Like

to talk with you where you are sure nobody can hear what we are saying."

Morley took him into the apple orchard back of the house. "All right," he told the sheriff. "Let's have it."

"This man East came to me last night and told me about Allen. He said he was reneging about killing the fellow. I don't blame you much, Morley. He ought to be put out of the way before he destroys anybody else. But why not let the law do it legally? Before a jury he wouldn't have a prayer if they thought he was guilty. And I reckon he is, from what you told East." Herrick's voice was amiable and friendly. He had the manner of one who hoped the ranch manager would approve of what he said.

Morley thought fast. He had to make a decision, and it must be the right one. For the moment he played to get more time. "Did East tell you I had some evidence against Allen?" he asked.

"Yes, and that Allen means to kill you. East doesn't want that. Neither do I. What I want is enough evidence to justify me in arresting Allen at once. I'll lock him up so tight he won't have a chance to get at you. This country will be grateful to you, Morley, for getting the evidence to convict a killer so cold-blooded as Allen. It must have taken guts for you to stand up to him and tell him you had found him out."

The sheriff had made Morley's mind up for

him. There could be no evidence against him except Allen's word, and that would have no weight at all under the circumstances. He had better be the good citizen fearlessly denouncing crime and standing valiantly with the law. One suggestion he offered, since he would far rather have the killer dead than captive.

"Allen is one of the most desperate villains alive. He doesn't fear man or devil. I doubt if you can arrest him without somebody being killed. If it is anybody, it should be Allen. Don't take any chances, Herrick. The fellow is chain lightning on the draw."

"I'll take him by surprise if I can," the sheriff said. "Now about the evidence against him."

The ranch manager repeated the story he had told East and supplemented it with more detail. After Herrick had gone he wondered if he had gone too far. It might be a good idea to warn Allen the law was reaching for him. This would divert the killer's animosity from him to the sheriff and might be a shield against the fellow's anger. Also he would fight rather than be taken and very likely get killed.

CHAPTER THIRTY-TWO

STEVE SANBORN WAS A LATE RISER. The sun was high in the blue sky when he came out of the hotel to stroll up the street to Chung Wing's restaurant for breakfast. He met Nell Herrick coming out of the butcher shop.

"How are you this glad morning, Mistress Nell?" he asked.

"I'm very well, kind sir," she said. "And happier than when I saw you last."

"No doubt because your soul is shriven." He smiled at her reproachfully. "Confession wasn't necessary. I would never have told."

"Charles knew all the time. I might have saved myself much worry. I'm so glad he knows."

A man on a claybank horse rode down the street and tied in front of The Good Cheer. Nell watched him walk into the saloon, her attention wholly absorbed.

"You are interested in Mr. Rodney Allen more than I would expect so happy a wife to be," Steve mentioned lightly.

The sheriff came out of his office and walked toward them. In his wife's cheeks the color faded.

She cried as he came close, "You're not—not going to—"

He said, "Please go home at once, Nell. Don't worry. It will be all right."

"Not now, Charles," she pleaded. "Wait till Jerry is with you."

"What's all this about?" Sanborn inquired. "If he's going to arrest me, Nell, you needn't worry. There will be no trouble."

"It's not you, Steve, but the phantom killer," Nell explained, fear in her low voice.

Excitement gleamed in the gambler's eyes. "I was your deputy the other day, Herrick," he reminded the officer. "Cut me in on this deal, too. Who is the fellow?" The answer jumped to his mind before either of them could answer. "Allen, by thunder!"

"I would be obliged if you would take Mrs. Herrick home, Steve," the sheriff said.

"No, I'll go alone," Nell promised quickly. "Stay with Charles, Steve."

"Do we cut this fellow down, Chuck? Or do you want him alive?" Sanborn asked.

The sheriff shook his head. "I don't need your help, Steve. I'll take him by surprise. But I want Nell away from here."

"I'll go—alone. I don't need Steve." She flung a look of appeal at Sanborn.

"Run along, Nell," he said cheerfully. "I'm in this whether Chuck wants me or not. You know how crazy I am about supporting law."

Herrick lifted his shoulders in a shrug. "All

right. I'll go in first. You can follow me. Don't make any sign to show you are a deputy unless trouble starts. I don't think there will be any. Before he knows what is up I'll cover him."

The sheriff passed through the swing doors into The Good Cheer. Before the doors had stopped moving Sanborn followed. Gus Rillings, behind the bar, nodded at the sheriff and said, "Mornin', Chuck." At the rear two men sat in a pitch game. Allen was just seating himself, with a dirty pack of cards in his left hand, at a table close to the wall. He was a solitaire addict. Cad Withers filled a chair as near to the bar as he could conveniently set it. Somebody might come in and stand treat, in which case he did not want to be overlooked. He was to the right and slightly in front of the table occupied by Allen.

Sanborn sauntered to the wall and leaned against it negligently. He observed that Allen's gaze held fast to the sheriff. His face was expressionless, the features frozen hard as those of a plaster statue. He had laid the cards down in front of him very gently and shifted his position slightly, pushing the chair back from the table.

"Like to talk with you, Rod," the sheriff said pleasantly. "If you can give me a minute."

"Don't come any nearer," Allen ordered coldly. "Talk from where you are at." His eyes were narrowed, his body taut as a coiled spring.

Herrick knew that he could not surprise Allen. The man was sure he had come to arrest him. Somebody must have warned the killer.

The officer called sharply to him. "Keep your hands on the table, Allen. You're under arrest."

Cad Withers got out of his chair very fast for a fat man. He was almost in the line of fire. His flabby face paled as he stumbled back toward the wall. During the second when he was between the two men Allen closed on Withers swift as a cat and encircled his great belly with an arm.

"If you want me, come and get me," the killer snarled.

"Don't shoot," Withers screamed.

Herrick pushed his .45 back into the holster. The huge barrel body of the fat man shielded the stock inspector completely. If firing began Withers would almost certainly be hurt.

"I don't want you that bad, Allen," the sheriff said.

"Shall I blast him, Chuck?" Sanborn asked quietly.

He was standing about eight feet from Allen, his weapon covering the killer.

"No, Steve," Herrick answered. "An innocent bystander is in danger. Allen gets away this time."

"All right. I'll give the orders." Allen did not raise his voice, but it was hard and cold as steel in below-zero weather. "Sanborn, move over to the lower end of the bar. You, too, Herrick. Rillings will take your guns."

"He won't take mine," Sanborn said.

"Keep it then, but don't use it. Now, Withers, we're backing out of the front door. You'll stay with me till I'm in the saddle. No funny business from any of you or I'll put a hole in this barrel of pork."

The badman and his shield moved through the swing doors. Allen dived for his mount, pulled the slip knot, and vaulted into the saddle. He swung the claybank and with a touch of the spur lifted it to a gallop. The sheriff and his temporary deputy crashed the door to the sidewalk. Each of them fired one shot, though the range was too far for accuracy. The killer disappeared around a bend in a cloud of dust.

The sheriff met Sanborn's wide grin sheepishly. "Don't say it," he begged. "I know I'm a hell of a sheriff. But will you tell me what I could do with a wide yard of Withers between me and him?"

"Oh, I'm in it, too," Sanborn admitted. He leaned against the wall and laughed till the tears ran down his cheeks. "The boys won't ever get over ribbing us for this."

Gus Rillings came to the door and looked up and down the road. "Where's yore prisoner, sheriff?" he asked in apparently innocent surprise.

"He said he had another engagement," Herrick

answered. "And I reckon he had, judging by the way he lit out."

"What did you want him for, anyhow?" Withers wanted to know resentfully, not yet fully recovered from the chill that had run up and down his spine.

"I wanted him because he is the phantom killer.

"Jumping Joseph!" Withers yelped. "And you tried to arrest him with me where I couldn't help getting killed."

"You hadn't ought to let yoreself get so fat you fill a whole room, Cad," the saloon keeper reproved.

"How do you know Allen is the killer?" Sanborn asked.

"There isn't any doubt of it, but I don't want to go into the evidence just now." A smile both grim and whimsical touched the sheriff's lips. "Since you have elected yourself my deputy suppose you come into my office for instructions, Steve."

Sanborn walked into the office with him, sat down, and lit a cheroot. "You don't want a stage robber for a permanent deputy, do you?" he asked. "Or am I not an outlaw any longer?"

"I'm not getting ahead very fast in proving it," Herrick admitted. "If I can't that will be fine with me. Now I'm deeper in your debt than ever. You're a nuisance, Steve. Why can't you stay inside the law?"

"It's not proven yet that I haven't. Let's forget

269

that just now. If you can convince me that Allen is the fellow they call the phantom killer I would like to stay your deputy until we land him."

"I can't use you while there is a cloud hanging over you. How would I feel if I had to arrest you later? I'd have my tail in a crack with the door closing on it."

"No hard feelings if you go ahead and do your duty." Sanborn gave the sheriff his most persuasive smile. "I'll count it a big favor if you will let me help get this killer."

Herrick promised reluctantly that if he saw a way to use him he would.

"Aren't you going to organize a posse and get after this bird before he gets out of the country?"

"Yes, but I have something else to do first. Allen won't leave—not unless he is crowded. He is going to stay and kill a man if he can—the only one who has any real evidence against him. That way he would be safe, but if he runs away he would be caught and dragged back."

"Who is this somebody with evidence against him?"

"I think I'll keep that under my hat for a little while." Herrick picked up his hat to go. "On second thought, Steve, I'll promise this, that when I make up a posse you'll be on it."

The sheriff walked home. He found his wife

waiting anxiously on the road in front of their gate. She was relieved to see him coming.

"What happened? Did you arrest him?" she asked.

Her husband grinned ruefully. "No, we didn't arrest him. He wouldn't let us. Steve and I stood there like wooden Indians and watched him go out of The Good Cheer big as Wild Bill Hickok. We took a couple of wild shots at him as he galloped away."

"But—why? I don't understand."

Herrick explained how Allen had made fools of him and Sanborn.

CHAPTER THIRTY-THREE

ALLEN KNEW EXACTLY what he meant to do, but he had not yet contrived a way to bring it about. If he could kill Morley secretly, leaving no evidence that he was the assassin, there would be no convincing proof that he was the man who had shot the homesteaders, though there would be a strong enough feeling against him to make it advisable for him to depart for Arizona or Texas. The difficulty was to get into contact with Morley. He could not go to the ranch house, and Morley certainly was not going to come to him without an assurance of safety.

He had arranged with Bill Roper to meet him again back of the Twin Buttes, but he knew the cowpuncher would shy off from him as soon as he learned Allen was accused of being the phantom killer. Bill was not going to run the risk of being tied up with one who was the object of so much hatred. Yet Roper was the only means he had to get a message to his boss, and he must carry a story that would bring Morley to him as fast as he could travel.

A plan flashed to his mind, and the more he considered it the more foolproof it seemed. To protect himself Morley would have to come without a companion.

While he was still a mile and a half from the Buttes he came on two calves grazing in a small draw. At his approach they looked up, startled, and turned to run. His glance swept the landscape to make sure nobody was within sight. He raised his rifle and fired. One of the calves stumbled over its front feet and collapsed. Dismounting, he tied the claybank to a scrub oak, then moved down into the draw. With his hunting-knife he made a deep long gash in the side of the dead animal. In the palm of his hand he scooped up the flowing blood and drenched the front of his white shirt with it, then took the bandanna from his neck and soaked it in the wound. He tied this around his head, making sure that his face was stained and his hair matted with the animal's blood.

The claybank snorted with alarm at the smell of the blood when Allen started to mount, but the cattle detective quieted the horse and swung to the saddle. He rode to the rendezvous and again picketed the horse without removing the saddle or bridle. From the horn he took a coated canvas water bottle. He lay down under a cottonwood and sloshed water on his stained shirt to give the appearance of blood still oozing from a wound. His preparations complete, he waited with what patience he could for the arrival of Roper. If the man failed him—and he probably would not come if he had heard that Allen was wanted for the murder of the homesteaders—the trap he had carefully prepared for Morley would be useless.

Inside of fifteen minutes Roper came into sight. What the cowboy saw shocked him. Allen lay soaked in blood, arms flung out, eyes closed. The rider swung from the saddle and moved closer.

"Someone has killed him," he said aloud.

The eyes of the prostrate man opened slowly. "That you, Bill?" Allen asked weakly.

Roper knelt on one knee.

"Who did it, Rod? How bad is it? Lemme have a look at the wound."

Allen waved him back feebly. "Give me a drink," he said.

The cowboy supported his head while he drank. "Listen, Bill," he murmured. "Don't touch me. Herrick and Sanborn got me. I'm shot through and through. Get back to the house and tell Morley I'm dying. I had a kind of a row with him but that doesn't matter. Hurry, or I won't last long enough to tell him that—that—" The thin voice died away.

"I can't leave you here like this, Rod," protested Roper,

"Go—go. It's all you can do for me. Tell Morley I've got something to say to him alone."

Roper left him reluctantly. He jumped his horse at once to a gallop. When he was out of sight Allen rose and stretched himself. There was one angle of this that would not look too good.

Roper would report him a dying man. He could not wait to let them find him perfectly sound. His best chance would be to take refuge in the Hole-in-the-Wall after destroying Morley. The fellows living there would not welcome him very warmly, since he had been hard on rustlers, but he could put up some kind of story they would swallow.

But that was in the future, something he did not need to worry about now. There was a fair chance that he might fall into the trap he had set for Morley. If the sheriff got in touch with Morley before Roper reached the ranch house, the manager of the Diamond Tail would know there was something wrong about the cowboy's story, and he would bring armed men with him to the Twin Buttes. That was a risk Allen had to take. It did not trouble him too much. Danger he accepted as a matter of course. It had ridden with him when he stalked his victims. It had lain down at night with him at his lonely campfires. He was a tough hard-bitten scoundrel, and it was in the back of his mind that he would someday go out with the roar of guns in his ears.

The day grew older, and the sun began to slide down toward the western horizon. Time was running out for him. If Morley came alone, it would have to be soon. He had nerves of steel, but the long wait was a strain. To fill the dragging minutes he busied himself with details.

He shifted the picketed horse to a new feeding-circle, wound his watch, examined rifle and six-shooter to make sure they were ready. From his pocket he took a small notebook and wrote in it with the stub of a pencil. If some of his hunters rubbed him out, they would find an account of his dealings with Morley that the ranch manager would not be able to explain easily.

A rider topped a rise and was for a moment silhouetted against the sky. He disappeared and presently came into sight again nearer than before. From back of a tree Allen watched the approaching man, field glasses fixed on him. The horseman was no stranger to him. He grinned malevolently.

CHAPTER THIRTY-FOUR

WHEN JERRY EAST RODE into the yard of the Diamond Tail the manager of the ranch was standing on the porch. He had lost the cocky assurance habitual to him, though it did not show in his manner. He still looked like a strutting little bully, but inside he was shaken by doubt. If this crisis should break against him he was lost. The sight of the Texan set anger and fear stirring in him. If this man had carried through as he had promised he would have been out of his troubles. Sullenly he watched the Southerner dismount, trail the bridle reins, and start for the bunkhouse.

"Come here," he snapped, his voice sharp as the crack of a whip.

East walked to the porch. "I know what you are going to say," he anticipated. "I don't blame you. But it was this-a-way, Mr. Morley."

His employer cut the explanation short. "You didn't have the guts to tackle Allen," Morley told him contemptuously, black anger in his face.

"That's your way of putting it," East mildly protested. "Fact is, I got to thinking it over and I figured we weren't going at this the right way."

"Who paid you to think? You claimed to be a tough guy from Texas who would do anything if the price was right. To hear you tell it you

277

wrestled with grizzly bears before breakfast and fought desperadoes at the drop of a hat."

"Now, Mr. Morley, I didn't claim all that."

"And you turn out a chickenhearted fourflusher who ran blabbing for the sheriff to do what you hadn't the nerve to do yourself."

"It looked to me both of us would be better off if we went at the job legal. I'm willing to be one of a posse out after the fellow. When we get him he can be tried and hanged high as Haman."

"You threw me down," Morley snarled bitterly. "It was my place to decide how I wanted this handled. I was paying the freight. You made a bargain and reneged because you daren't face the killer for all your big talk. If you found you were too much a rabbit to take on the job why didn't you come back to me and say so? I could have found the sheriff if I had wanted him."

"Might be you are right, but the way I got to feeling was that if Herrick arrested Allen he would be hanged and you would be shet of him."

"Pack your stuff and get out, East. You are not working for the Diamond Tail any longer. It can't use men like you—fellows who promise but don't perform. Here's your check, made up until today. Hit the trail pronto. Better go back to Texas where you can still swagger around and play tough."

East put the check in his pocket. He mumbled something about being sorry Morley was not satisfied. At the bunkhouse he rolled up his belongings and tied the roll back of the saddle, after which he mounted and rode up the lane to the main road.

Before reaching it he caught sight of a man cutting across the south pasture toward the ranch buildings. He was riding fast. As the horseman drew nearer he saw it was Bill Roper. Their paths did not cross, but from a distance Bill shouted something he could not make out. East waved a hand, an indefinite answer that would do as well as words which could not be heard.

The Texan cut across country to the Slash 72. His ostensible errand was to drop a casual word to Truesdale that he would be glad to accept a job at the ranch if one was still open. Another reason for going there flitted through his mind. He wanted to see Amy Truesdale.

Truesdale and Hal Carruthers were at the horse corral watching two bronco peelers break some colts to the saddle. East joined them. The young Englishman asked him how things were shaping at the Diamond Tail.

"The stock looks good and fat," he said, and added, "I've just been fired."

Truesdale looked at him coldly. He could understand that. From what he had gathered the Texan spent too much of his time loafing in town to suit any ranch manager.

"That's too bad," Carruthers said. "What for?"

"Failed to satisfy the boss," East said. "It's quite a long story, and I'm not free to tell it all yet. But I can say this much—that something big is going to break inside of twenty-four hours, a piece of news that will surprise you."

"News that has to do with Morley?" Truesdale asked.

"Yes, Morley comes into it." The Texan decided it might be wise to say more. "We know who the man is they call the phantom killer."

"Who knows this?" inquired Truesdale, his voice sharp.

"Morley and the sheriff and I. The man is Rod Allen."

"I don't believe it," the ranch foreman said bluntly. "Not that I like Allen. I don't. But I would bet he isn't that kind of killer."

"You would lose your bet," East said quietly. "I've been working on this case ever since I came here. We've got him spotted at last."

"Who are you working for? Who is paying you?"

"I'm working for myself, Mr. Truesdale. Henry Carlton was my brother. His real name was East. I came to find out, if I could, the man who murdered him."

"And you think it was Allen?"

"I'm sure of it."

"Has he been arrested yet?"

"No. That is why I'm telling you. He might be

seen around this way. The chief witness against him is Morley. Herrick and I are afraid he may be out to get Morley to save himself."

"If he is guilty he might," Carruthers agreed.

"What is in my mind is that if you would care to invite Morley here for a day or two until we have Allen in custody, and if he would come, it might protect him from this killer."

"I'll do that," Carruthers promised.

"What evidence have you against Allen?" Truesdale wanted to know.

"For one thing he banked money in a Cheyenne bank right after each killing. Morley found that out. There is other evidence."

"If you are on Morley's side why did he give you your time?" Truesdale inquired suspiciously.

"We had different ideas about how to work this out. Allen had threatened to kill him for accusing him of these crimes. Morley was worried about his own safety. He thought the thing to do was to shoot the man down on sight. I didn't want to do that and took the matter to Herrick. The trouble is that though there is no doubt of Allen's guilt there may not be evidence enough to convict him."

Carruthers neither liked nor trusted Morley, but his feeling about the man ought not to prevent him from harboring him while there was danger. The Englishman said, "I'd better write a note to Morley and invite him over, then send it by one of the boys."

He walked to the house to write the invitation.

With some embarrassment East mentioned that he had a message for Miss Truesdale from Mrs. Herrick. The truth was that the message was a flimsy one. He was speaking for himself and not for the sheriff's wife.

"Amy went out with one of her brothers riding the line," her father said. "Likely she won't be back till evening. I'll tell her what Mrs. Herrick says."

"Only that she has finished making the blouse and wants your daughter to come in and try it on," East explained.

While they were still talking Dick Stuart rode down the ranch road from the main one. He was on his way home from town. With him he brought news. It seemed that Rod Allen was accused of being the phantom killer. The sheriff and Steve Sanborn had tried to arrest him at Rillings's place and he had escaped by using Cad Withers as a shield while he backed to the door. It was believed he had headed for the Hole-in-the-Wall.

Jerry East did not think that was his immediate destination. Unless he was crowded closely he would not leave without trying to destroy the main witness against him. It would be wise of Morley to remain always among those who would guard him, until Allen was safely under custody. He took this up with Carruthers. If

Morley was coming to the Slash 72 a guard ought to ride with him. Carruthers added a postscript to his invitation urging Morley not to ride alone.

By a judicious question Jerry East learned that Miss Truesdale and her brother Ralph were riding the Twin Buttes country to push back strays wandering to the Diamond Tail range. He cut across the plain in the hope of meeting them. His story would be that he had run across them by chance. It was all right for her to guess that he was interested in her, but he was not yet prepared to admit that he had ridden fifteen miles out of his way to say, "Good morning, Miss Truesdale."

The long range lay in front of him, snow still in the seamed gulches below the sun-kissed crests. Rooted in the nearer foothills rose the Twin Buttes, sentinel peaks overlooking the undulant land waves stretching to the far horizon. He dipped into small valleys and emerged from them to ridges where the windmills of the Diamond Tail could be seen, their blades glinting in the sun as they revolved.

Faintly there came to him the sound of shots, two of them, fired so closely that the reports almost merged into one, and scarcely a minute later a third. Some sure instinct told Jerry that the breeze had brought to him notice of a death in the desert. There was no sensible reason for it, but for a moment the heart died under his ribs.

Somewhere in that waste in front of him Amy Truesdale and her brother were riding the line.

He was already heading for the Twin Buttes when the report of a fourth shot beat across the plain to him.

CHAPTER THIRTY-FIVE

MORLEY SAW BILL ROPER galloping across the pasture and wondered what was causing the man's wild haste. He hurried from the house and met the cowboy at the gate. Roper flung himself from the horse and cried out his news.

"Rod Allen has been shot."

"Shot?" Morley stared at the man, hope already churning in his heart. "Who shot him?"

"Herrick and Steve Sanborn. He's lying in the cottonwoods back of Twin Buttes. Hit two—three places. How he ever stuck in the saddle to get so far God knows."

"Is he dead?"

"Dying. They plugged him in the belly and the head. He wants to tell you something before he kicks in. I doubt if you get there in time. He's sure a goner."

"Wants to tell me something?" Morley repeated.

"That's right. I'll fling a saddle on Big Ben and take you there."

Morley thought fast. Within an hour or two a dozen men would be at the Twin Buttes. But he must get there first—alone. It sometimes took a mortally wounded man days to die. During that time he could talk enough to damn somebody

285

else. Before the sheriff or anybody else got there Allen must be dead.

"Did he say anything else to you, Bill?" Morley asked. "Say how they came to get him—or why?"

"No. He was mighty weak. Just said they had shot him and asked me to get you."

"This is a bad business, Bill," the ranch manager answered. "I don't understand it. Saddle Big Ben for me. I can go alone to the cottonwoods. Soon as I take off you had better get a fresh mount and ride to town. Tell Herrick where he can find Allen. You had better bring a doctor back there with you."

"I'll get Doc Norris. But it will be too late. He's limp as a rag doll now—if he's still alive."

As Morley rode through the pasture he felt the beat of confident excitement in his blood. Fear had ridden him for days and he was now free of it. This was a tremendous stroke of luck. It was easy to guess what had occurred. Herrick had sworn in Sanborn as a deputy to help him arrest Allen. They had probably surprised the killer and he had fought rather than be taken. Nothing could have suited Morley better, for as a prisoner the man would have been a constant menace to him. Evidently the wounded man had managed to get away on his horse. The one danger was that the sheriff might pick up the trail and get to his victim before Morley. But that was not likely. No doubt the battle had been fought on foot and

Herrick had been forced to find and saddle a horse. Otherwise they could have followed him at once to the Twin Buttes without losing sight of Allen.

Nonetheless Morley rode fast. He slackened pace only once to make sure his revolver lay light in the holster. Allen was a desperate man and might be dangerous even with the life ebbing out of him.

In the distance, while still two or three miles from the Buttes, he saw a slim cowboy in chaps moving through the brush. This was a slight mischance. The boy might hear a shot and later talk of it. But the sound of it would not reach him unless he rode a good deal closer to the Buttes, and at present he was not heading in that direction.

Morley kept well away from the brush along the foothills. Allen might not be as badly wounded as Roper had thought. He could be lying there waiting to get a shot at the man who had hired him to kill others. Approaching the Buttes, the Diamond Tail man made a wide circuit to by-pass and swing around them in order to reach the cottonwoods from the south in case the wounded man might be watching for him. Very cautiously he moved forward and presently caught sight of a prostrate figure lying back of a tree. There was no sign of life in that slack huddled form.

When about fifty yards distant Morley dismounted and walked slowly toward the clump of trees, the revolver in his hand. The bloodstained shirt and bandanna heartened him. He guessed that Allen had died since Roper had been here. But he was a cautious man, one who did not care to take risks. It was in his mind to make sure as soon as he was within range, though he felt that would not be wise. Unless necessary, it would be better for him not to fire a shot. An extra bullet hole in the body might raise a question.

The poor doomed coward took the last steps he was ever to take in this world. While he was still thirty yards distant the bloodstained figure leaped to its feet, rifle in hand. The shock of it drove the blood from Morley's flabby face. He knew the beating clock inside him was about to be stilled forever. A dreadful fear paralyzed him.

"So you came, Mr. Morley," the hardy ruffian jeered. "I thought the news that I was dying would bring you—to finish the job your friends had left undone."

"I—I—came because you sent for me," Morley faltered.

"So I did. Nice of you to come. I've been wanting to see you, you double-crossing yellow coyote. I know all about your talk with East after I left that last time and how you sent for Herrick

288

to throw the hooks into me. You're crooked as a dog's hind leg. You've come to the end of your last rotten mile."

"Listen, Rod," Morley cried desperately. "Listen, it isn't the way you think at all. I came to you because I thought you were hurt. We've been friends. I wouldn't turn against you."

"We've been friends, have we? What do you know about friends? Or I either? We're both damned murdering scoundrels. The difference is that I admit it and you don't. You've got a gun in your hand, Morley. Start using it." The killer laughed. He knew that at that distance there was not a chance in fifty that the poor wretch holding it could hit him, even if his nerves had been steady and had not set his cold flesh to quaking with fear.

"No, Rod. Listen—please."

"Sure, I'll listen. Get down on your hambones and beg."

The butt of Allen's rifle still rested on the ground. There was no hurry. He was enjoying this. With the years the lust to kill had grown in him. To blast the life out of men against whom he had no personal feeling gave him a terrific sense of power. In the case of Morley was added a hatred of the man that had been dormant even before he found out his employer intended to betray him.

"Let's talk this over, Rod," Morley implored.

"We're partners, you and me. I came to help you. Don't—don't do anything that—"

Again Allen's callous laughter sounded. "You can dish it out, but you can't take it. Who ordered Radway rubbed out—and Carlton—and Chapin—and young Baxter who was just fixing to get married? It's your turn now, you damned double-crossing murderer."

"No, Rod—no!" the doomed man cried.

"I'll give you a chance for your white alley. Come three steps closer and then cut loose. You can have first shot." He added harshly, "Last call before you go to hell, Morley."

Without hope Morley raised the revolver in his slack shaking fingers. The two shots rang out almost at the same time. Morley pitched forward. He lay on the ground face down, a faint trickle of smoke rising from the barrel of his revolver.

The killer walked slowly forward and flung another bullet into the prostrate body. He looked at his victim a long time, an exultant excitement in his eyes, then turned away to walk to his horse.

Abruptly he stopped. A slim figure in chaps was watching him from a ridge two hundred yards distant. He flung up his rifle and fired. There was no chance for another shot. The rider had swung the horse and disappeared in the hollow back of the ridge.

CHAPTER THIRTY-SIX

THERE WERE TIMES when Amy Truesdale became tired of trying to act like a lady and reverted to her earlier life as a tomboy. This day was one of them. She looked at her dresses resentfully and rejected them in favor of dust-stained boy's jeans and an old checked shirt. At breakfast she announced that she intended to ride the line with Ralph.

After pulling on a pair of leather chaps worn slick by time she roped and saddled her favorite pony Sonny Boy. They headed for the Twin Buttes country.

Ralph was fond of his younger sister. She was a good kid and could ride and rope as well as the average boy of her age. The conflict in her due to adolescence amused and interested him, and he took an older brother's privilege of teasing her. He looked at her slim immature figure and her tousled hair flying wild in the wind. A stranger might have guessed her about fifteen.

"How in the world did Jim Baxter ever fall in love with a harum-scarum kid like you?" he asked. "He must have got the idea that you were going to grow up and be a woman."

"It was at a dance," she explained. "I was wearing that red dress Father bought for me. We

291

were partners in a quadrille and all of a sudden I saw his eyes get big while he was looking at me. He must have thought I was sort of nice. I was so pleased. It made me feel grown up."

"You get tired of feeling grown up, don't you?"

"I can't be in a kitchen all the time or sit in a parlor with my hands folded. All my life I have loved to ride and work stock. So sometimes I still break over. Isn't that all right?"

"Sure it is. Do you miss Jim a lot?"

"Not so much as I did." She was a little shocked at herself for being so fickle. "We were both awf'ly young, Ralph. I'm not sure I was in love with him. It scares me sometimes now when I think of it."

"I had a notion it was kid stuff," Ralph said. "Take a full-grown man next time, Sis. You're the kind that needs one who will wear the breeches— till you quit being so doggoned impulsive, anyhow."

A tide of pink beat up through the tan of the girl's face. "Maybe there won't be a next time," she answered, and put her mount to a canter to turn back a bunch of grazing cattle. It would be embarrassing if Ralph guessed from her confusion what full-grown man had jumped to her mind.

When she rejoined him her brother's thoughts had shifted to another subject. "Looks like Father will sign up this week to buy the Barford ranch and brand," he told her. "Hope he does. He'll be getting the outfit at a whack-up price."

At the higher ground where the Twin Buttes were rooted they pulled up for a moment. Here they separated, to meet later at the mouth of Sand Creek Canyon. Ralph was to ride the undulating country of bunch grass to the left, his sister to circle the Buttes and push back any Slash 72 stuff that might have wandered into the hills. There was good feed there, but scattered in the grass was a lot of poisonous locoweed.

Amy swung wide around the Buttes to comb the slopes back of them. One old bull persisted in leading his followers into the pockets below the cliffs and every two or three days a rider had to push the stock back to the plains. The girl sighted the bunch and started it toward the Buttes.

As she jogged along behind the cattle her mind was on the advice Ralph had given her, to marry a man more mature and stronger than she was. Of course he had no idea how much her own inclination leaned the same way. She wondered if it was unmaidenly to have a man so much in her thoughts as she had this easygoing Texan who had so much strength back of his friendly smile. Already she knew it would have been a mistake to marry Jim Baxter.

A hundred times a day Jerry East pushed into her consciousness. She was a fool, no doubt. He had been nice to her out of kindness and she had been silly enough to fall in love with him. With youth's swift judgment she decided that no woman ought to care about any man until she was sure he wanted her more than anybody else in the world. You just laid up grief for yourself if you did, for a girl was so completely helpless when she gave her heart to a man. As a young girl she had been much distressed because she had not been born a boy. That regret had vanished and left another injustice rankling in her. This whole business of being in love was so unfair. The man could speak out what he felt, but a woman had to hide love in her heart, pretend she did not care, and pray that some day he would turn kind eyes on her.

The cattle emerged from the tangle of hills and debouched into the lowland back of the Buttes. They topped a rise, and Sonny Boy followed them lazily snatching here and there at a clump of grass. Amy looked down on the setting of what was to be the most shocking scene in her life. A man with a drawn revolver was moving soft-footed toward the cottonwoods back of the Buttes. Something in the way he crept sent a chill through her, for she saw another man lying as if dead in the clump of trees. The man with the pistol was Morley. His eyes never shifted from the prone figure. Amy wanted to cry a warning, but the sound froze in her throat. Very carefully Morley drew closer. Unexpectedly the man in the grove leaped to his feet. She saw that he was covered with blood, and that he had a rifle in his hand.

Morley stopped in his tracks. Words passed between them that she could not hear, but she realized Morley was petrified with terror. She recognized the rifleman now, Rodney Allen the stock detective. He was taunting his victim savagely and cruelly. It was plain that Morley did not have a chance. He was out of revolver range and could be cut down by a rifle bullet easily.

The weapons blazed almost simultaneously, and Morley fell instantly. Allen came out from the trees, stood over the fallen man, and sent another bullet crashing into him.

The murderer looked up—and caught sight of her. Amy was wheeling her pony to go when a bullet slammed into her shoulder. Before there was a chance for another shot she was out of sight in the hollow. That her reprieve was short she knew. She had caught a killer in the act. To save himself he must destroy her.

But he had to get to his horse. That would give her a minute or two, and if he was as badly wounded as he seemed to be he might not have the strength to follow her far. Already Sonny Boy was dashing up a draw with bunched muscles standing out as he took the slope. It brought them to a ridge from which they plunged down into another hollow.

A wet, red stain was soaking her shirt. The first impact of the bullet had not been very painful but now every leap of the horse brought a knife stab to her shoulder. The sight of the blood frightened Amy. A sick faintness she had never felt before was stealing through her. To steady herself her left hand clutched the saddle horn so tightly that the knuckles stood out white from the brown flesh. She must not fall off. She must keep going until she was lost in the hills where the killer could not find her. Her body lurched in the hull. The hills tilted violently, and the ground rose up to meet them. She was sliding in a deep gulf of space.

At sight of the slight unconscious figure Allen dragged his horse to a halt with an oath. He slipped from the saddle and moved warily forward, unwilling to accept the evidence of his eyes. That tangle of bright hair shining in the sun belonged to no cowpuncher but to a girl in boy's clothes. This was damnable luck. The thought of what he had done appalled him. If he had killed her there would be no place for him alive in all this Western country. He would be hunted down like a sheep-killing wolf.

The girl was the wild hoyden daughter of Cliff Truesdale, known to everybody within fifty miles and liked by most of them. He could not have picked a worse target for his shot. It was her own fault, of course. She ought not to have been traipsing over the range wearing a man's togs. But he would get all the blame.

He knelt down, opened her shirt, and examined the wound. It was a relief to see that the bullet had struck no vital place. The lead had torn through the flesh without touching a bone. Given the proper care, the wound would heal nicely. Though he was anxious to be on his way, he could not leave her here. They might not find her for days, and then perhaps not alive. Sullenly he set about giving her first aid.

From the saddle he brought his canteen. He untied the bandanna hanging loosely around her throat and soaked it with water. As he started to wash away the blood the girl opened her eyes.

To orient herself took a moment. Fear came into her eyes. She shrank back from him.

"I'm fixing you up," he told her ungraciously. "You don't need to be scared."

"You shot me," she charged feebly.

"Why do you wear men's clothes?" he demanded, his voice harsh and angry. "How could I tell you were a girl?"

She was still afraid, but not so much. He would not be taking care of her hurt if he meant to kill her. "Is it—bad?" she asked.

"No, a scratch. The bullet missed your lungs. This is going to hurt some. Don't start yelping." He pushed the shirt back from her breast.

The picture of what she had seen him do was

vivid in her memory. She wanted to tell him to go away and leave her alone. He read the horror of him in her mind.

"He came to kill me. I had to defend myself, didn't I?" The callous coldness of his voice was shocking. "He was a yellow coyote—better dead. Hold back your shirt and let me get at this."

He was gentle as he could be, but she groaned at the touch of the wet handkerchief brushing the wound.

"The bullet went clear through," he told her. "You are lucky. In a couple of weeks your shoulder will be well as ever."

After he had done what he could for her he swung to the saddle.

"Are you going to leave me here?" she asked.

"I'm going to bring your pony," he answered.

Sonny Boy was grazing a couple of hundred yards distant. Allen caught the animal and brought it back.

"Can you make it to the Buttes?" he wanted to know.

"I'll try, if you can get me into the saddle."

He lifted her into it and saw that her feet found the stirrups.

"We'll travel slow," the killer said. "I'll go first and pick the easiest way."

Most of the time he rode beside her, watching to make sure she was not going to fall off. She gritted her teeth and did not make any complaint, though the knife was stabbing at her shoulder again.

"Not much farther," he promised. "Just a couple of hundred yards more."

She stuck it out. When they reached the grove he lifted her from the saddle and laid her under a cottonwood. He had carried her so that her back was toward the dead body of Morley.

Amy said, "I'd like a drink, please."

He brought the canteen and held it while she drank.

"What are you going to do about me now?" she wanted to know.

He frowned down at her, annoyance in his leathery face. That he could not leave her here alone and forget her he knew, and he was trying to decide what was best for him. The nearest ranch was the Diamond Tail. There he dared not go. The KZ was about seven miles and not in the direction he wanted to travel. He could drop in there and tell of the girl's plight. It might be dangerous, but perhaps that was the best thing he could do. The news that he was the phantom killer had probably not reached that ranch yet, though it was surprising how quickly gossip spread in the thinly settled cattle country. Maybe he might meet a rider on the range and give him a pointer about her. It was a piece of rotten luck that she was here at all, but the fact was that she would be a far greater danger to him dead than alive. Roper's story would tie him to her death.

"I've got to let somebody know you are here," he said sourly. "Get this straight, girl. Morley laid a trap to murder me. I thought he had brought you along to help him do it. When you tell what happened get it right."

"Yes," she promised. "I wanted to cry out and warn you. Was it Mr. Morley that wounded you?"

"That's right. He came back to finish the job." The man ripped out an oath. "Why did you have to come buttin' in?"

"I'm sorry. Ralph and I were riding the line."

"Where's he?"

"We separated to meet later."

"All right," he snapped. "I'll send somebody to you."

Amy cried, "Look!"

A man was rounding the lower end of the Buttes at a gallop.

Allen glared at him for a split second, then swung to the saddle and was off. Before Amy discovered that the arrival who had driven him away was not her brother the killer had disappeared in the hill folds.

CHAPTER THIRTY-SEVEN

AS JERRY SWUNG AROUND THE LOWER END of the Buttes into the little valley back of them he saw a man vault to a saddle and jump his horse to a gallop. The rider-in-a-hurry had vanished into the hills before East caught sight of the body lying close to the edge of the cottonwoods. A split second later he became aware of somebody in distress sitting propped against one of the trees in the grove, and almost simultaneously his eye picked up Sonny Boy. He sprang to the ground and ran past the dead man, his stomach knotted into a tight ball. He knew who it must be under the tree.

"Jerry—Jerry," Amy cried, a throb of joy in her voice.

"You're hurt," he exclaimed, and dropped to a knee beside her.

"He shot me," she answered. "It's been so dreadful, Jerry." Her voice broke to a sob. "I—I saw him kill Mr. Morley."

"Shot you?" He asked tensely, "Where are you hurt?"

"In the shoulder. He bandaged it and said I would be all right in a few days. Oh, I'm so glad you came."

"Who bandaged it?"

301

"Rodney Allen. After he had shot me. He thought I was a man, on account of the clothes."

"Good God! The murdering devil might have killed you. Where is Ralph?"

She explained that they had separated to drive back the strays. He would probably wait for her at the mouth of Sand Creek Canyon.

He got his water bag, moistened his bandanna and wiped her hot face. "Are you in much pain?" he asked gently.

Amy smiled wryly. "I don't mind it now, since you are here. I've been so awf'ly afraid. But after he knew I was a girl he did all he could."

Jerry gave her a drink and offered to rearrange the bandage if she wished. She said she would rather leave it as it was and wanted to know how he was going to get her home. "If I have to I can ride, but I'd rather not," she added. "It joggles the wound and starts bleeding."

"I don't think you ought to move," he told her.

"Don't leave me," she pleaded. "I'd rather not stay alone."

He was distressed. It would be cruel to leave her after the shock she had been given, but a doctor ought to look after the wound as soon as possible. "Maybe somebody might hear if I give a signal for help," he suggested.

Three times he fired his revolver in rapid succession, then loaded and sent into the air three more shots.

Though Amy was in pain, she was not so unhappy as Jerry. The one man in the world she most wanted to be with her was here. He sat beside her, the tumbled head of hair resting on his shoulder.

"Is this lesson number two, big brother?" she presently asked in a small voice.

"What you need, little girl, is someone to take care of you," he said grimly. He was thinking how dreadfully empty his life would have been if Allen had shot straighter.

"I have a father and two big brothers, not counting you," she mentioned.

"Yes? Where were they today when you needed them?"

She sighed. "You came." Almost she said, *And that was wonderful.*

"Hurting a good deal?" he inquired.

"It's easier when I rest on your shoulder. I'll be all right. I'm not afraid now. Why did they want to kill each other?"

"Allen was paid by Morley to kill the homesteaders. They were caught in a trap and were afraid of each other. Don't think about that now." He put his head down and let his cheek rest against hers.

She said, and laughed a little tremulously, "You're dear—to be so nice to a little sister."

"To the girl I love," he corrected.

A pain shot through her shoulder as she raised

her head, but she paid no heed to it. "A man *ought* to care for his sister a little," she told him doubtfully, her eyes anxiously on his. "That's what you mean."

"And much more for his sweetheart," he said.

"A man once told me that flirting is making love to a girl without meaning it," she quoted, trying to keep her voice light.

"I aim to put a wedding ring on this girl's finger—if she'll let me," he declared in a low Texas drawl.

"You're not just—sorry for me?"

"I'd be sorry for myself if you wouldn't have it that way."

"I've been so afraid you wouldn't like me much," she confessed happily. "I thought maybe I was a fool for hoping."

He tilted her sweet mouth up and satisfied her on that point.

"Hey! What's going on here?" a voice demanded. Ralph Truesdale had come up on their blind side and was swinging from the saddle.

"You told me to choose a full-grown man when I got married," she reminded him.

"I didn't expect you to take me at my word the same day." The grin went off his face like the light from a blown candle. He was staring at the body of Morley.

"Allen killed him and lit out," East explained.

"But he didn't go until he had slammed a bullet into your sister's shoulder."

Ralph dropped the bridle reins and came forward swiftly. "Great Jehosophat!" he cried. "How come he to do that, Sis?"

"He thought I was a man and did not want to leave a witness alive," she answered. "But I'm going to be all right. It's just a little flesh wound."

"What's the matter with the fool?" Ralph cried. "Has he gone crazy? I thought he and Morley were friends."

East explained the relationship between the men in two sentences, after which they discussed the best way of getting Amy to a doctor. It was decided that Ralph would ride back to the Slash 72, send somebody for a doctor, and return to the Buttes with a rig for his sister.

While they were still talking there came to them the sound of moving wheels. A rider came into sight and just behind him a light wagon. The horseman was Bill Roper. The two in the wagon were Sheriff Herrick and Doctor Norris. They had come to pick up a dead or dying man. They found one dead, but nonetheless were surprised. The body they found was not that of the man they had expected to discover.

CHAPTER THIRTY-EIGHT

BEFORE BILL ROPER REACHED HERRICK with word that Rod Allen was lying mortally wounded at the foot of Twin Buttes the sheriff had sent out two posses to cut off the escape of the killer in case he sought refuge in the Hole-in-the-Wall. Herrick did not go with either of these man-hunting parties because he did not expect Allen to leave without first attempting to shoot Morley. Steve Sanborn was in charge of one group, Chris Dunn of the other.

With Sanborn rode Nick Fox. He was not a member of the posse but had been given his freedom to take a message to his associates in the Hole. He was to impress on the night-riding gentry living there that Allen must be turned back at the gateway and given no harborage. It would not be difficult to convince them of the wisdom of co-operation with the law. Their sympathies were already with the small cattlemen and against the hired assassin whom they suspected of being employed by the big ranches. An even more potent argument was that the feeling of the district against this killer had become so intense that any attempt to befriend him would probably result in a community invasion of the outlaws' habitat.

Allen did not know of these preparations to trap him, but he was very well aware that within a few hours this whole country would be alert to kill or capture him. There would be no safety for him in any place where cattle ranged.

He rode fast, twisting through the low folds of the brown hills, up small canyons to the rims above, down into watered parks, until at last he crossed the divide that took him into the desert that stretched far across to the rougher land that marked the retreat of the outlaws.

There might be danger here, if Herrick had started the hunt for him. His eyes searched the land waves for any sign of a posse. So far as he could tell he was alone in that great waste of wilderness. If his luck held he could cross it to the gateway of that mountain sanctuary where other scoundrels wanted by the law lived safely in a hunter's and fisherman's paradise. He would get a very reluctant welcome, but he did not care a rap for a hostility that would probably take the form of having nothing whatever to do with him.

From the top of a rise he saw far to the left a billow of dust. Through his glasses he watched it for several minutes. He knew that moving animals were making that cloud, and that the animals must be bunched horses. Cattle did not travel so steadily unless driven. A shift in the wind showed him riders, five of them, headed in his direction. He judged they were looking for him. If it had not been for the eyewitness of his latest crime, the girl he had left in the cottonwoods back of Twin Buttes, he would have ridden to meet them and bluffed it out. They might suspect, but they could not prove. But no denial would serve him now, not after what Amy Truesdale had seen. He hoped they had not seen his dust. It would go hard with him if they had and later stumbled on him where he was hiding. For it was plain he could not cross the wrinkled floor of the plain in front of them, leaving behind him in the quiet air a thin cloud of dust to mark his progress.

Through ravines and draws he worked back to the divide he had traversed, fastened his horse out of sight behind it, and lay down among some scrub-oak brush to watch the posse. He picked the riders up with his glasses as they topped a rise and watched them disappear into the bed of a dry stream. After that he saw no more of them. They had vanished in the defiles of the huddled hills far to the right.

His business as stock detective had been one requiring infinite patience. Many a time he had lain back of cover for the better part of a day without stirring, on the lookout for any rustlers who might be at work. Now he waited until dusk began to fall over the land before taking to the saddle again. By the time he came to the valley night had blanketed the earth. He did not hurry, but he held his horse to a steady gait. The stars came out, and the moon was high in the sky when he unsaddled and picketed his mount for rest and feed. Allen was a hungry man. He had not eaten since morning. There were ranches within a few miles of him, but he dared not show face at any of them. Twice he had seen game without firing. The sound of a gun's explosion might draw his hunters to him.

Though the terrain was as crisscrossed with washes, draws, gulches, and cattle trails as the palm of a man's hand is with fine lines, Allen could have traveled it in the blackest night without getting lost. He knew every pocket and hogback in it. His knowledge stopped at the gateway to the Hole-in-the-Wall. Beyond that lay enemy country forbidden to him because he had been an employee of the Cattlemen's Association. Making for the entrance of this outlaws' paradise, he cut to the right, his way deflected by brush, dips, and hill scarps around which he circled to take up anew the trail to his destination. It would be well for him to be inside before sunup. A few more miles would bring him to temporary safety.

At the top of a rise he looked down into a gulf of semidarkness. Thin streaks of gray were already beginning to sift into the sky. He could not see the wall of hills beyond, but his gaze clung to the far, faint light of a campfire. It must be in the little valley just this side of the gateway.

He did not need to be told that a posse was camped there to cut him off from the Hole.

There was no use blundering about in the night. He decided to wait the situation out. Come morning the posse would either be on its way or would keep its present camp. He could make up his mind then what to do.

He loosened the saddle girths and again picketed his horse. From a post on the ridge he watched day come over the land. The smoke of the campfire rose into the light air. Some member of the posse was cooking breakfast. The sun rose on the far horizon and climbed higher. Long experience in the outdoors informed him that the fire had been put out when he no longer could see any smoke. Presently a small moving dust streak gave information that the campers were on the move.

They might not all be gone. The leader could have left a couple of men to look out for him if he appeared. At this distance he could not be sure. He mounted and rode cautiously closer to the site of the camp. From a screen of willows beside a creek he searched the country with his glasses and let them come to rest on the spot the posse had occupied. There was no sign of either horse or man. The only way to find out was to go and see whether a trap had been laid for him, taking very good care not to blunder into it if there was one.

It was a nice question at what point he had better leave his horse. He did not want it near enough to betray his presence as he wormed his way to the rim of the valley, nor did he want it too far away for him to reach the saddle in case there was pressure on him. Back of a brush clump about a quarter of a mile from the gap he tied his mount.

No Apache could have taken better advantage of such cover as there was in his advance to the rim. He moved noiselessly, light-footed as a cat. From the rimrock he scanned the small park, combing it yard by yard with his probing gaze. That there were no horses and no men there, he was sure. Opposite where he lay was a break in the saucer-shaped rim. An upheaval of nature had cleft an opening with huge gate posts of gneiss and porphyry into a dark canyon beyond. Within that narrow rock-split men might be waiting for him.

He kept vigil for a long half hour, motionless as a lizard on a rock. No sign of life appeared. Just as he was starting to bring his horse two riders came out of the gash. One of them was a tall, lank man, Sink Curry, against whom he had gathered evidence of rustling several years before. The jury had found him not guilty. At the time there had been bitter words between the two men.

That the whole posse had gone was plain. Otherwise Curry would not be here. He and his companion were examining the campground with its litter of empty cans, broken remnants of food, and cold charred bits of wood. Allen thought, *Beggars can't be choosers. I'd better fix up a peace with Sink.* The stock detective did not like the layout. Curry was a vindictive devil, and it might be hard to persuade him that his former enemy was now a fugitive wanted by the law. But it was a chance he had to take.

He rose and waved a handkerchief. "Hi, Sink! Want to talk with you," he shouted.

By common consent the horsemen moved apart with no discussion. The second rider was a short heavy-set fellow with shoulders so rounded he was nearly hunchbacked.

"Come on down," jeered Curry. "We been waitin' for you, Mr. Phantom Killer, with a fatted calf all ready. Ain't that right, Shorty?"

"You've done said it, Sink," his companion agreed. "Pleased to meet up with you, Mr. Allen. Hands in the air as you drift down, please."

Allen's heart chilled. Both of the men carried rifles. That did not disturb him so much as the certainty that the sheriff had already closed the Hole to him. These men were here to guard the entrance. Even if he could force a way in he would find himself in a nest of enemies.

He did not stop to argue the matter. A bullet whizzed past him as he turned and ran, crouching, back from the rim. His objective was a rocky outcrop from the ground that topped jaggedly a low ridge. As the horses clambered over the rim he reached the sandstone barrier.

His first shot was good. Sink Curry ripped out an oath and dragged his horse to its haunches. "I'm hit," he yelped.

Shorty pulled up. Allen was behind cover and could drop them as they came forward. "Let's get outa here," he cried.

The outlaws wheeled their horses and left at a gallop. Allen fired a second shot at them as they went.

He walked to his horse, mounted, and rode back into the desert from which he had come. The outlaws of the Hole had served notice that there would be no refuge for him there.

Allen was tired and hungry. His shoulders sagged. The horse he rode was weary and would be easily overtaken if it came to a race. He swung into the foothills and skirted them as he rode toward the west. Before he had traveled a mile he saw the dust of another posse perhaps two miles distant.

He was being hemmed in, and if he did not get out of this district would soon be trapped. Swiftly he came to a bold decision, to ride straight for Powder Horn, come into the outskirts from the south, pick up a fresh horse and some food, then strike for the Wind River range. If his luck stood up he might make it.

CHAPTER THIRTY-NINE

DOCTOR NORRIS AGREED with Ralph that a flesh wound in the shoulder ought not to prove too serious when the victim was a strong healthy girl like Amy. What she would need primarily was rest and good nursing. Since there was no other woman in her father's house it would be well to get somebody from town to care for her.

She was in a good deal of pain. The jolting of the wagon on the way home had set the wound to throbbing fiercely. The fever grew with the hours, and the girl tossed restlessly. She talked, delirious fragments. Once she murmured, "He told me he didn't need that finger, anyhow." And later, "I want a nice dress, so I can be a lady."

Her father asked her gently, "Are you all right, honey? Anything you want?"

She told him fiercely, "I'm not, either, ugly. He said—he said—" Her voice thinned out, and the sentence died.

East had stayed for the night. At breakfast Truesdale said anxiously to him, "I wonder who is the best woman we can get to nurse Amy."

The Texan suggested Mrs. Herrick. "She is very competent, and Amy is fond of her. If you like I'll stop in and ask her to come. I'm pretty sure she will."

"That will be fine," Truesdale agreed, and named one or two more in case Mrs. Herrick could not come.

Already reports about the killing of Morley were drifting in to the Slash 72. Bill Roper's story showed that Allen had laid a trap for the dead man. The calf killed by the stock detective had been found. It was unlikely that the man had been wounded at all. Both the sheriff and Sanborn were pretty sure their bullets had not touched him. There seemed to be no doubt that the two men, Morley and Allen, had been responsible for the death of the four homesteaders and that they had quarreled later. Each had been afraid of the other. Morley had hurried to the Twin Buttes to make sure his accomplice was dead and had fallen from the fire of the more desperate villain.

Before East left the ranch a cowboy rode in from the Diamond Tail with news of the hunt. Three posses at least were out, two of them combing the rough country below the Hole-in-the-Wall. Early in the morning Allen had tried to slip through the gateway to the Hole and had been stopped by a pair of outlaws waiting there for him. In the gun fight that followed, Allen had wounded Sink Curry and made his escape. He was hemmed in by the posses, and the chances were that within a short time he would be killed or captured.

"Not captured," East said. "If they bring him in it will be dead."

Truesdale thought that probable. The fellow was a desperate villain and would prefer to go out to the roar of guns.

Ralph came out from the house to join them. "Amy would like to see you before you go, Jerry," he said.

East tightened the cinch of the horse he was saddling, ground-tied the reins, and went to Amy's room. The delirium had passed and the fever had dropped a degree or more.

"I don't believe you have been to bed all night," she accused. "If you are worrying about me you can stop it. The doctor says I'm doing fine."

"That's why I'm singing 'Glory, Hallelujah' inside," he told her cheerfully.

"I sent for you to make sure I'm not imagining you said something I think you did after you found me yesterday."

"If you mean about me caring for you, why just make it double and then some," he reassured her.

"That's fine," she said, and moved her small hand toward his.

She looked so little and so helpless lying in the bed with gifts in her eyes that emotion swelled in him. He knelt and kissed her. "That must be all for now," he whispered. "You must rest."

Amy nodded. Her eyes drooped. Presently she

fell asleep. He freed his fingers gently from hers and tiptoed out of the room.

Jerry East rode across the cowbacked hills to town in the golden sunshine, his heart high within him. He felt sure his sweetheart would soon build up the blood she had lost. Truesdale would not stand in the way of their marriage. His changed manner showed that. It had become warm and friendly. Hal Carruthers had dropped down to the old house to inquire about Amy and had said plainly he wanted Jerry to ride for the Slash 72. The task that had brought him to this district was almost completed. He saw peaceful years for him and Amy, a long procession of them. There would be children and prosperity, herds of cattle carrying the JE brand. It was a good world. A snatch of a proverb heard in his Sunday school days flashed to his mind. *The wicked shall fall by his own wickedness . . . The righteous is delivered out of trouble.* He did not reckon to qualify as righteous, but anyhow he was not wicked.

Since he had been a cowboy and was distrustful of softness due to sentimentality he broke into trifling song, a friendly mockery of his emotional state of mind.

"Oh, I'm going home
Bullwhacking for to spurn,
I ain't got a nickel
And I don't give a dern;

317

’Tis when I meet a pretty girl,
You bet I will or try,
I’ll make her my little wife,
Root, hog, or die.”

He knew Nell Herrick would be pleased with the news. He would tell her nonchalantly, with drawling indifference, and watch the glad surprise come into her lovely eyes. Maybe he would pretend to be afraid of marriage and act as if he had been trapped into it, so defending himself against the teasing which he foresaw.

When he left Cap and his rifle at the corral he exchanged news with Karl. Herrick had just pulled out of town with a fourth posse, the owner of the wagon yard mentioned. There was a rumor that Allen was surrounded in a pocket just below Black Eagle Prong. Some of the boys were sure to get him soon. That would be fine. This country would sleep easier with the killer under the sod. Powder Horn sure owed Mr. East a lot for clearing up this business.

Jerry sauntered up the street and turned in at the gate of the Herrick place. He walked between the jonquils bordering the path to the porch and rapped on the door. There had been a murmur of voices in the house, he thought, but now it had died away. Nobody answered his knock. Presently he tried again. After another long silence he heard the faint rumor of talk again.

Then Nell spoke, her low throaty voice strangely unlike the one he knew. "Go away, whoever you are. I—I'm dressing."

He answered, "All right, Nell. I want to see you. Be back in a few minutes."

"Make it half an hour, Jerry," she replied.

That something was wrong he knew. Nell was in trouble of some sort. If she had not been the coolest and most self-contained woman he knew he would have read fear in the ragged voice. Certainly she was agitated. Who was in the house with her? Neither Herrick nor Sanborn. Both of them were out with posses.

"Half an hour it is," he said, and went down the steps.

He stood in front of the porch, uncertain as to what he had better do. To go away and leave her in distress would be no friendly act. *Nell did not dress in the front room.* She had flung out the first excuse that had come to her mind. Swiftly he decided to take a hand in this, though she might think him a brash fool for interfering. Jerry tiptoed up the steps and flung open the door.

CHAPTER FORTY

WHEN BILL ROPER CAME to the Herrick house with the urgent news that Rodney Allen was dying back of the Twin Buttes of wounds inflicted by the sheriff and Steve Sanborn, the law officer knew there was something queer about this. He was reasonably sure that neither he nor Sanborn had scored a hit on the escaping killer. But Bill stuck to his story that he had seen Allen lying under a cottonwood desperately wounded.

Nell feared this was a plant to ambush her husband and said so. Though Charles promised to be very careful, she was uneasy until she saw him driving into the yard late that night. Before he was out of the wagon she was hurrying across the yard to meet him.

"I'm glad you're back," she told him. "I've been worrying."

"No need to worry." He put an arm around her shoulder and gave her a little hug. "We found a dead man, but not the one I was looking for. And we found Amy Truesdale too, shot in the shoulder."

"Amy!" Nell exclaimed. "What was she doing there? Who shot her?"

"She had been riding the line with her brother.

Allen shot her. Took her for a man. Doc says she'll be all right."

"There's no woman at the Slash Seventy-Two. I must go out in the morning and look after her." Her face retained its look of shock. "Was the dead man her brother Ralph?"

"No. He and Amy had separated to comb the brush for strays. Amy happened to be back of the Buttes when Allen killed Morley."

"Killed Morley?" she repeated. "You were afraid he would do that."

Herrick explained how the cattle detective had laid a trap for Morley and the ranch manager had walked into it. There was a good chance that Allen would be taken or killed since three posses were out after him, two of them in the terrain where he had disappeared. If Allen eluded them he would be forced to cut south, but he would not try that until they were closing in on him. In the morning, the sheriff said, he was going to get another posse in the saddle to prevent him from breaking through to the settlements below.

When Nell spoke of supper he told her he had eaten at the Slash 72 but would like a cup of coffee. While she was making it he mentioned another piece of news. Jerry East and Amy Truesdale had evidently come to an understanding. After reaching the ranch Jerry had carried her to the bedroom, but before putting her down he had kissed her while Ralph and he were in the room.

Nell was agog at once. What kind of kiss was it? Just a brotherly brush of the cheek given out of sympathy? Or did he act as if it meant more? And how did she take it?

"She didn't seem anyways mad about it," her husband said. "Her arm was mighty tight around his neck and she turned her lips to his real willing. I'm not very good at describing such things. Maybe I had better show you the kind of kiss it was."

Which he did. She said, smiling at him, "It must have been a very satisfactory kiss, but I think you overemphasized it a little."

After breakfast Herrick organized, armed, and mounted his posse. On his way past the house he waved a good-by to his wife. She watched the riders leave the road and disappear in the land swells. When she had done the housework she went uptown to buy a few supplies.

She heard plenty of rumors about the hunt but very little news. One of Sanborn's men had come in to report to the sheriff. Neither of the posses operating in the north had contacted the hunted man, but it was known that the outlaws of the Hole-in-the-Wall had blocked the gateway and driven him back after a battle in which one of their men had been wounded.

Nell was baking bread and when it had risen

enough she put the pans in the oven. As she was testing a loaf with a straw to find if it was done the kitchen door opened and a man walked into the room.

Nell looked over her shoulder and chill fear swept through her. The muscles of her legs went weak and a knot tied in her stomach, but even in that moment of dread she was thankful her husband was not here.

The man was Rodney Allen. He carried a rifle, and his usually neat clothes were wrinkled and travel-stained, his face unshaven and dust-streaked. The sunken harried eyes were chill and hard.

"Don't tell me you are not pleased to see me, Mrs. Herrick," he jeered. "And with me so popular that half the men in town are looking for me."

The woman rose from her crouched position. She thought, *I must not show I am afraid or even disturbed.* "Did you come to the sheriff's house to give yourself up?" she asked. "My husband is not at home."

He was relieved at the quiet coolness of her challenge. There would be no trouble in dealing with her. She would not scream for help and have to be knocked in the head.

His jangled laughter held no mirth. "I knew he wasn't here. An hour or so ago I met him."

"Met him?" she cried.

"Not exactly. I was lying on a brush-covered rimrock with my rifle trained on him. Lucky for him he did not turn my way. Seeing him gave me an idea. I want a fresh horse and food, so I figured I could get them here. We killers have to stand together."

So he knew she had shot Henry Fallon and was putting her in his own class. That might have been a small influence in bringing him here, but the major one was that the Herrick house was on the outskirts of the town where he was less likely to be seen and that there was always a horse in the pasture.

"I can't prevent you from taking anything you want," she said.

"That's good sense. We'll get along. First off, fix me up breakfast—some food that is already cooked. And make some coffee. I'm hungry as a wolf."

"Somebody may come," she suggested. Already she was on the way to the cupboard to get dishes and food.

"That would be too bad for him," he told her grimly. "I'm not feeling friendly to other visitors today."

She set before him a cold roast of beef left from yesterday's dinner, a loaf of the new bread, butter, and presently a cup of coffee.

"Sugar and cream?" she inquired.

"Straight."

He ate rapidly, almost wolfishly, seated at a place where he could watch both doors.

"Don't try to make a break to get away," he warned.

"I'm not a fool," she answered curtly. "All I want is to get you away from here as fast as I can."

"My idea, too," he agreed, his mouth twisted to a sneer. "I'm here only for a short visit. Before I leave I'll have to tie you up and gag you. I'm sure you won't mind that."

He cut himself another thick slice of beef and tore the loaf in two. "Excuse my manners, Mrs. Herrick. I'm a gent in a hurry." While he was slapping the meat on the bread he ordered her to pack into a gunny sack all the cooked food there was in the house.

Nell did as she was told. "Shall I put any coffee in?" she asked.

"No. I won't be lighting any fires. I notice two horses in the pasture. I want one. Can you rope?"

"It isn't necessary. My horse Pete is so gentle I can bridle him in the open pasture."

"I don't want a lady's pony, but a horse with speed and stamina."

"Pete has both, but if you want to walk down to the pasture you can take your choice."

"I'm not going into the pasture. You'll get the horse and bring it to the house. I'll be covering you with a rifle every second of the time. Don't bother about a saddle. I'll pick mine up where I left it in the brush."

"Am I to go now?" she asked.

"Yes. You can finish packing the stuff after you come back. If you make a move to run I'll pump lead in you."

Her scornful eyes rested on him. She was not afraid any longer. He would not harm her unless it was necessary to save himself. That would be suicidal folly.

"Yes, I know," she said quietly. "The way you did with Amy Truesdale."

"The little idiot was wearing a man's clothes. How could I tell she was a girl?" He reached for his rifle and picked up the sandwich in his left hand. "Get going—and don't make a mistake." His chill, rasping voice held a threat more potent than the words.

"I'll have to step into the stable to get the bridle," she explained, her eyes meeting his directly. "Get this into your twisted brain. I am not going to give you any excuse for killing me. Another thing, I don't want you shot here but to get you off the place soon as I can."

"That's fine. But don't play any tricks."

From the window of the kitchen he watched her go into the stable and come out with a bridle. His gaze followed her to the pasture and rested on her while she caught and bridled the pony.

Leading it, she came back to the house and trailed the reins on the ground.

"Did you see anybody?" he demanded.

"Mrs. Dennison is taking in her laundry from the line farther down the road," Nell said. "She ought to be through in a minute."

He handed her the carving-knife. "Cut down your clothesline and bring it in."

"To tie me with?"

"Yes. I don't want you screaming out that I've been here."

She went into the yard and cut the rope, then brought it into the house. Without waiting for further instructions she put the remainder of the roast in the gunny sack.

"How about a can of tomatoes?" she asked.

"Yes," he agreed, and added grimly, "You think of everything."

If he should be on the desert out of reach of water the juice might be lifesaving. He was a man impatient of women and usually indifferent to their charm, but it flashed across his mind that she was one he could have gone all out for. Few men would have accepted this situation with the cool unfluttered nerve she was showing. Yet every graceful motion she made, every expression of the lovely disdainful face, was wholly feminine.

He made a slipknot in the rope. "I'm going to tie you to a chair," he explained. "I hope you are going to be smart and not make a fuss."

"Would it do any good?" she asked contemptuously.

"No, and it might do a lot of harm."

She stood motionless while he slipped the loop over her feet and tightened it. "You've got more sense than any other woman I ever met," he said bluntly. "Most of them would have thrown a fit."

He dragged a chair toward them. "Sit down," he ordered.

His body stiffened abruptly. A crisp step sounded on the walk leading from the gate.

The killer picked up his rifle. "If the fellow knocks don't answer," he snarled, the wolf look in his face.

"Let me handle it," she answered in a low voice.

There came a rap on the door. Nell sat very still. Perhaps he would go away. The caller knocked again. She prayed he would not walk to a window and look into the room.

"Tell him to go away," Allen murmured. He had put down the rifle and drawn a revolver. The man looked as venomous and dangerous as a rattlesnake.

CHAPTER FORTY-ONE

FEAR CHOKED NELL'S THROAT. The only ray of comfort she had was that the man on the porch could not be her husband. He would not have knocked. Whoever he was, to save his life she had to send him away ignorant of the presence of her unwelcome guest.

Her throat quavered when she called to this second visitor to go away, that she was dressing.

She recognized the voice that answered. The man at the door was Jerry East. He said he wanted to see her and would be back in a few minutes.

"Make it half an hour, Jerry," she told him.

Nell breathed easier when she heard him going down the steps. He had been very close to death, she thought.

"You did fine," the killer said in a low voice. "Lucky for him you kept your head." The revolver he slid back into its scabbard.

He passed the rope around her body and the back of the chair, her arms inside the circle. Before he could tie another knot the front door opened swiftly.

Jerry East stood in the doorway, his right thumb hitched in the sagging belt close to the hilt of a .45. All three of them were swept into instant violent action. As the killer straightened from his position his six-shooter leaped from its holster so quick the eye could scarcely follow, but no more swiftly than Nell had freed her hands from the rope and reached for the plate from which Allen had been eating.

The guns crashed almost at the same time and each bullet hit its mark. From Nell's hand the plate sailed like a discus, and the sharp edge of it caught the killer in the throat. He staggered back, his second shot plowing into the door jamb. While he was still off balance from the shock a bullet tore into his belly and another just below the heart. As the man was sinking, his twitching finger flung a slug through the floor. He dragged the tablecloth down with a clatter of dishes.

The inert body of the killer lay sprawled, his outflung arm still holding the revolver. Without conscious volition his fingers tightened, and the .45 roared again. Lead ripped a scar in the floor two feet long. Before the sound of the explosion had stilled, Allen was dead. Jerry's eyes did not lift from the motionless figure until he was sure of that.

He turned to Nell. "You're all right?"

"Yes." Her voice shook, and her face was ashen. "And you?"

He put his weapon on the table, a thin wisp of smoke still rising from the barrel, then knelt and undid the knot fastening her ankles. She saw a trickle of blood oozing from under the shirt sleeve to his wrist.

"You're wounded," she cried.

"In the arm. Might have been a lot worse. If you hadn't flung the plate he probably would have got me."

She helped him slip off the coat and rolled up the shirt sleeve. It was a neat flesh wound, not deep. After washing it in cold water she tied one of her husband's handkerchiefs around the arm.

"I'll bring Doctor Norris," she said.

Jerry told her dryly, "I reckon I can make out to walk that far if I take it right easy."

"I'll go with you," Nell replied.

He thought that a good idea. It would not be pleasant for her to stay there with the body of the killer on the floor.

As they walked up River Street they saw people pouring out of every building to learn the cause of the shooting. A dozen of them crowded around East and his companion.

"Please let us through to the doctor's office," Nell said. "Mr. East has been wounded. He killed Allen. You'll find his dead body on the floor of our front room."

The crowd turned and hurried to the Herrick place.

Doctor Norris made light of the wound. "You're lucky, Mr. East. This ought not to bother you much if you take care of it."

"You don't know how lucky, doctor," the Texan answered. "Allen's first shot was a little hurried but his next would have stopped my clock if Mrs. Herrick had not crashed a plate into his neck and staggered him. While he was still groggy I finished him."

"The town will celebrate tonight," the doctor prophesied, "but I don't think you had better join in the revels, Mr. East."

"I'm going back to the Slash Seventy-Two," the wounded man said, and remembered the errand that had brought him to town. "Since there is no woman at the Truesdale place, Mrs. Herrick, Amy's father wondered if it would be convenient for you to come out and nurse her for a few days."

"Of course it would," Nell replied. "I meant to go anyhow this afternoon. Charles won't mind being alone for a few days."

While Jerry was being driven by Nell to the ranch in her husband's buggy he explained that this nursing job was a special one since Amy was expecting to get married soon. Nell wanted to know if the lucky man was a nice peaceable person who would look after his bride well and not always be getting into trouble. Jerry assured her that the guy from now on was going to be strictly a family man and could be depended upon to run a mile in the opposite direction if any difficulty appeared on the horizon.

Nell put her hand gently on Jerry's arm. "I hope you will be as happy as Charles and I are," she said. "And I think you will."

The Texan knew that Nell was much easier in mind than she had been a few weeks earlier. The brittle tenseness had gone out of her and left her more relaxed and gentle. Jerry felt there must have been some adjustment in the life of the Herricks that had removed the strain. The sheriff had told him two days earlier than he had given up any hope of proving that Sanborn was one of the stage robbers. East was glad of that, but more glad that Sanborn was no longer a threat to the happiness of his friends.

At sight of Nell and Jerry the face of Amy brightened.

"Where have you been all through my engaged life?" she asked East.

"He was jealous of all the attention you were getting," Nell told her with a smile. "So he went to town and picked up a scratch of his own he calls a wound."

Amy's quick eyes rested on Jerry. "Tell me," she said. He told her what had occurred at the sheriff's house. She drew a long breath of relief.

"We're lucky, you and I, aren't we?" the girl replied happily. "We might both have been dead, and it's so good to be alive."

He agreed with her that it was good. And through the years, after he had become a prominent cattleman with a well-stocked ranch, a charming wife, and a houseful of spirited children, he was still of the same opinion. His later life, though an active one, was peaceful. Sometimes he looked back, almost with surprise, at the saddlebum who had been the center of such wild and dangerous adventures, and he reflected cheerfully that this was what came to a man who settled down and gave hostages to fortune. Youth had flown on feathered foot and he was only a substantial citizen.

Center Point Large Print
600 Brooks Road / PO Box 1
Thorndike, ME 04986-0001 USA

(207) 568-3717

US & Canada:
1 800 929-9108
www.centerpointlargeprint.com